# GALAXY UNSTABLE

### FORGOTTEN GALAXY
### BOOK 2

## M.R. FORBES

Published by Quirky Algorithms
Seattle, Washington

This novel is a work of fiction and a product of the author's imagination.
Any resemblance to actual persons or events is purely coincidental.

Cover illustration by Tom Edwards
Edited by Merrylee Laneheart

# CHAPTER 1

"Ish, does this thing have external comms or does everything go through the collux network?" Caleb asked, looking through the Nightmare's flight deck transparency. Looming overhead, the starship Glory's rusted and scuffed hull occupied the entire top half of the view.

Peeling his eyes off the damaged hull, he stared out at the spacetime compression field surrounding both ships like a translucent white blanket, allowing both ships to travel through the Manticore Spiral at faster-than-light speed. While he doubted any manner of comm signals could penetrate it, he figured signals should work just fine inside the field, just as long as the Nightmare had gear to support it.

"I want to talk to General Haas."

*I doubt he wants to speak to us.*

"Too bad. I don't really want to speak to him, either. Especially if he's the one who brought the Legion down on the planet. But I'll get to that in due time. Right now, we need to set the record straight so we can get on board. Haas thinks we killed the Empress."

*We did.*

"Technically, yes. But not really."

*How do you intend to convince him of that?*

"I don't know yet. We'll figure something out. First step is to open a comms channel."

*There appears to be the appropriate equipment on board. It is intended for external operation.*

One display mounted to the central control column switched away from the feed from the Nightmare's hull to a comms control display. Sliders provided the controls to select channels, bands, and frequencies.

"Great. Now all we have to do is find a setting Glory can hear us on. That shouldn't take too long."

*Are we in a hurry? We can't exactly go anywhere. With the amount of compression surrounding us, I would imagine exiting the field would leave us instantly pulverized to microscopic particles.*

"I've known men like Haas before," Caleb replied. "It's only a matter of time before he realizes we tagged along for this ride, and once he does—"

"Ish, evasives!" Caleb ordered as two of Glory's hull-mounted gun turrets swiveled toward the Nightmare.

*Evade to where? We only have about four hundred meters of open space around the barge.*

"So use it!" he shouted just as Glory's guns opened fire, sending projectile rounds into the Nightmare's shields.

Ishek did his best to avoid the attack by firing vectoring thrusters and pushing the Nightmare sideways beneath Glory's hull, forcing the turrets to recalibrate and track their firing solutions. As soon as he reached the edge of the starboard side, he slipped back the other way, absorbing a few more seconds of fire as their path again crossed over the line of fire. It worked for now, but like any kind of repeated evasive maneuver, they'd eventually end up obliterated.

Meanwhile, Caleb adjusted the dials, trying to hail the barge. "Glory, this is Nightmare, do you copy? Glory, come in." He repeated the statement each time he switched to a new comm setting.

*Can't we take out the guns?*

"No," Caleb snapped. "We're trying to help them. Destroying their already pitiful defenses won't accomplish that goal."

*What if they destroy us with their pitiful defenses?*

"Just stay out of their targeting vectors until I can talk to them."

*Easier said than done.*

Ishek guided the Nightmare back and away from the turrets, dipping dangerously close to the bottom of the hyperspace field. Over-correcting to avoid being smashed to atoms, he climbed right into the gunfire. A few of the rounds penetrated the shields, digging into the fuselage beside the flight deck.

"Damn it, Ish!" Caleb complained, changing the comm channel again. "Glory, this is Nightmare. Please stop shooting at us. Glory, come in."

*I think I'm doing well considering this is my first time piloting a starship.*

"It might also be your last if we don't stay out of their gun sights."

The Nightmare continued its climb, leaving the line of fire and gaining a moment of peace before the top guns swiveled to track them. Firing starboard side vectoring thrusters, Ishek pushed the Nightmare hard left, dipping back behind Glory's thruster exhausts, all of them still burning lightly inside the field.

*They can't get an angle on us here.*

Caleb nearly allowed himself to feel relieved, only to have the thrusters flare suddenly, the heat of the massive push of ions blasting against the Nightmare's face. Not only did Ishek need to duck away from the makeshift flamethrower, he had to adjust their velocity to match. The unexpected shift almost pushed them out of the back of the field. Only the Nightmare's superior thrust allowed them to overcome the differential.

"Glory, come in," Caleb repeated. "We need to talk. Glory, do you copy?"

*Perhaps if we can get in close to their bridge. They might reconsider destroying us if the debris may puncture their defenses.*

"That's not a terrible idea."

*Unlike your typical plans.*

Ishek launched the Nightmare toward the front of the vessel, taking another bead of fire in the process. A few more rounds penetrated the armor, puncturing the rear cabin. Caleb immediately heard the air begin leaking out into space.

*That's not good.*

"How long until we can't breathe?"

*The holes are relatively small, so we may be able to patch them. If we can't, perhaps an hour.*

"I don't intend to be out here that long."

*Even if you can convince Haas to allow us onboard, which seems highly unlikely right now, there's no guarantee the barge has a suitable docking mechanism compatible with this ship.*

"You keep throwing all these complications at me, Ish. First things first. We need to get Haas to pick up his damn comms!" He shouted the last part, growing frustrated with the situation. Trying a few more channels without success, he growled in exasperation.

Ishek guided the Nightmare past the bow, making a quick maneuver to carry them back up over the top of Glory before Haas could try to cut them off. He couldn't spin the ship around for fear Haas might try to out-accelerate them and knock them from the field. Instead, he fired the retro-thrusters, slowing the Nightmare enough to bring them in line with the transparency fronting the barge's bridge. They were lucky whoever had built the craft hadn't bothered to bury the control center in the middle of the ship, like Centurion shipbuilders were required to do.

Even so, it took a few more seconds of cannon fire and some quick ducking and jinking by Ishek before someone must have told Haas what the consequences of blasting them apart so close to the bridge might be. The guns went silent just as Caleb was about to try another comm channel. A different frequency began flashing on the display. He had failed to hail Haas, but now that they had moved into a better defensive position, Haas was hailing him. He tapped on the flashing comm channel, opening it up. "This is—"

"Card, you son of a bitch!" Haas shouted, his voice coming through a speaker hidden somewhere in the display. "You've got some nerve slipping into our hyper-space field like that!"

*I told you it was a hyperspace field, not a warp bubble.*

"With all due respect, General," Caleb spat, ignoring Ishek. "I saved your life, and the lives of every single person on board your ship."

"After you got the Empress killed. Without her, we're already dead. You just extended the misery of the rest of our lives spent on board this garbage barge, running from Crux's Legion."

"The Empress would never have been in a position to be killed if a traitor on that ship hadn't tipped off Crux where to find you. Which I'm not even close to convinced isn't you."

"Me?" Haas roared. His vitriol was so full of fire he was either an actor worthy of an award or he wasn't the mole. "How dare you insinuate I had anything to do with it. You're the one who showed up out of nowhere, and two days later the Legion came in right behind you. If anyone looks guilty, it's you, Card."

"Except I didn't need the Legion to kill the Empress," Caleb shot back. "I had a knife to her throat, remember?"

The comment gave Haas pause. The comms fell silent for a long stretch before he spoke again. "I intend to look into your accusations personally," he finally replied, his voice still hard, but at a much lower volume. "I'm not the traitor, Card." He paused again. "Maybe you aren't either. But that doesn't change the fact that you're indirectly responsible for the Empress' death."

Caleb's jaw clenched at the statement.

*Don't say it.*

"Maybe not as indirectly as you think."

*Why did you say it?*

"What are you talking about?" Haas asked.

*He's not going to let you on board when you tell him that your hand is the one that drove the sword into the Empress' chest.*

*What am I supposed to do?* Caleb questioned. *Lie?*

*Yes!*

*I can't.*

*Of course you can. It's easy.*

*Damn it, Ish. It would be easy, but I can't help these people if I can't build trust with them, and how can I build trust with a whopper of a secret like that?*

*You do remember we're venting atmosphere, right?*

"Card? Explain yourself." Haas demanded.

Caleb could sense Ishek's immense displeasure with his desire to come clean. The little worm was probably right, but he couldn't live with himself perpetuating such a huge lie. "When we were down in the support tunnels, a powerful Relyeh seized control of Ishek, my Relyeh symbiote, and through him, me. The Relyeh used my body to stab the Empress. I didn't kill her by my volition, but she did die by my hand."

"I see," Haas replied, followed by another long pause.

"This does…complicate things. I was almost ready to believe I was wrong about you."

"I'm being up front with you so there are no secrets or hidden agendas. We didn't get off to a good start, but we're on the same side."

"I don't know what side you're on, Card. You showed up out of nowhere, and forty-eight hours later we're running for our lives. Traitor or no traitor, we lost two APCS and too many good Guardians dealing with you."

"That wasn't my fault. I tried to talk to them. They wouldn't listen."

"It doesn't matter now. Your hand slayed the Empress. I wouldn't have told me that if I were you."

*See?*

"But you can't unsay it, and I can't unknow it. Which leaves me in a tough spot."

"General, thanks to your shoot first, ask questions later approach to dealing with me, this Nightmare is venting air. Why don't you bring me onboard, throw me in the brig, and we can talk about it later? Work something out."

"No," Haas replied, simply and forcefully.

"Why not?"

"Even if I completely trusted you, which I don't, you're way too much of a risk for me to allow on this ship. You claim a Relyeh seized control of your khoron and forced you to kill the Empress. Even if I believed you, which I'm not sure I do, how can you assure me the Relyeh won't repeat his assassination methods a second time, maybe when we're alone in a passageway together? You're like a walking time bomb, ready to go off at any moment. The more I think about it, the more galling it is to me that you would even ask to come aboard. How can anyone trust you right now when you can't even trust yourself?"

Caleb's jaw remained clenched, hands tight on his armrests. There hadn't been time to give the situation much thought between the race to save Glory from destruction and his desire to stop Haas from firing on him. "You're right, General. Maybe I'm not as much of an ally as I want to be. I am indeed a risk. But the fact remains that in less than an hour, I'll be out of air. Like I said, throw me in the brig. Leave me there while we figure out what used me and how to prevent it from happening again. You have my life in your hands."

"I'm sorry, Card. Everyone on this ship is on edge. Beyond the Empress, beyond the Guardians we lost on the surface, the hit to the bow killed nearly three hundred people. All it would take to finish breaking us would be for you to lose control as soon as you stepped on board."

"I could lose control right now, and slam my Nightmare into your bridge, General."

"Then you should move away from the bridge, Card. I won't resume shooting at you. I give you my word."

*Ish, do it.*

*You could have played this a lot better.*

Ishek guided the Nightmare up and away from the bridge, taking position between the upper edge of the field and Glory's highest point.

"Better?" Caleb asked.

"Much. I appreciate your act of faith, Card. I can't let you on this ship, but I do have an idea."

"What kind of idea?"

"In twenty minutes, I'll have Glory brought out of FTL. You'll distance yourself from my ship, and then we'll resume our travel without you. The system we're currently in is remote, but it isn't so remote that a distress call will go unnoticed. The only question will be how well you can conserve your oxygen supply."

"You've got to be kidding," Caleb said. "How is that a fair deal?"

"Who said anything about being fair? I appreciate your

desire to help, if it's sincere. But I won't let you onboard. You have a better shot at survival with my plan than you do tagging along in a leaky boat. If you do survive, and you are sincere, I trust you'll find a way to make yourself useful to those who still support the Empire under the rule of Empress Lo'ane's designated successor."

Caleb finally loosened his jaw, releasing a resigned exhale. "It's not like I have much of a choice."

"No, you don't."

"What about Abraham? He got you into hyperspace alive."

"He did, and there may be a place among us for him because of it. For now, he's in the brig, waiting for a fresh round of questioning. I expect he'll be more forthcoming this time."

"He's a good Marine. He deserves your respect."

"If he earns it, he'll have it."

"And Private Marley?"

"She'll be court-martialed and sent to work in the galley for leading you to our base. I'd consider having her executed, but we need every hand we can get right now, and she's not a true enemy of the people, just an idiot who made a bad choice."

"Once I figure out who used me and ensure it can't happen again, how will I find you?"

"I don't know. But you seem like a resourceful man. The kind of man who stops at nothing to get what he wants. Assuming you don't asphyxiate."

"Suss out the traitor, General. Or there might not be anything or anyone left for me to find."

"Count on it, Card."

"Then I won't ask you to tell Ham and Marley I said goodbye. Please tell them to hang in there and I'll see them later. And tell Ham I still intend to find a way to get him home to his family. Can you do that for me?"

"You did help us escape Galatin, mostly in one piece. I'll let him know what happened to you."

"Thank you. Until next time, General. Card out."

He tapped the disconnect on the display before leaning back in his seat.

*Well, that went exceedingly well.*

# CHAPTER 2

"This should buy us at least two more hours," Caleb said, reviewing the quick patch job he had done on the bullet holes in the Nightmare's fuselage. He'd used Hiro's sword to cut pieces out of the dead Legionnaire's armor, holding them in place with the Legionnaire's magboots. Without a welding machine, the seal wasn't completely airtight, but it would have to suffice.

*Time's up.*

In response to Ishek's comment, Caleb turned his head back toward the flight deck. The white blanket began losing its distorted threads, the stars spreading out in front of them as compressed space expanded. He still didn't love the idea of being dropped off in the middle of nowhere, but it had to be better than getting captured by Crux's warships or being stranded on Galatin.

And Haas was dead on in his assessment. Now that he'd solved the asphyxiation problem, at least temporarily, he could fully focus on completing his mission. It didn't matter that he still wasn't sure where to start. One problem at a time. One step at a time. He would work it all out.

Noticing the comms display flashing from the rear

cabin, he headed forward to answer. One benefit of the collux-based control network for the Nightmare was that he didn't need to be in the pilot's seat for Ishek to keep tabs on their position and heading. Of course, he couldn't fly the ship very well from anywhere else because he needed Caleb's eyes to see, but it had allowed them to effect the repairs to the hull without crashing into Glory or veering out of the hyperspace field.

Regaining his seat, he pulled the safety harness down and locked it in before answering the hail. "This is Card."

"I'm sure you've noticed we're dropping out of hyperspace. The system is called Agni. It's a cluster of four habitable planets within a two hour hyperspace jump of one another, which means they have plenty of traffic crossing through the area. Ships in hyperspace can't receive distress signals, obviously, but you should be in range to have your call picked up by someone who either dropped early for a longer sub-light approach or needed to make some minor repairs of their own. I know thirty minutes isn't a lot of time, but I think you'll figure something out."

"I already did," Caleb replied. "The patch isn't perfect, but it'll buy us another couple of hours."

"I think you'll do well in the Spiral, Card. You have the right mindset."

"That reminds me, General. What is it with this place?"

"What do you mean?"

"I understand this side of the universe was settled by the colonists on board the H.M.S.S. Pathfinder, a generation ship from Earth, about four hundred years ago. What I don't understand is why you have an Empress instead of a Queen, or even a President or Prime Minister."

"I don't know much about our origins. When it comes to history, my focus has always been on the military side of things. What I can tell you is that we weren't always rooted in feudalism. It developed over time as the original colony on Atlas evolved. New planets were discovered and settled, and the human population exploded. With early hyper-space tech limiting the initial reach of our exploration and the vastness of space limiting interplanetary communica-tions, it didn't take long for different factions to splinter off. They declared their independence from whatever form of perceived tyranny they were under and formed their own individual governments. It didn't take much longer than that for the different groups to desire expansion and start picking fights. You're clearly a seasoned fighter with a head for war. You don't need me to explain any more than that."

"Are you saying there's more than one Empire?" Caleb asked.

"About a hundred years ago, the seven major kingdoms agreed to unite under a single leader and form a single Empire. They were tired of the constant fighting, and advances in hyperspace fields had opened up a new fron-tier for them all to explore. With plenty of fresh opportuni-ties, there was little reason for them to squabble, at least until the second Age of Expansion came to a close. Then came Lord Crux. He was the first to betray the Empire and re-declare his independence. At first, we believed we could quell any such act of rebellion, but between his deal with the demons and the new alloy his researchers invented, he not only defeated our enforcement of the laws his ancestors agreed to, he proceeded on the offensive. And as his victo-ries piled up, the other houses questioned their allegiance as well.

Yesterday, I believed that if we could rally the houses who still believed in the idea of a unified Empire, we could restore Empress Lo'ane to her throne and put an end to twenty years of war. Today, you crushed all of my hopes of preserving the Empire and restoring peace when you murdered the last link to unity we had left."

*You probably shouldn't have asked.*

Caleb swallowed hard, momentarily unnerved by Haas' explanation. He had come searching for a lost colony ship and instead found a galaxy at war.

"The only upside is the war should end soon," Haas continued. "With the Empress dead, it won't take long for Crux to consolidate power and hunt down what remains of the pockets of displaced loyalists. I've heard rumors he made a pact with the demons to gain their help in the fight. That he promised them a percentage of annual population growth as payment, I assume so they can infect them and continue to expand their own population. If that's true, I can only wonder how long it will take before Crux is converted from master to slave."

*He's already a slave. Whoever his puppet master is, he's producing khoron at an impossible rate. We will need to find out where, so we can destroy the source.*

"He's already a slave," Caleb repeated, passing on Ishek's words. "Even if he doesn't admit to it yet. Have you heard of people being shipped out to them? Do you know where they're being sent?"

"No. I told you, it's only a rumor. I would think with the number of bodies the Legion has claimed on the battlefield and the number of planets that have fallen under Crux's rule, the demons have had plenty of humans to infect. Anyway, we're out of time, Card. There's no telling who might be in the vicinity, and where their loyalties may lie. We can't afford to be captured again. Not now."

"Where will you go?"

"I don't know yet. With the Empress gone..." He trailed off before continuing, voice shaky. "We can only hope one of the few nobles still loyal to the throne will risk taking us in. If not, there are other places for us to hide."

"Forget hiding. You see where that got you. What about fighting?"

"We're in no shape to fight. Not right now. Maybe never.

I hope you succeed out there, Card. You may be the only chance we have."

"Just keep Ham safe for me. I'll be back for him."

Haas chuckled. "I believe that. Good luck. Glory out."

The comms disconnected. Almost immediately, the hyperspace field again began forming around the barge. "Ish, bring us out of range of the field."

The Nightmare rose away from Glory, ascending above the field as it spread, forming a distortion in space that slowly formed into an oval surrounding the ship.

And then it was gone.

Caleb stared for a few heartbeats at the spot where the ship had been, wondering if he would ever see his friend and comrade again. He was ready to do whatever it took to make that happen. "Ish, do we even have a distress beacon?"

*I have activated it.*

"What about nearby planets?" He looked out through the forward transparency, searching for something solid. A sensor projection activated from the pilot column, revealing a map of the area. The closest rock was estimated at four days travel time at maximum burn.

*And here we are with only a few hours of air.*

"We've been in worse situations."

*When?*

"I was almost dead three hours ago. And you were almost dead about eighty minutes earlier. Which means we both almost died twice pretty recently."

*Third time's a charm?*

Caleb couldn't hold back his grin. "Okay, now that time you were funny."

*I wasn't trying to be.*

"The question is whether we should start burning for that planet, in case our oxygen supply lasts longer than we think. Or do we sit here and hope someone curious pops in to check on our distress call?"

*We won't seem very distressed if we're moving at maximum velocity toward the nearest hard place.*

"Is that a vote for waiting it out?"

*Do I get a vote now? Who breaks the tie?*

"I do."

*So even if I vote against you, then we still do what you want.*

"I *am* the dominant consciousness."

Caleb could feel Ishek's resigned annoyance.

*I vote to remain here. Haas believed someone would happen upon us before too long. Enough so that he was in a hurry to return to hyperspace and flee the area.*

"I agree. It's unanimous. My only question is what sort of someone he was expecting, considering he left in such a rush."

*What do you mean?*

"I don't think General Haas would have been too worried about a random trawler or salvager dropping in. Glory was beat up, but she still had functional guns."

*Did we escape Crux's warships, only to be captured by Crux's warships?*

"That remains to be seen. I sure as hell hope not." Caleb's eyes drifted to the dead Legionnaire. "He's starting to smell."

*In this case, I'm thankful to be able to disable my ability to share in your senses.*

"I wish I could do that. Looking at him gives me an idea."

*I don't like any of your ideas.*

"If you put me to sleep and slow my heart as much as possible, leave me as close to death as you can, we can save another four hours of air, at least."

*It isn't without risk. I don't know if I'm well enough to sustain you.*

"And I don't know if two hours is enough time. We can triple it, but the longer I'm breathing like a fully awake human, the less we can stretch out what we have."

He could sense Ishek's hesitation. Finally, the symbiote relented.

*You should put your helmet back on. The armor will protect you from the increasing cold, at least for a while.*

"Good idea," Caleb said, picking the headgear up from the floor beside the pilot's seat. He shoved it on, locking it into place with a soft click.

*I will alert you when the ship's sensors pick up anything nearby. Or when we're about to run out of air.*

"Sounds like a plan." Caleb leaned back, resting his head against the seat and closing his eyes. He did his best to let his body hang limp, fighting to release the gathered tension. "Okay, Ish. Hit me with the good stuff."

A sudden warm tingle formed at the base of his brainstem, quickly beginning to spread. Within seconds, the chemicals Ishek poured into him left him unable to open his eyes. In thirty seconds, he was sound asleep. By a minute's time, his heart rate had slowed to only twenty-four beats per minute, his breathing shallow, his body cool.

Almost dead. Again.

*Maybe the third time will be a charm.*

# CHAPTER 3

*Caleb, wake up!*

The jolt of adrenaline and other chemicals Ishek pumped into Caleb immediately roused him from his slumber. Eyes popping open, blinking to focus, he straightened in the pilot's seat of the Nightmare, his attention fixing on the sensor projection. A contact was approaching from a few thousand kilometers distant. Decelerating to a docking speed, it was still too far away for him to get a read on its size, shape, or potential armament, but it was here, and it was coming their way.

*It arrived out of hyperspace twelve seconds ago.*

"How long was I out?"

*Six hours.*

Caleb breathed in. He could tell right away that the air was thin. They wouldn't run out of air and die an ignoble death, but they didn't have much time left. At least his estimate was off in the right direction. His idea of having Ish put him in pseudo-stasis had saved their lives. "Give me the comms screen."

The left-side display switched to the comms view. He

had thought perhaps the incoming ship would hail them, seeing as how they were transmitting a distress call. There was no sign of an attempted transmission. It immediately raised the hairs on his arms, his gut feeling turning in a negative direction.

*If they have sensors to detect life signs onboard, they may not have been sensitive enough to pick us up before now. Don't rush too quickly to judgment.*

Caleb waited for the comms screen to flash an incoming hail, splitting his attention between it and the sensor projection. "Give us a little burn, so they know we're operational and alive." The Nightmare's thrusters activated.

The comms finally flashed, registering the channel and frequency. Caleb tapped on the screen, establishing the connection. He opened his mouth to speak, unable to get a word out before a gravelly voice snarled through the link.

"Identify yourself."

*He sounds like he's military.*

*Hopefully not Legion,* Caleb replied. "My name is Captain Caleb Card. My ship is damaged and losing oxygen. I have only ten to twenty minutes of air remaining. I need immediate assistance. Please help."

"Captain? The Legion doesn't put officers in their killing machines."

"I'm not a Legionnaire," Caleb answered.

"You're in a Legion ship."

"It's a long story that I'd be happy to share with you once I'm aboard your vessel."

"That ship's metal is worth decent coin. If I bring you in, the claim is mine."

"I'll need a ride."

"Where are you headed?"

"To be honest, I don't know."

The deep voice crackled laughter over the comms.

"What do you mean you don't know? Space ain't the kind of place one goes a'wanderin'"

"I just told you, it's a long story."

"Right-o. Like I just told you, if I bring you on board, your ship is mine. I'll carry you to our next port, you can hitch a ride wherever you want from there."

"Deal."

"Okay, mate. Hang in there. I'm going to send you coordinates. It'll save us some time if we coordinate velocity and heading."

"Copy that."

A line of text appeared on the comms display:

RECEIVING DATA TRANSMISSION. ACCEPT / DECLINE

Caleb tapped ACCEPT. The sensor projection changed, displaying a suggested course and velocity. "Ish, can you match that?"

*I will try.*

He breathed in, already becoming light-headed from the thinning air. The Nightmare changed course again, putting the incoming vessel behind them. He tracked it through the second screen, displaying the rear view. With the profile nearly dead on as the distance closed between the two craft, Caleb couldn't get a good look at their rescuer's ship. What he could see suggested it was a salvage or cargo ship, its grimy gray metal surfaces scuffed, faded, and worn. A wedge-shaped face led back into a diamond configuration nearly one hundred meters across. Scaffolding jutted out from somewhere behind the diamond, connecting the main fuselage to large thruster nacelles on either side of the craft. What appeared to be gun turrets were mounted to the scaffolding, two top and two bottom on either side, confirming the ship was ready for a fight.

But with who and under what circumstances?

The ship's captain had correctly identified the Nightmare as a Legion ship, but he was still willing to bring Caleb on board and provide safe passage.

*Money talks. This ship is too valuable for him to destroy it without provocation.*

*Agreed. We have no reason not to trust him, but I'm not ready to blindly trust anyone in this galaxy. If he tries anything out here, either now or once we're docked, our goal is to get on that ship and stay on that ship. Alive.*

*Even if that means violence? I hunnnngggeerrrr.*

Ishek's tone was hopeful. Maybe a little too hopeful. "If it comes to that. I hope it won't."

*I hope it will.*

The ship continued its approach, slowly gaining on the Nightmare, drifting over the much smaller ship once they converged. The changing position revealed a long, flat hull that went back close to five hundred meters. The seams of a hangar or cargo bay were visible near the center, leading Caleb to believe the ship would swallow them up in its belly once it was in position.

"Still breathin' in there?" the captain asked.

"For now," Caleb replied, though his head was throbbing, and his heart thumped rapidly.

"Five more minutes, yeh?"

"I'll make it."

The ship continued closing on them, slowing as the tip of the bow overtook the stern of the Nightmare. Caleb's attention diverted from the rear view to the sensor grid as another contact suddenly appeared on the projection. He saw it live in his peripheral vision as a second ship appeared almost directly in front of them.

"Oh, hell," the first ship's captain growled. The comm link disconnected, his rescuer pulling away from them as blue energy poured from the thruster nacelles.

*I don't like this.*

"Me, neither," Caleb said. The newcomer was slightly larger than the first ship, with a shape that vaguely reminded Caleb of the original Space Shuttle. Like the other vessel, it had a wedge-shaped bow, but it spread back into a squarish fuselage that quickly became a delta-winged pyramidal pattern toward the stern. Its surfaces were in better condition than the first ship's, the metal clean and undamaged. Gun batteries were placed regularly across every part of the hull, and while they were smaller than the first vessel's, they were much more numerous.

All at once, the Nightmare was forgotten.

Which would have been fine with Caleb if he could still breathe normally.

Flashes of energy crossed the gap between the first ship and the second as the first vessel opened fire. Heavy ion blasts pounded into the newcomer, their shields absorbing the blows as the ship accelerated and maneuvered. Giving the first ship its broadside, it returned fire. A spew of projectiles ripped across space, smacking into the first ship's shields as it too began evasive maneuvers.

Caleb's air continued to thin as it leaked out through the damaged hull, making it difficult for his body to draw in enough oxygen. He didn't have time for these two ships to duke it out over who would get salvage rights.

The two ships angled away from him, exchanging fire. The first vessel benefited from its separated thrusters, in that it had a lower profile, the open scaffolding more difficult for the other ship to hit. The second ship, considering the number of guns it was firing at a higher rate than the first ship's ion blasts, would no doubt run out of their conventional rounds more quickly. The first ship simply needed to survive the onslaught long enough for the second to run out of ammo.

A minute passed. Then two minutes. Caleb's head

pounded, making it hard to concentrate. The two ships had moved into the distance, still slugging it out. The first ship's larger, less numerous guns landed heavier blows on the second ship's shields even though it had a more concentrated, less furious rate of attack. Despite the differences in appearance, the two ships seemed evenly matched.

The comms display flashed, two hails coming in nearly simultaneously. Caleb tapped on both, open channels to the fighting ships. They both began talking simultaneously, though Caleb was able to sort out their individual statements.

"Friend," the first captain said. "If your weapons systems are still operational, I suggest you use them. The ship attacking us is a pirate vessel, and I guarantee they'll take your craft and throw you from an airlock first chance they get. Help us against it, and I'll give you ten percent of the value of your scrap metal."

"Distressed starship," someone on the second ship said. "This is Commander Roger Graystone of the starship George's Shield, an escort ship to the Star Line Transport Company. As your ship appears to be operational, I respectfully request that you assist us in defeating the pirates with whom we are currently engaged so that we may come to your aid. Failure to open fire on the wretched scum or provide reasoning why you cannot do so will leave us no choice but to target you as an accomplice."

*Did I just hear what I thought I heard?* Caleb asked silently.

*They're both calling each other pirates.*
*Yeah, that's what I thought I heard.*
*One of them is clearly lying.*
*Obviously. But which one?*
*That's not really up for debate, is it?*
*Appearances can be deceiving.*
*Not in this case. Graystone is civilized. A company man. His*

*ship is newer and cleaner. Since when do space pirates have clean ships?*

*When have we ever encountered space pirates before to know that? In any case, Graystone threatened to kill us if we don't comply. The other guy did no such thing. He even offered us compensation to help them out.*

"Friend, we really need your help," the first captain said, filling in Caleb's initial moments of silence. "If those bastards win, you can kiss your keister goodbye."

"Distressed starship, you have ten seconds to comply," Graystone said.

*Graystone can afford to threaten us because he can likely call for backup. Perhaps he already has. He said his ship is an escort, probably one of a few. I doubt our so-called friend can do the same.*

Caleb watched the two ships exchange another round of fire. The first ship took a direct hit to the port side nacelle that created a sudden chain reaction. The thruster exploded in a brief ball of flame, throwing debris out in every direction. He tapped on the first ship's comms, disconnecting them. *Ish, engage the target of your choice.*

*I knew you would come around.*

*Not for the reasons you might think.*

"George's Shield…this is Captain Caleb Card…" The lack of oxygen forced him to gasp out his response in halting phrases. "…on board the distressed starship. We're targeting…the pirates…but we'll require immediate pickup…as soon…as this is over. My ship is…operational… but it's leaking…and dangerously low on air… I am running out…fast."

"Understood, Captain Card," Graystone replied. "We are prepared for immediate pickup the moment the threat is eliminated."

The Nightmare shot toward the first ship, slipping up underneath it as it continued firing and taking fire. As one of the first ship's heavy ion blasts broke through the other vessel's shields, ripping a chunk out of several decks, Ishek opened up the Nightmare's guns on one of the damaged sections of the ship above them. With its shields already weakened in that spot, the blasts burned through the hull, digging deeper into the wound and breaking through secondary emergency seals.

Ishek slipped the Nightmare hard astarboard as one of the first ship's ion cannons turned toward them and opened fire, sending huge blasts of charged ions in their direction. Avoiding the return fire, he made a loop over the ship, maxing the throttle out to gain velocity in the opposite direction. Caleb tightened his stomach against the heavy Gs, struggling to stay focused as he gasped for oxygen in the increasingly thinning air. The hard burn slowed their velocity enough that the pirate gained a solid firing solution, hitting the Nightmare with three cannon blasts in rapid succession. The last one penetrated the shields, shearing off the starboard wing.

"Ish!" Caleb shouted, annoyed with the symbiote's flying.

*It couldn't be helped.*

The Nightmare shot back toward the pirate, successfully evading the defenses once more and returning fire the entire time. George's Shield added to the firepower, and together they inflicted more wounds on the other ship's hull. Rocketing past the bottom of the pirate ship, Ishek repeated his turn one more time, pointing the Nightmare's nose toward the original gaping wound in the pirate's side and triggering their cannons. Drifting backward put them in position to continue firing on the damaged part of the hull unabated. Ishek sent dozens of blasts into the chasm.

Sensing the kill, George's Shield joined the attack, all of its guns unloading into the same gash. With the combined firepower, they could pierce all the way to the ship's reactor core, puncturing the power source and knocking the pirate's remaining thruster offline. Graystone could have halted the attack right there, letting the crippled pirate limp away. Instead, he continued firing thousands of rounds into the ship, only stopping once the ship broke apart, debris and bodies pouring out of both ends of the tear.

"Target eliminated," Graystone announced. "Your aid is greatly appreciated, Captain Card."

"Please," Caleb said, a tightness growing in his throat, his lungs beginning to burn, his head pounding from lack of air. "I need...evac."

"And you'll have it for a job well done," Graystone said. "Hold tight, Captain."

George's Shield changed course, the Nightmare's backward momentum leaving the escort ship approaching from the bow. Caleb did his best to slow his breathing as the ship neared, though his pounding heart made it difficult to manage. The burn in his lungs steadily increased, his head slumping as he fought to stay conscious.

"Captain Card, please deactivate your shields," Graystone said.

*Shields...deactivated.*

Ishek's thoughts were weak, his consciousness equally affected by Caleb's lack of air.

"Shields...are down," Caleb announced, his voice noticeably weak.

"Standby," Graystone answered.

Bay doors opened amidships of *George's Shield*. Twin harpoons launched from the gaping darkness, crossing the short distance and stabbing through the flight deck's transparency, sinking into the deck in front of Caleb. The cables winched tight, and he expected George's Shield to reel him in. Instead, the Nightmare remained dangling while the seconds ticked past.

"Commander Graystone," Caleb said, his voice raspy in

the thin air. "I'm almost...out of...air. I need to come aboard...now, or I...will die."

Graystone's voice was bitter when he replied. "That's the idea, Captain Card. Haven't you heard? Dead men tell no tales."

# CHAPTER 4

Graystone's gloating tone ignited a fire in Caleb's gut.

George's Shield had answered his distress call, but not to rescue him from trouble or save him from pirates. If the first ship had even been a pirate after all. Like the other captain, he had come to see if there was any profit to be had, and if so to claim it. No wonder Haas had been so eager to leave the system. It was crawling with scum.

Caleb didn't reply to the remark. Not with words, anyway. The fact remained that they were nearly out of oxygen, and if he wanted to survive, there was only one way out. He was staring right at it through the transparency, holding the Nightmare like a fish on a hook.

In case Graystone had cameras monitoring him, Caleb feigned imminent collapse to the deck. On hands and knees, head pounding, and his lungs able to draw only half breaths of air, he had a destination in mind. He had secured his rifle in the cabin, too far away to reach, but he still had his sidearm and Hiro's sword. In a world of guns from conventional to plasma, a melee weapon like the sword seemed obsolete, but he understood now why the former Emperor-in-waiting had carried it. Made of the dark alloy that had given Crux the edge he'd needed to seize control of the galaxy, it definitely had its uses. Given enough time, maybe Caleb could make him regret ever gifting any of the material to the Emperor.

*Ish, please tell me…you have enough left…to give me a boost.*

*I…I'm so…tired.*

*Knuckle up. It's do or die time… Literally.*

*Then…let's do it.*

Warmth began spreading from the base of Caleb's skull and down his spine to his extremities. His oxygen-starved body regained a majority of its strength, though he knew it wouldn't last for long. He needed to act quickly..

*When I give the thought, turn off the gravity.*

He didn't wait for Ishek to confirm. And he couldn't be sure what he planned would work, but it was the only chance they had to survive.

In one fast, smooth motion, he grabbed the sword from his back, sealed his helmet ventilation with his free hand, and from his crouch, lunged at the forward transparency..

*Now!*

Gravity disappeared just as he pushed off the floor, careening toward the flight deck transparency. He swung the sword into the clear polycarbonate, the blade's dark alloy sinking through the transparency. A spider web of cracks snaked between the breaches created by the two harpoons. Jerking the sword back, Caleb turned his shoulder into the damage, crashing through the transparency as though he were jumping through a glass window.

The remaining oxygen inside the Nightmare quickly escaped with him. Before he could drift out into space, he returned the sword to his back and grabbed onto one of the tug cables, pulling himself hand-over-hand along the taut line toward George's Shield.

With the last of his oxygen depleted, his lungs burned

like a bonfire, his strength of will alone all that kept him going. If George's Shield had armed guards ready to meet him in what had to be the cargo bay, he was probably already a dead man, but there was still a slim chance he could catch them by surprise.

His armor wasn't intended to be spaceworthy, but it held up well against the vacuum, protecting him from instant death in the vacuum as he crossed the gap between ships. The lack of resistance was the only boon to his progress, his speed increasing as he pulled himself forward.

Halfway to the ship, the hangar doors began closing on the cables, the crew of George's Shield hoping to trap him dangling in the vacuum until he suffocated. Caleb doubled his efforts, his muscles complaining with every movement. He ignored the pain. He had to make it onboard. Had to give himself one last chance to keep fighting. For Ham. For the Empress. For humankind and for vengeance. He had no intention of dying like a damn tuna at the end of a fishing line.

With gritted teeth, fighting the blackness creeping in around the edges of his vision, he focused on the end game,his strength waning. He heaved himself forward as fast as he could. concentrating on clenching his fingers tightly around the cable with each handhold. Gaining velocity, he yanked himself forward three final times before pulling his legs up and letting go. He shot across empty space, his path carrying him toward the cargo bay doors, the panels only eight feet apart now. His attention shifted from the doors to the cable and the distance he had left to reach the back of the cargo bay. It would be close.

He also knew he would make it.

Until his vision started to dim. He was on the edge of losing consciousness, his entire body a mass of pins and needles.

Barely aware, he slipped through the doors with little

room to spare, passing through the one-way shield that held the atmosphere in. Artificial gravity grabbed him, and he landed flat on his back beside the bay doors, held open only just enough now by the cables. He reached up and opened the air vents on his helmet. Immediately, he began sucking in oxygen in huge gulps. Fully expecting the plasma bolts that hissed past him,he rolled away from the doors, the crackling heat of the blasts passing so close he could feel the heat prickle his skin.

He rolled laterally across the deck, quick bursts of blurry vision suggesting the cargo bay was relatively small and messy. Plastic-encased crates of varying sizes were scattered among a hodge-podge of other random items, including something his still-dazed brain saw as the statue of a large golden dragon.

His evasive maneuver ended in a dead stop when he collided with a crate. Still sucking in air as fast as he could, the burning numbness in his muscles was fading fast, his body recovering quick thanks to Ishek, who was no doubt already fully recovered.

The loss of motion left Caleb a temporary sitting duck, but his armor served as his one saving grace. Plasma bolts sizzled into it, dissipating upon contact against the hardened alloy plates.

He jumped to his feet, finally getting a slightly better look at his surroundings. The harpoon launcher was mounted to a track that ran along the top of the bay, currently positioned a third of the way across, the cables still clinging to the Nightmare. An operator sat behind the controls, though he had traded the levers for a pistol. The man fired on him, the blast sizzling harmlessly against his armor. He spotted four other people in the bay, dressed in what were obviously civilian clothes, simple shirts and pants made of a coarse material he'd never seen before, magnetic boots and coats he assumed offered some level of protection against gunfire. They fired a barrage of poorly aimed shots from scuffed plasma rifles at him. Only twenty percent of the bolts hit him, and those did minor damage to his armor.

*This feels unfair...for them.*

Caleb smirked slightly at Ishek's comment as he drew his sidearm. With the shooter's weapons underpowered, the initiative remained his. He didn't waste it, rushing toward the nearest shooter, aiming his pistol at him. The defender, having finally realized his rounds weren't having the desired effect, lowered the weapon to adjust the dial on the side while simultaneously trying to retreat behind cover. He failed at both. Caleb's rounds dug into his chest, eliminating him.

*Nine o'clock.*

Pivoting in response to Ishek's warning, Caleb dropped to his knees and fired off four rounds to the chest of a man who'd popped out from behind the cover of the harpoon launcher. As the man writhed and fell, Caleb rolled to the side, coming to his feet and angling for the dragon statue. He ducked behind it just in time to avoid the next round of plasma bolts, the energy output enough to melt the artwork's gold shell.

Staying low, Caleb swung out around the other side of the statue, catching another enemy by surprise. Loosing a half dozen well-grouped rounds, he was confident his aim was good and didn't wait to see the man fall. He dashed across the deck, heading for a stack of cargo crates draped in heavy tarps. He flinched when a round from overhead hit the top of his helmet. Looking up, he swung his sidearm toward the harpoon operator's direction and sent a volley toward him. Even though the operator ducked away, Caleb's errant rounds still gave him time to duck behind the crates.

*They fear for their lives. I can taste it. I hunnnnggeerrr.*

For once, Caleb was glad Ishek hungered. Feeding on the crew's pheromones would speed up the symbiote's recovery, allowing Ish to continue energizing Caleb.

"They think they're afraid now," he growled, retrieving his sword, "wait till they see us at our best."

Moving around the back of the crates, staying in a crouch to remain out of view, Caleb heard a door slide open off to his right. Looking toward it, he spotted a hatch beside the crates as it closed, the armed crewman crouched there drawing his aim. Just as her eyes found him, his shots found her. She dropped to the deck as he rushed toward her position.

Yet another crewman moved into the open as he reached the dead woman's body, his rifle pointed at Caleb. His eyes widened an instant before Hiro's blade sliced cleanly through his throat. The man dropped his rifle and fell to his knees, both hands clutching his gaping wound. Blood gushed through his fingers, his fear palatable.

*Yessss. Sooo tasty!*

Ishek's greed as he gorged himself and his own rage over Graystone's betrayal washed through Caleb on the rush of oxygen to his brain. He sprinted for the door, running past the dying crewman and reaching for the lift bar on the hatch.

He suddenly had second thoughts, deciding against leaving the cargo bay early. Whoever these people were, whether they really were escorts for some transport company or pirates themselves, their training left a lot to be desired. With their lousy aim and pathetic armor, the cargo bay was a shooting gallery.

His shooting gallery.

He slapped the pistol to his thigh and returned the sword to his back. Scooping up the dead woman's rifle, he turned the dial all the way up. Shouldering the weapon, he moved along the side of the crates to the end of the stack.

He cornered out, sweeping the area before locking onto a target. They traded fire, but only his shots connected, eliminating another man.

*Three o'clock.*

Caleb wheeled to his right, spotting a head sticking out past what appeared to be a small transport ship. The man ducked back behind cover when Caleb opened fire and sprinted across the open room. He ceased fire a few seconds before he arrived. The man's head poked back out just in time for Caleb to crack the stock of his rifle across it, knocking the man out. He didn't slow more than necessary to duck around the man, a barrage of bolts chasing him behind the small transport.

Advancing past it and through the cargo, he stopped at a break in the piles. Leading with his rifle, he caught another shooter by surprise. By his count, there were only two remaining, plus the harpoon operator. Remembering him, Caleb backpedaled as he aimed his rifle toward the launcher, only to find the man had guided the machine back to its original spot and was fleeing through an upper-level hatch.

*Well, he got away.*

"For now. Let's finish clearing this room."

Caleb moved back toward the center of the bay. Stepping behind the single huge crate for cover, he peeked around the edge of it to find the last two crew members standing in the open, rifles lying on the deck in front of them, hands in the air.

"We surrender," the woman said. "Please don't hurt us."

"It's not our fault," the man with her said. "I knew the commander shouldn't have messed with one of Lord Crux's ships. But he said the salvage is worth a lot of coin, at least on the Dark Exchange. And what the commander says, goes. It's written in our contracts."

"You were supposed to suffocate," the woman added. "Not swoop up in here like Death hisself."

"You're pirates then?" Caleb asked.

"That's one way to put it," the man replied.

"Graystone told me the other ship was a pirate vessel."

They both laughed. "It probably was," the woman said. "Pickings have been slim in these parts the last few months. Blood in the water always brings sharks."

Caleb shook his head while lowering his rifle. It figured both ships were pirate ships. "Which way to the bridge?"

"What are you planning to do?" the man asked, slowly lowering his hands.

"Find Graystone. Have a little chat with him. Anyone who attacks me, dies. Anyone who surrenders and stays surrendered lives. Understood?"

"Y…yes, sir."

"Good. Don't think about trying to sneak up on me. It won't work."

"I believe that," the woman said, glancing at one of the bodies on the deck. "We'll be waiting right here for you. If you decide to come back, you won't get any trouble from us."

Caleb nodded. "Which direction did you say the bridge is in?"

# CHAPTER 5

A pair of pirates were already running toward Caleb as he left the cargo bay and entered the passageway. Armed with the woman pirate's fresh plasma rifle, he surprised the two men with his sudden presence, leaving them slow to bring up their ion blasters. The hesitation cost them their lives as Caleb sank a pair of plasma bolts into the chest of one and two more to the other's head. Though the corridor behind them remained clear, approaching footfalls echoed off the bulkheads.

It figured Graystone would send more people his way. The man had made his intentions and his treachery crystal clear. It was the second flaw in the man's line of thinking within the last ten minutes. First, he'd underestimated Caleb's ability to get on board his ship. Now he was overestimating his crew's capacity to take him out. They were spacers, not soldiers, and their lack of cohesion and coordination would ultimately be their undoing. The only question was how many of them he would have to take out before Graystone got the message.

*I'm feeling much better.*

"So am I," Caleb replied softly, peering down to the end

of the corridor as he stepped over the two dead pirates. The passageway was wider and more open than the corridors on Glory, with clean metal bulkheads and soft lighting emanating from the ceiling. He was cynically amused because the pirates had a better ride than the galaxy's Empress. It spoke to the condition, decline, and desperation of her people.

*It's also a warning about how difficult it may be to challenge Crux, whoever he is. Perhaps we should forget about the Empress' people and consolidate our focus on finding a way back through the wormhole to Proxima.*

*And just let the Relyeh have this galaxy?*

*Yes.*

*No. We came here because Pathfinder was in trouble. We aren't leaving this place to the enemy.*

*Caleb, we're one symbiotic partnership. How are we supposed to win a war that's already been lost? Especially when whoever made us kill the Empress and almost killed us in the process might derail us again.*

*Now that you're feeling much better, you can start trying to figure out how to stop him from overwhelming you again.*

*That's the point. I cannot stop him. He's too powerful. He blasted right through my defenses that have served us so well since we bonded.*

*Whoever he is, you reached out to him first to protect us from being discovered. Maybe he learned something during that interaction that allowed him to get past your shields.*

*I drew too much attention to us. And now there's little I can do to stop him if he shows up again.*

*I don't accept that,* Caleb pushed forcefully. *He's the reason Haas ultimately couldn't trust us. Hell, we can't fully trust ourselves! To avenge the Empress' death and aid her people, we have to find and deal with this enemy. You have to find a way for us to do that.*

*I will try.*

Caleb slowed as he reached the end of the passageway. The pirates were close now. Peeking around the corner, he jerked back as a mob of at least a dozen, all carrying guns, rushed into the passageway

All headed his way.

He paused, considering his options. While he didn't have any qualms about killing pirates, he wasn't eager to kill anyone, unless he absolutely had to. Right now, he had the element of surprise and the beginnings of an intimidation factor. He could fall back to a more defensible position in the cargo bay and let the pirates come to him. It would be easy pickings as they moved into the open, and their lack of organization would leave them slow to train their weapons on him. Plus, he was sure their aim would be as bad as the others he had downed in the cargo bay. He could absorb their attack for long enough to put them all on the deck. His second option was to set them back on their feet by charging ahead and barreling through them like a tornado.

*A veritable smorgasbord. I still hunger.*

It didn't surprise Caleb that Ishek voted for option two. In this case, he agreed with his symbiote. The crewmen were close enough now for that surprise to work.

Swapping the plasma rifle for his sword and sidearm, he bolted around the corner and crashed into the first man at full steam, cracking his bare head against the bulkhead. The man slid to the deck, out cold. Caleb pivoted cleanly away from him, swinging Hiro's blade in a long arc across the bellies of the next two. They dropped, writhing on the deck with minor belly wounds, and the next two, one a woman, tripped over them, the pair going down in a tangle. The rest stopped before they ran into Caleb's buzz saw. He shot two of them at close range before an ion blast caught him in the chest, accomplishing nothing but knocking him back a step. He rushed forward again, whirling to kick another man hard in the chest. The man collided with the bulkhead, knocking himself out.

In less than five seconds, only four of the reinforcements remained on their feet. Too slow in bringing their rifles up to fire, Caleb lunged at them, his sword cutting across the chests of two, another taking a glancing blow off his cheek. The last one scrambled backward, avoiding the blade by mere inches.

"Mercy!" he shouted, throwing his hands up and dropping to his knees.

Caleb quickly realized it was the operator of the harpoon launcher. Keeping him in sight from the corner of his left eye, the blade still at his throat, he turned his gun on the two who had tripped and fallen, waiting as they untangled themselves. They immediately put their hands behind their heads and rose slowly to their feet. One was a tall, red-haired woman.The man, he noticed, had wet his pants.

"The bridge is this way?" Caleb casually inquired, tipping his head to the left.

The woman nodded. "Yes, sir."

"My beef is with Graystone. Stay out of this, and I'll have no reason to kill you."

"Commander Graystone will kill us if we don't do what he says," the woman answered. "He's done it before."

*Caught between a rock and a harder rock. Their fear is divine.*

"He won't have a chance to kill any more of you," Caleb replied. "I'll see to that."

Behind the pair at the end of Caleb's gun, one pirate Caleb had knocked out slowly found his way back to his feet. An older man, lean and wrinkled, with two days' worth of stubble adorning his chin and stringy white hair dangling from the back of his otherwise bald head. "Don't believe him," the man growled, his eyes narrowing on Caleb. "He can't kill all four of us at once. I say we rush him now." He took a step forward.

"Bones, I think we ought to stay out of this," the pirate at the end of Caleb's sword said, stopping Bones in his tracks. "Don't you recognize that armor? He's royal blood. We kill him, and mark my words, we'll come to regret it."

"Don't be ridiculous," the woman said. "Everyone knows the royals are all dead, save for Empress Lo'ane. His gear's fake."

"I heard we were about to nick a Nightmare." The man who'd wet himself finally had something to say. "That don't sound fake to me."

"You idiot. What would a royal be doing on board a Nightmare?"

"I can make this easy," Caleb spoke up. "Contrary to what Mr. Bones here said, I can indeed kill all of you right here and now. After all, there were twelve of you. Now, there are just you four."

They stopped bickering immediately, all of them going stone still as they stared wide-eyed at Caleb.

"We're good," Bones finally said, suddenly changing his tune. He pointed down the corridor. "Gorgon's bridge is amidships. Turn right, then left, go halfway down that corridor and turn left again. Go through the hatch and take the lift to deck six. Once you come out, go straight to the second passageway, you'll be looking at the port bulkhead of the bridge. Follow it around to the hatch. It'll be sealed tight. Graystone, he likes to send us hired help to do all the dirty work while he…"

Bones went silent as a pair of pirates came around the corner in the direction he had pointed. They came to an abrupt stop once they spotted Caleb standing there with four of their crewmates under the threat of death. When they noticed the number of crewmen already lying dead on the deck, their hands went up as well.

"Good choice, mates," Bones said. "This bloke here

wants some words with Graystone. Best not to get in his way."

Caleb glanced at him. "Thank you."

"Of course, sir. Pleased to be of service to you."

Caleb walked past the man still on his knees and then by the two latecomers, picking up speed again once he rounded the corner. He made the next left into a long, clear passageway that traveled most of the length of *George's Shield*.

*Bones said the ship's name is* Gorgon*. Graystone lied about that, too.*

"Right," Caleb agreed. "Well, soon enough, he won't be telling any more lies."

He sprinted to the intersection halfway down the corridor, slowing at the corner and moving more cautiously into the left-hand passageway. The lift was twenty meters away, a pair of guards positioned in front of it. They reacted to his sudden appearance with shocked surprise, making them slow to reach for their guns. He put two rounds into each of them, dropping them where they stood.

Crossing the remaining distance to the lift, he tapped the call button, waiting only a few seconds for the cab to arrive.

*Anything Graystone has left will be there to ambush us the moment we arrive on Deck Six.*

"Obviously," Caleb agreed. "Should we take the stairs?"

*Are there stairs?*

"I didn't think to ask. Lift it is."

*This should be fun.*

# CHAPTER 6

Hands and feet maglocked to the walls at the top of the lift cab, Caleb waited as the doors slid open on Deck Six and plasma fire poured into nothing but thin air. The barrage slagged the back of the cab, melting through to the bulkhead behind it before the pirates realized there was no one there.

"What the?" one of them said. "It's like a ghost rode it down here."

Caleb released the magnetic clamps on his boots and gloves, allowing *Gorgon*'s artificial gravity to pull him down out of hiding. Drawing his legs up, he landed cleanly in a crouch, finger already depressing the trigger of his plasma rifle. While the pirates tried to make sense of his sudden appearance, he targeted them, taking down three of the eight standing behind a stack of tables and chairs blocking the entire corridor. It didn't take long for the survivors to take cover behind the makeshift barricade.

Caleb burst from the lift, his weapon trained just above the barricade, The moment one pirate lifted his head into view, he fired, sending a bolt whizzing past the man's ear.

"That was a warning shot," he shouted. "I'm here for Graystone, and only Graystone. There's no reason any more of you need to die today."

"You're only one man!" another pirates shouted back. "You can't fight us all."

"I made it down here, didn't I?" Caleb asked. "And you're the ones hiding behind a barricade. Not me."

"He has a point," one of the other pirates muttered.

"After Graystone answered my distress call, he ordered you to leave me in my ship to suffocate. He double-crossed me, and now he needs to suffer the consequences. You can either let me through, or I can kill you all and then deal with him. One way you survive. The other you don't."

*Spoken like a true Relyeh.*

*Except I'm trying to intimidate them so I don't need to fight them. You would intimidate them just to intimidate them.*

*For their fear. Yessss.*

"You have five seconds," he added. He could hear the murmurs of the defenders speaking among themselves. "Four. Three. Two…"

"Wait!" one of them said, putting his hand up over the barricade. "We'll let you pass. Just hold on."

The others in the group began moving aside the tables and chairs, creating a narrow aisle through the center. Once they finished, two of them waited at the front of the barricade with their hands up. One stood on the left of the barricade, the other on the right, their hands also up where Caleb could see them.

He walked forward, nodding to the two at the front when he passed between them. They nodded back at him, their features tense. Caleb couldn't help but notice how tired and wane they looked, as if they'd all seen better days.

*They're going to go for it.*

*I know.*

*Stupid.*

*Yes.*

As he reached the midpoint of the barricade, the man standing furthest away shouted, "Now!"

A moment later, they all scrambled away, and explosives inside the barricade detonated. Caleb didn't know which one of them had pressed the button. He didn't care. What mattered was that he was already diving onto his stomach to avoid the firestorm of heat and flying shrapnel that tore into the bulkheads on both sides of him. It was too much to hope he could escape it all. Red hot pain sliced into the back of his right shoulder where a small piece of shrapnel found its way through a gap in his overlay.

Gritting his teeth against the pain, Caleb leaped up, bursting through the miasma of smoke and bits of debris still fluttering to the deck. With a sweep of his sword, he cut the throat of the pirate directly in front of him before he could bring his weapon to bear. Pivoting, he swept the blade down, lopping off another man's hand. Before he could scream, Caleb shot him twice in the gut.

Catching a sudden flash of movement out of the corner of his eye, he swung his gun around, clocking a pirate in her temple before she could fire her handgun point-blank at the vulnerable back of his neck. She stumbled backward, finding her balance and swinging her gun back at him, her intention obvious. To blast him through his faceplate. Caleb dropped his gun and grabbed her throat, lifting her with one hand and driving her back into the bulkhead. While he knocked the breath out of her, the hit didn't force the gun out of her hand. She brought it back around to take her shot. As much as it bothered him to do it, he drew his arm back, and grimacing from the pain of his wound, he sank his sword deep into her gut. Her eyes went wide, the gun falling from her suddenly limp hand as she stared at him, her expression registering shock for a fleeting moment before all life drained from her eyes.

Releasing her, she hung there. His sword had gone all the way through her, undoubtedly severing her spine before penetrating the bulkhead. Unable to pull it out, he claimed the pirate's gun from the floor, turning it on the remaining two pirates in one smooth motion. Rather than fight, they made a break for the lift, desperate to escape.

Letting them go, he looked over his shoulder to see the shrapnel embedded in his shoulder, close to where Ishek clung beneath his arm.

*Too close.*

Wincing, he grabbed the metal and ripped it out, leaving a powerful flow of blood pouring from the wound.

*Close that as quickly as you can.*

*Already on it.*

Warm numbness surrounded the wound. The bleeding stopped by the time he finally wrenched the sword free of both the bulkhead and the woman's body. Unable to just let her fall, he caught her in one arm and lowered her body to the deck, leaning her back against the bulkhead, her legs stretched out in front of her. He took a few moments to stare down at her. He regretted having to kill her. All the killing, so much of it needless, sickened him.

*Knuckle up, Caleb. It is what it is.*

"I know, but I don't have to like it."

He continued forward to the bridge's outer bulkhead, cautiously following it around to the double-wide entrance. Bones had warned him the doors were secured, a panel with a retinal scanner and keypad attached confirming the older pirate's honesty.

*How long do you think he can hide in there before he starves?*

"Longer than I'm willing to give him," Caleb answered. He stepped up to the keypad, entering Pathfinder's master passcode. A red light flashed when he stopped typing, the doors refusing to budge. At least he'd confirmed this galaxy had moved on from the colony ship's original base software.

*You also confirmed we have no way through these doors.*

"I'm getting through these doors," Caleb insisted.

*How?*

"Boost me."

*Caleb, I can't continue to—*

"A veritable smorgasbord, remember? You should be plenty strong enough to boost me. And don't tell me it's bad for my health. Dying is worse for my health."

Ishek remained reluctant, but Caleb felt the next jolt of adrenaline and other stimulants course through his veins. Stepping up to the blast doors, he slid Hiro's blade between the two panels, trusting that Crux's alloy was strong enough to work like a pry bar. Leaning into the blade's grip, he created a gap wide enough to wedge his hands into. Letting the weapon fall to the deck, he overpowered the locking motors, separating the two doors. Kicking the sword ahead of him, he lunged through; the doors slamming closed behind him.

The entire bridge crew, standing behind the cover of their individual stations, opened fire.

Plasma bolts and ion blasts burned into his armor in a fierce barrage that would have melted any other combat armor, including, he believed, his Centurion overlay. The alloy protected him long enough to scoop up his blade and rush the female crewman crouching behind the edge of a terminal a few strides away. She panicked at his approach, tossing her pistol aside and falling to the deck, hands over her head.

Caleb turned away from her, still taking fire as he grabbed his sidearm and swung it toward the front of the bridge to where three stations lined the area in front of the empty command seat. Four spacers hid behind the stations, ducking out of view as he pointed his gun at them. He had no intention of firing on them if he could avoid it. Not in here. Not when he might damage not only vital electronics but the forward wraparound screen as well. Currently, it displayed space forward the starship's bow, including a view of the Nightmare still dangling from the harpoon cables.

He needed a ship, and Gorgon would do.

He charged the stations, coming around one side faster than normally possible on his chemically enhanced legs. The crewman there froze in response, his weapon falling from his hand. He might have surrendered, but one of the other pirates shot him in the back while also firing on Caleb. The wounded pirate stumbled into Caleb's grip, eyes pleading for help before they glassed over. Caleb dropped the man's body and turned his attention to the shooter.

Graystone, no doubt.

Younger than Caleb expected, with a handsome-but-greasy look, a short beard, and bright blue eyes, he was fashionably dressed in a white shirt and black slacks beneath a long, dark red coat. Still crouched behind the nearest station, he didn't stop firing; the blasts doing little to faze Caleb as he took the last few steps to him. Grabbing the man's gun hand, he broke his wrist in one quick motion and then tossed Graystone into the bulkhead below the surround. He fell to a knee, barely pausing before reaching into his boot with his good hand and pulling out a knife.

He lunged at Caleb. A flash off to the right and the soft thunk of an ion blaster sent a ream of energy through the air, hitting Graystone in the temple. His body made it two more steps on his brain's prior messages before he collapsed to the deck and didn't move again.

Caleb turned to face the man who had fired the shot. Older, with a square jaw, short gray hair, and a scar on his forehead, he had the look of a soldier.

"Oops," the pirate said, turning the blaster around in his hand, and holding the grip out toward Caleb. "I guess my aim isn't what it used to be." His smirk drifted to Graystone. "Son of a bitch turned on his own. I don't care what kind of dishonest bastard you are, that's crossing a line."

"I agree," Caleb said, turning his head to check for any other attackers. There was a second crew member on the starboard bulkhead opposite the woman who had surrendered, but he'd already dropped his weapon too.

"There's no need to worry, sir," the pirate with the blaster said. "It's over." Since Caleb hadn't taken his gun, he tucked it back into a holster on his hip. "I know that armor. I served with Prince Hiro not long after Lord Crux gifted it to him. Hiro was a good man, and a better leader. It's a shame what the Legion did to him."

"Be quiet, Damian," the woman standing behind him hissed. "He was stranded in a Nightmare. He may be a Legionnaire himself."

"He's no Legionnaire," Damian replied, meeting Caleb's gaze through his faceplate.

"How do you know?"

"For one, Empress Lo'ane wouldn't let one of those inhuman monsters get their hands on her brother's gear. She'd melt it first. For another, I can see it in his eyes. He doesn't have the icy stare of an infected."

"You've fought the Legion before," Caleb surmised.

"Aye," Damian replied. "In one of the first battles of the war, a long time ago. On Atlas, the night after the Empress escaped."

"You're a Guardian?"

He smiled. "No. Only the ones who fled with her took that name. I stayed to fight. I planned to die. But the stars had other ideas."

"Are you loyal to the Empress?"

Damian laughed. "Now that depends. I can see you're

not with the Legion. And since you're wearing Hiro's armor, I assume you know the Empress, and she trusted you enough to loan it to you. What puzzles me is why you were on board a Nightmare. And you are out here all alone, with no sign of Her Majesty. Why is that?"

"I'm the one asking the questions here."

"You look like you have a lot of questions. But you aren't as in control as you think you are. That spot on your armor, just over your heart. It looks like one more blast will punch right through it." Caleb looked down to see how beaten and slagged the plates in the area were. Damian wasn't lying. By the time he looked up, the man had his pistol again in hand, aimed at the spot. "I had a choice between shooting you or Graystone. I decided on Graystone. But I'm not convinced I shouldn't—"

Caleb pivoted his shoulder toward Damian. The pirate's blast hit his armor, wide of the original mark. He didn't have time to fire a second round before Caleb grabbed his wrist, pushing his arm aside and kicking him in the ribs. Damian groaned as he fell onto the deck. Caleb stood over him, his sidearm aimed at the man's forehead.

"I guess I had that coming," Damian said, laughing. "Yeah, I'm loyal to the Empress. But loyalty doesn't get you anywhere these days, except locked up in a prison somewhere uncomfortable, mining ore in blazing heat. I got off Atlas by selling my soul. Thousands of my comrades weren't as lucky."

Caleb stared at Damian for a long moment before finally returning his gun to his thigh and offering the man his free hand. Damian accepted it, letting Caleb pull him back to his feet.

"I wish I could give you better news," he said. "Empress Lo'ane is dead. What's left of her Guardians are on the run. My friend and pilot, Abraham, is with them."

Damian's face fell. "So all hope is lost." His voice was

weak, his bravado vanishing. He squinted at Caleb. "So you ran away? What else could you do, right?"

"I'm not running away from the fight," Caleb replied. "I never have, and I won't start now. I intend to start a war of my own against Lord Crux."

"Oh yeah? You and what fleet?" Damian asked.

"Well, I started with that Nightmare out there…" He nodded at the forward surround. "…and in eight hours, I've already added the Gorgon."

Damian's grin spread wider. "So you intend to seize control of this ship?"

"Unless you or someone else on board wants to try again to stop me, I think I already have seized control."

"It's not quite that simple."

"Isn't it? It's a pirate ship. Don't tell me it has papers."

"I'll tell you something. You don't lack in confidence; that's for sure."

"I don't lack in motivation either. What I do lack is a second. Someone who knows their way around the galaxy. Especially the dark underbelly."

"You also lack funds," Damian said. "I may care if you want to preserve the Empire. Honestly, I haven't decided yet. But most of these spacers…" He gestured around him. "They're in it for the coin."

"I have a Nightmare I can sell. How long will that last me?"

Damian stared at him, an amused look on his otherwise hard face. "Long enough to do some damage, I imagine." He bit his lower lip before nodding to himself. "That you made it from your ship up the tow lines and all the way down here has given me a sense of hope for the first time in months." He considered Caleb a moment longer before taking a knee and bowing his head. "Master Sergeant Damian Uehara, at your service, uh…" He tipped his head back up just enough to meet Caleb's gaze, one eyebrow raised in query. "Who the bloody blazes are you, anyway?"

"Card. Captain Caleb Card."

"Captain Card," Damian raised his head and nodded. "When do we get started?"

# CHAPTER 7

Damian quickly introduced Caleb to the other three members of the bridge crew. Sasha, the comms operator who had been the first to surrender. Naya, from engineering, and Rufus, one of Gorgon's four helm officers. As a former Royal Marine, Damian had served under Graystone as tactical officer, handling the weapons systems and shields. It was primarily his work, with Caleb's help, that had allowed them to defeat the other pirate ship, who was a known entity to Graystone and his crew.

While the other crew seemed wary of Caleb, they approached him with what he perceived as a sense of relief. From what he had learned of Graystone from the other pirates and from what he had witnessed himself when the man shot his own first mate in the back, it was obvious he had been a heartless coward. They seemed glad to be rid of him.

"Judging by the condition of your armor, I'm sure you're itching to take a breather," Damian said once he had finished the introductions. "But I think it would be prudent for us not to linger here too long. While Graystone enjoyed pretending to be an escort for the Star Line Transport

Company, which clearly we are not, there are proper company escorts that move through this part of the system, running sweeps against outlaws like us. I'm sure that since we picked up on your distress call, they did too. We don't want to get into a scrap with them, especially in our current condition."

"What do you recommend? I know there's a planet a few days sub-light years from here."

"That might work for a ship with all its affairs in order. While Gorgon's records aren't tainted yet, every check against her identifier adds to the risk that the databases will sync and flag us for destruction."

"Is that how it works then, to steal a starship?"

"There's more than one way to steal a starship. But its the most common method for pirates. I wasn't with Graystone when he acquired Gorgon."

"I was," Rufus said. A younger man with a mop of blonde hair and dark brown eyes set in a cherubic face, he seemed unbothered by the memory. "That was about a year and a half ago. We were in a modified decommissioned freighter before then. A real rust bucket. We actually lured this ship in the same way you brought us here. Sent out a distress call. Reactor trouble. Failing life support. We practiced the ruse for a month before we ran it. Once a ship comes to help, you fake comms trouble, convince them to come on board. They're nervous the whole time but they also want to help, so they push past their hesitation. Once they're committed…" He raised his hand, snapping his fingers closed like the prongs of a trap. "And you've got 'em. You storm the samaritan, kill all souls on board, and stake your claim. It's a pretty common scam, so it takes a real convincing act to pull it off. Graystone actually shut off the engines and the oxygen flow to sell it. Two spacers died during the exercise, but we came away with a better upgrade than we ever imagined."

"Preying on a captain with a conscience," Caleb said.

Rufus shrugged. "Graystone was a monster, but he was a successful monster. You can pass whatever judgment you want, Captain Card. We all do what we need to do in order to survive. I doubt you're any different."

"I try to be different," Caleb replied. "But I've done some things I'm not proud of. Anyway, I'm not in a position to judge anyone right now. I don't care what you did under Graystone's command. As long as you follow my orders, I'm satisfied."

"As long as you keep paying me, I'm satisfied," Rufus shot back.

Caleb turned to Damian. "You say we should clear out of the area. Where do you suggest we go?"

"Space is a big, mostly empty place. The further you get from occupied planets, the more privacy you have. With that being said, if you aim to sell that Nightmare, your best bet is Aroon."

*Are you sure we can trust him?*

*You're raising an objection now?* Caleb asked silently, after Ishek had been mostly silent since they had entered the bridge.

*Better late than never.*

*I'm not sure we can trust anyone. But we also don't know enough about this place to get by without a little faith. He recognized the armor. He says he's loyal to the Empire. Is there a reason I shouldn't give him the benefit of the doubt?*

*Maybe because he's a pirate?*

*I doubt there are many job openings in Crux's society for people like Damian.*

*Possibly. But he's still a pirate. They're all pirates.*

*And we need them for the foreseeable future. I would think you'd feel right at home surrounded by killers and thieves.*

*I blame our bond.*

*You would.*

Caleb noticed Damian's expression shift during the moment of silence while he held his mental exchange with Ishek. He got the feeling the man had identified that he was carrying a symbiote after all, and he tensed, waiting for Damian to call him on it.

He didn't, remaining silent while Caleb helped himself to the command seat. "How long to Aroon?"

"Thirty-six hours," Rufus replied. "Give or take."

"What are we giving or taking?"

"Hyperspace travel isn't pinpoint, though I hear Infinity Cruises is looking into starting a racing league where timing and accuracy will play a hand in determining winners and losers. If they pull it off, I'll watch it. Anyway, pirates make their margins on the margins, if you know what I mean."

"I think I do. Thirty-six hours should give me plenty of time to get situated here."

"Captain, you may want to address the entire crew," Damian suggested. "So they know to stand down, if nothing else."

"I was getting to that, but thank you for the reminder." He glanced over each of the bridge officers. "Return to your stations. Rufus, set a course for Aroon."

"Aye, Captain," Rufus said, as each of them took their places.

Caleb sat back in the command seat, looking over its layout. A pair of swivel arms allowed him to bring a pair of touch displays into his lap, which snapped together magnetically once they were fitted together, creating a single wide view. A curved display rested just overhead, also on a swivel arm he could use to pull it down in front of his eyes, though for now he didn't know why he would want that.

"Damian, I'll need you to teach me how to use this interface when we have time."

"Aye, Captain," he replied. "Though you don't need to use it at all. If you bark the orders, we'll take care of everything you need."

"I still intend to learn. I don't mind delegating, but I don't like feeling helpless."

"I think you've already proven you're far from helpless, sir."

"Sasha, open shipwide comms," Caleb said.

"Aye, Captain." She turned away from him to tap on the interface at her station. "Comms open, Captain."

Caleb drew in a deep breath. What he'd accomplished by reaching the bridge and replacing Graystone hadn't fully sunken in yet. An hour ago, he'd been on a damaged ship, struggling to conserve air with little prospect of survival. Now he was the captain of a pirate ship. He hadn't decided whether that was a good thing.

*Would you rather be dead?*

*I'm just not sure how effectively I can counter Crux as an outlaw.*

*I think our best chance of countering Crux is as an outlaw. Knuckle up, Cal. This can be fun if you let it.*

Caleb smirked. In a more chaotic environment, he was better off relying on his symbiote's instincts. "Attention all hands. Attention all hands. This is your new captain speaking. I repeat, this is your new captain speaking. Some of you already know me. You surrendered to me in the cargo bay and passageways on my way to the bridge."

*Great start. Keep going.*

"Graystone is dead. I have control of the bridge, and the support of the officers to continue as his replacement. I understand you may feel confused by this sudden turn of events. First, a warning. Put any thoughts of mutiny out of your heads right now. If we crossed paths on my way up here, then you already know I can put down any insurrection. I will meet any efforts to seize control of this ship from me with harsh retribution. I reached the bridge on my own. I'm prepared to put down any challenges to my authority the same way. Rest assured, you'll continue to be paid under the terms of the agreements you made with Graystone, which I expect you to honor. That doesn't mean things won't change. Graystone and I don't share the same goals or desires. Nor the same methods to achieve them. For now, return to your regular stations. We'll be departing for Aroon shortly. I'll address you all again before we arrive."

Caleb looked at Sasha and nodded. She nodded back after she cut the comms.

*How was that?*

*Not bad. You didn't tell them your name.*

*They don't need to know my name. Not yet. The lack of familiarity will keep them from getting too comfortable.*

*True. You warned them, but someone will still try to take your place.*

*I know. We'll be ready for when they do.*

"Captain," Rufus said. "I've locked a course for Aroon. We're ready to go on your command, sir."

"Execute."

"Aye aye, Captain."

Caleb watched the hyperspace field form around Gorgon. The way the universe seemed to compress and bend had impressed him from the Nightmare's flight deck, watching from the outside. It mesmerized him now, eyes wide and jaw slack as reality curved around the starship.

"Hyperspace field complete. Thirty-six hours to drop."

"Damian, can you confirm the destination?" Caleb asked.

"What?" Rufus said, looking back over his shoulder. "Are you suggesting—"

"He doesn't know you from a pile of dung," Damian

said, coming to Caleb's defense. "He'd have to be an idiot to trust us right now."

"He asked you to check it. He trusts you."

"Maybe he does. Or maybe he's setting me up, too. He might not know how to work this ship's interface, but I'm pretty sure he knows how to read a star map. Don't you, Captain?"

Caleb nodded. "If either of you lie to me, I'll kill you before you can utter a pathetic excuse."

*Well spoken. You're a natural.*

Damian tapped on his station interface. A projection of the star map appeared in front of the forward surround, showing their course to Aroon. Most of the route would apparently carry them through empty space. "It looks good to me, Captain."

"Me, too," Caleb agreed. "Naya, I need full access permissions to all of Gorgon's systems, including secured hatches, data storage, and anything else that's currently locked down."

"Aye, Captain," she replied, turning her seat toward him, giving him his first good look at her. Waifish thin, with pale skin, hair dyed deep red, dark eyes and a sly smile. "You'll need to provide a retinal scan."

"No," Caleb answered. "I'll use a passcode."

"Retinal scanning provides faster, easier, and more secure access. There are no codes to remember."

"Passcode," he insisted. "With a three retry lockout."

She made a face as she turned back to her station. A moment later, the display across Caleb's lap changed, offering a numeric keyboard and a passcode entry field. "Enter whatever code you want, sir. It's encrypted from your station, so only you will ever know it."

"And you can't bypass it?" he asked as he typed in a six-digit code and saved it.

"I'm the systems officer. It's essential that I have root access."

"Did you give me root access?"

"No, Captain."

"Give me root access."

"Captain, it's unwise—"

"Do it," Caleb barked.

She tapped on her terminal. "I've given you root access, Captain."

"Good. Lock out navigation, accessible only with root access."

"You're locking us out of the helm?" Rufus questioned.

"I may not understand everything about flying a starship at faster-than-light speed, but one thing I know is that humans can't do it. Only computers can. Which means we're on autopilot right now. You don't need the helm. Damian, what's standard operating procedure for the bridge crew during hyperspace travel?"

"Graystone liked to give us other duties, depending on his mood and how much he hated us at the moment."

"Like scrubbing the heads?"

"That's one example."

Rufus' chin dropped to his chest, waiting for the order. He flinched when Caleb said his name.

"Rufus, Sasha, if your duties are complete, you're dismissed. Enjoy some time off."

"Really?" Rufus asked, his head snapping up in surprise.

"Unless you'd like to be part of the cleaning detail." He pointed to where Graystone and his first officer lay dead on the deck. "Someone needs to take out the garbage."

Rufus shook his head as he stood. "Permission to be dismissed, Captain?" he asked.

"Granted," Caleb replied.

Sasha stood as well, nodding to him before joining Rufus, exiting the bridge.

"This isn't your first command," Damian stated.

"No, but it is my first civilian command," he replied. "It's not the same."

"It's not that different, when you break it down. You usually get a little more lip from the subordinates, but I'm sure you can keep them in line."

"I need a detail to take care of the mess I made getting up here."

"I'll take care of it. Just a minute." He tapped behind his ear. "Bones," he said, pausing for a moment. "Our new captain asked me to put together a detail to dispose of the dead. See that it's done." He tapped behind his ear again before looking at Caleb. "It'll all be spic and span by chow time, Captain."

"I thought they called him Bones because he's so thin," Caleb said.

"Oh, you met him on the way up? That, too. He's a jack-of-all-trades, owing to the number of years he's been a pirate."

"How many corpses did Graystone create as commander?"

"Only a few. Mainly spacers who wanted to break their contracts and wouldn't take no for an answer."

"It seems strange to me that pirates would have legally binding contracts."

Damian smiled. "There's nothing legal or binding about them. But they help minimize ambiguity, which reduces conflict, which leads to a less chaotic working environment. Which ultimately benefits the captain."

Caleb returned his smile. "Right. I'll review a sample of the contracts later. Like you said, I'm itching to get out of this armor and clean up. I assume Graystone's quarters will meet my needs."

"The nicest quarters on the ship, of course," Damian answered.

"Captain, what would you like me to do?" Naya asked.

"How good are you at hacking?"

"Hacking is illegal, sir," she deadpanned, drawing a laugh from both Ishek and Caleb.

"But are you good at it?"

"I've dabbled, but I'm no professional."

"Do you think you could break into Graystone's private electronics? Maybe find your way into his bank accounts?"

Her sly smile spread wider, becoming even more sly. "Possibly. It depends."

"On what?"

"Two things. One, how much of the take I get to keep. Two, how you feel about me cutting out a dead man's eye."

He grinned back at her. "Does thirty percent sound fair?"

"Forty sounds more fair."

"Thirty-five?"

"Thirty-seven."

"Deal."

"No guarantees, Captain. I'm just as liable to get his accounts locked."

"It's zero risk from my perspective. Nothing ventured, nothing gained."

"I like the way you think. Thank you, sir."

Caleb turned back to Damian. "I'm eager to see Graystone's quarters. Lead the way."

# CHAPTER 8

"You'll learn the layout pretty quickly once you've been here a day or two," Damian said as he led Caleb and Naya off the bridge. They worked their way around the corner on the port side, opposite to the way he had approached. "Gorgon has twelve decks, eight at the aft, split above and below the reactors and internal thruster components, plus the hyperspace drive. You probably noticed the bow is wedge-shaped. The nose is a single compartment that houses most of the sensors, including one of the four high-speed arrays that allow quick triangulation and estimation for the targeting computers. Obviously, Gorgon has too many guns for any human to operate efficiently, so as tactical officer, my job is to ensure the equipment is functional and the solutions are optimal."

"How do you do that?" Caleb asked. "You just said targeting is automated."

"With an override so we can adjust tactics. It's more useful in scrapes involving smaller spacecraft or swarms."

"Swarms?"

"Drone ships. Pretty self explanatory, I think."

"Yeah, I get it."

"Anyway, crew quarters are amidships, lower decks for grunts, upper decks for officers. But we aren't military, so don't let the descriptions fool you. Quarters are determined by pay grades, seniority, and superiority."

"Superiority?"

"It's not uncommon for the crew to challenge one another for racks," Naya explained. "If they're challenge-able. My quarters, for example, aren't available to anyone else under any circumstances."

"Even if you quit or die?"

"If I quit or die, someone would need to replace me. They would get my quarters, not some uneducated deck worm."

"Should I expect a lot of fighting among the crew?"

"Not really. Most of these blokes know their place. The pecking order's pretty well established."

They turned the corner at the outside edge of the bridge's bulkhead, coming to a stop in front of a dozen crew members headed by a greasy brute a good head taller than Caleb. The group blocked the passageway, their eyes all fixed on Caleb.

"Speaking of pecking order," Naya muttered behind him.

*You only get one first impression.*

*Thanks for the reminder*, Caleb replied, locking eyes with the big man. "Can I help you?"

"We came to see the new captain. Me and my boys, we was thinking about making him the old captain." He grinned widely, revealing a row of metal where his bottom teeth should have been.

"I see," Caleb replied, looking past him. "You're going to need more boys."

The entire group laughed. "Is that right?" the behemoth asked, turning his attention to Damian. "You should back away, Sarge. You too, Nye. I don't want to get any blood—"

His voice faded as the ion blast from Caleb's pistol ripped through the front of his face, burning out his eyes and reaching his brain. He was dead before he hit the deck with a deep thud.

*Perfectly executed. I have been rubbing off on you.*

Caleb sensed Ishek's mirth as his eyes swept across the group of pirates assembled in front of him, returning the sidearm to his thigh with a quick flick of his wrist. "I warned you all about attempting to mutiny," he said, his voice soft and frigid. "Any of you want to join your friend here?" He casually kicked the sole of the dead man's boot. "Or are you more interested in earning coin?"

The pirates looked at one another, and as a group, they each lowered themselves to a knee, silently offering their allegiance.

"Don't cross me again," Caleb warned sharply. "I won't be so benevolent next time." He and Damian started to go around them, Naya close behind. Caleb stopped. Damian and Naya pulled up short, silently waiting for him as he turned back around. "And since you all helped make this mess," he added, the eleven spacers rising and turning to face him, "I expect you to clean it up."

"Aye, Captain," one of them said.

Smirking, Damian shook his head, obviously amused by their stupidity. He resumed leading Caleb and Naya down the corridor, turning right at the junction midway down. It was a mirror image of the other side, with a lift placed at the end of the short corridor. "You'll need to enter your passcode to open the doors," he said. "Graystone used this as his private cab."

Caleb approached the control panel, using the keypad to type in his code. The pad flashed green and the doors to the lift opened. "Where to?" he asked, stepping inside.

"Up one deck, then we'll come back around in this same direction."

"So Graystone's quarters are directly over the bridge?"

"Yes, sir. At the front of the officer's berthing, inside the EHZ."

"What does EHZ stand for?" Caleb asked, directing the lift up to Deck Five.

"Emergency Hardened Zone. In the event of a catastrophic breach, heavy blast doors seal off the interior of the ship, including the bridge."

"My ship had something like that," Caleb said.

"The Nightmare?" Naya asked, obviously surprised.

"No. My ship before that. It was destroyed, but the secondary defenses saved the lives of me and my crew."

"I'd like to hear more of that story."

"So would I," Damian agreed. "I'm more than a little curious about how you came to be stranded in a damaged Nightmare."

"It's a long story for another time."

"Of course, Captain. By the way, I'm impressed with how you handled that situation back there with Targan. It's a shame to lose one of our best boarding crew leaders, but you didn't give any quarter, and your response will have a ripple effect across the rest of the ship."

"I'm not looking for your approval, Damian," Caleb replied, a little more harshly than he intended.

However, the other man seemed to take it in stride. "Aye, Captain."

The cab doors opened on Five, revealing a passageway identical to the one on Six. Though he didn't need Damian to guide him, Caleb followed him around to the front. Instead of twin doors, the compartment had only a single thick hatch which again required his passcode to open. He typed it in and stepped back as the hatch swung outward on a silent hinge.

Looking inside, the living space was in line with his expectations. Comfortable but understated, a full suite complete with bedroom, galley, and head. Painted a slightly brighter gray than the passageway metal, there was a desk on one side, a sofa on the other, a small bar behind it with two rows of different alcohols, glasses, what he assumed was an icemaker, and a sink. A tablet computer rested next to the ship's terminal on the desk, the wiring suggesting they were connected to the same long, curved, semi-transparent display.

"Graystone was a slob," Caleb commented, his attention shifting to the floor, where food wrappers, empty booze bottles, dirty cups, and multiple articles of clothing littered a relatively plush carpet. The bed was unmade, and used towels blocked the threshold between the living area and head, preventing the door from closing.

"He never allowed anyone in his quarters unless he was present," Naya said. "And when he was here and didn't want to be alone, the only company he desired was female."

Caleb noticed after she said it that not all the clothes on the floor could have belonged to the former captain. "I see. Do you know who he was intimate with?"

"Is that important?"

"If they had an emotional attachment, they may be next in line to want to kill me."

"Anyone Graystone was intimate with got paid for the sacrifice. He didn't endear himself to anyone. I'm not even sure he knew how to feel or even show affection or allegiance of any kind."

"So how did he end up in his position?"

"Like Rufus explained, he was the best I've ever seen at pulling off a scam. He convinced the right members of the crew to support him and seized control with only a single shot fired."

"Right into Captain Jones' temple," Damian added.

"Let me guess, Targan was one of his lackeys."

Naya nodded. "Him and his away team, the Berserkers. They made sure no one complained when Graystone took over."

"That explains why they were unhappy about my emergence." Caleb entered the quarters, kicking the garbage on the floor into a heap as he passed it on his way to the desk. He picked up Graystone's tablet and tapped on the screen. Of course, it was secured.

"You and Graystone were the only ones with access to this suite, correct?" he asked Naya.

"That's right."

"He trusted you not to come in here uninvited?"

"He didn't trust anyone. I had to be on the bridge or verifiably in the officer's berthing whenever he wasn't in his quarters. Which was sometimes a real pain in the ass. I might have chosen a less traditional lifestyle than your typical sysops engineer, but I take my job seriously. I would never betray or break the trust of my captain or my crew."

"So you're suggesting I should trust you?"

"I'm saying that you can trust me. That doesn't mean you will."

"From my experience, it's challenging to make it through life trusting no one," Damian said. He had continued Caleb's process of gathering up the debris on the floor into a pile. "I can have a few spacers clean this place up for you, Captain."

"No, I'll take care of it," Caleb replied. "At least until I get to know more of the crew."

"Understood."

Caleb handed Graystone's tablet to Naya. "Your job is to get through the security and gain access to everything on this tablet, by any means necessary."

"Aye, Captain," she replied, taking it. "I keep thirty-seven percent of whatever coin I can recover, right?"

"I just handed that to you knowing that you could open

it up, withhold half of whatever you found, and then bring it to me claiming you hadn't taken half. What you don't know is whether I would know if you were lying. I'm willing to trust you, but you need to earn it."

Her face flushed, and he wondered if she had intended to do exactly what he had said before he said it. "Aye, Captain."

*Are you sure you weren't born to be a pirate?*

Caleb almost smiled at Ishek's comment. "With that said, I have nothing to hide, and if you're the only one with access to this suite, I'll know who's responsible if anything were to go missing. We can disregard whatever procedures Graystone had in place."

She nodded. "Thank you, sir."

"You're dismissed, Naya."

She nodded again and left the room with the tablet.

"Are you sure that was a good idea?" Damian asked once she was gone.

"To let her walk out with Graystone's personal device? Not one hundred percent. But since whatever's on it doesn't belong to me anyway, I haven't really lost anything."

"You have an interesting perspective." He paused. "Captain, I assume you wanted to speak to me privately. Perhaps you noticed—"

"We both know I'm a host to a Relyeh," Caleb said bluntly. "Ishek is my Advocate. A more advanced form of khoron. He's also my subordinate."

*I hate when you call me that.*

"That's impossible," Damian said.

"I thought you might say that. But you also said yourself that I don't have the look of someone who's not in control of their own faculties." He reached for the clasps on his combat armor, beginning to undo them.

"Who are you?" Damian questioned. "And where did you come from?"

"Are you familiar with Earth?"

"Only in legend. Some people say that's where we're originally from. There's a rusting hulk of a decommissioned starship on Atlas. They say it brought us to the Spiral."

"You don't believe it?"

"They say the ship carried a colony inside, and traversed the stars for hundreds of years. But it has no hyperspace drive, and there's no planet matching Earth's description within ten-thousand light years. So how could that be? Beyond that, there are no official accounts or records anywhere on the hypernet. Only stories and myths."

"And nothing more about Earth?"

He shook his head. "To me, its just another name for another planet. Nothing more."

"Your hypernet doesn't have photos from Earth? Archival footage from Pathfinder? Anything?"

"No. Nothing."

*Interesting. It seems as if someone is trying to erase the history of humankind's arrival in this galaxy.*

*But to what end? And why leave Pathfinder intact if that's the case?* Caleb wondered. *Could it have anything to do with Benning's discoveries and the presence of the khoron?*

*That seems likely.*

"Well, I can tell you that Earth is real," Caleb said. "And that Pathfinder originated from there, two hundred years ago."

"Pathfinder has been on Atlas for over two hundred years."

"Two days ago, I was millions of light years away, responding to a distress call from Pathfinder. We discovered evidence that the ship intentionally entered a wormhole, though we don't yet know why. The Relyeh attacked my ship. They forced us to enter the same wormhole to escape. It delivered us on the far side of a dwarf star orbited by the planet Galatin."

Damian didn't look convinced. "I'm familiar with the planet. You're telling me that Lo'ane was there all this time?"

"From the day she fled Atlas ahead of Crux's assault."

"If I had known, I could have joined her there."

"And possibly led Crux right to her."

"You said she's dead. It sounds like Crux found her, anyway."

"One of her own people betrayed her. Do you know General Haas?"

"Aye. He wouldn't turn against her, if that's what you're thinking."

"It crossed my mind."

"Uncross it. Haas is as loyal as they come."

"What about Colonel Chambers?"

"I don't know him as well."

"Help me with my armor?" Caleb asked, having finished undoing the clasps. He turned his back on Damian, who took hold of the armor, allowing Caleb to step out of it.

"Interesting choice of underlay," Damian said, seeing him in his stained and sweaty scrubs.

"Like I said, it's a long story," Caleb replied while the other man laid the battle-worn suit on the carpet. The stains it left would join the dozens of others already on the fibers. Turning to face Damian, he lifted his shirt. "This is Ishek."

Damian looked at the symbiote, flinching in obvious disgust. "I have to be honest, Captain. My instinct is to kill it, and you."

"That's understandable."

"You said some of the Empress' retinue escaped. Why didn't you escape with them? Come to think of it, the sector of space where we found you is beyond the range of a

Nightmare." His eyes remained glued to Ishek until Caleb lowered his shirt. "What aren't you telling me, Captain?"

Caleb's jaw tensed. "The truth is, I'm a stranger in a strange land here, Damian. I have so many more questions than answers, but I'm doing my best to catch up. I understand Crux is nearly finished usurping the Empire. What about the Relyeh and the khoron? Beyond forming the backbone of Crux's Legion, where do they fit in? How much do you know about them?"

Damian's brow furrowed. "You say khoron and Relyeh as if they're two separate things."

He had suspected the people here didn't know the difference when speaking to Marley. Now he had confirmation. "They are. Very different. The Relyeh conquered Earth. They're the reason Pathfinder even existed to bring your ancestors here. Khoron are only one of countless species under their flag."

The other man's face paled. "You mean there are more than them out there?"

"They've conquered huge portions of the universe. Destroyed unimaginable numbers of intelligent life forms. That khoron might be here without a more powerful Relyeh commanding them is hard for me to believe." He paused, having reached the moment of truth. "Even harder, because one of them seized control of Ishek and me back on Galatin. He used us to kill the Empress."

Damian stood there staring at him, obviously stunned. Caleb was ready to defend himself in the event the worn veteran attacked him. Instead, he seemed to age a dozen years in an instant, his shoulders slumping. "That explains why they left you stranded. You want Naya to earn your trust, but you can't be trusted yourself."

"I didn't have to tell you the truth. By being honest, I knew I might lose the only indigenous ally I have in this galaxy, but lying to you won't earn me your trust. My body killed the Empress. My mind didn't, and neither did Ishek's. I intend to set things right, and make up for what happened as best I can."

"But you don't know who this Relyeh is, or if he might possess you again."

"Which is another reason I needed you to know the truth. You need to monitor me. If I become a danger, you know what to do. Don't kill me if you don't have to, but if you do—"

"I will."

Feeling Ishek's shudder, Caleb nodded, his look grim. "Just keep in mind, if you kill me, I can't help either you or Haas. I was also hoping you might shed some light on who or what this being might be before I run into him or it again."

"I don't know. I wish I did. It would be easier for me to believe you. I want to believe you, Captain. We need help. A lot of help. And if you can give us that—"

"Then you should take what you can get." Caleb smiled. "Me and Ishek."

Damian grinned back. "Maybe you're right. What can I do to help?"

"Right now, use whatever pull you have with the crew to keep them in line while I get settled. I need to shower, eat, and sleep for starters. Does the ship have a data store with information I can pull on Lord Crux, the war, and the Spiral? I need to get up to speed on this place as quickly as I can."

"I'm afraid Graystone wasn't much of an intellect. The only thing he kept cached on the ship was entertainment, and not the kind I think you'd be interested in right now. But I can summarize things and get you off the ground."

"Like where I can find the mess and a change of clothes?"

"Since Graystone's clothes won't fit you, I'll have some

brought up. Your galley should have some decent snacks, but if you don't see anything you like or Graystone already ate everything, the officer's mess is out your front door and straight down the passageway about fifty steps, on your left. The communal head is on the right, next to the fitness center."

Caleb's eyebrows shot up. "We have a fitness center?"

"Two of them. The one up here is smaller, but it's also nicer. The officer's quarters surround the common areas. My quarters are on the starboard side. Just make a right out your door, I'm the first one."

"I'll try not to bother you when you're in your quarters."

Damien reached behind his ear, peeling off a small black disc Caleb hadn't noticed. "Take this. It's a comms device. Just say the name of whoever you want to talk to and wait a couple of seconds."

"Not bad," Caleb said, accepting the disc and placing it behind his ear. It stuck easily to his skin. "Don't you need it?"

"I'll have Naya transfer that one to you and pick up a new one of my own. I figure she's on the bridge by now, trying to position Graystone's eye in front of the tablet while Bones waits to collect the body."

"Then you better hurry down there before she finishes," Caleb said.

"I'll holler out to you when Naya's done with the setup. Is there anything else you need from me right now?"

"No. Thank you, Damian."

He nodded. "You seem like a good man, Captain Card. It's been hard to believe in anything these last few years, the last six months especially. But I find myself believing in you despite my reservations."

"I'll do my best not to let you down."

"Aye, Captain."

Damian saw himself out, leaving Caleb standing in front of Graystone's, or rather, *his* desk.

*Rags to riches.*

"We're just getting started."

*Hopefully, you didn't just get us killed.*

# CHAPTER 9

"Captain, do you copy?" Damian's voice echoed inside Caleb's skull, the transmitter patch conducting the signal directly to his inner ear.

"Loud and clear," Caleb replied.

"Obviously, your comms are active. Naya also wanted you to know that she's already bypassed the tablet's password protection. Apparently, Graystone liked passwords with lockouts too. Getting access to the sensitive data will be more difficult now."

"At least when it comes to his coin," Caleb said. "I'm not surprised. Am I going to have issues paying the crew?"

"We'll reach Aroon before it becomes a problem."

"Great. Besides the Nightmare, is there anything else we can sell when we get there? I noticed a big gold dragon statue in the hold when I slipped in."

"Aroon is more of a scrap hub. They won't have much interest in artwork. You can probably find a buyer but you'll only get a tenth of what it's worth."

"Where did Graystone get it?"

"We robbed a private luxury yacht six weeks ago. The

owner was foolish enough to send it through the sector unaccompanied."

"I still don't understand how pirating in space works, exactly. Given the distances and velocities."

"I assume you don't have piracy where you come from."

"Not in space. We only have a handful of ships, and they only travel between Earth and Proxima Centauri, which is where I live when I'm not being thrown across the universe in a wormhole."

Damian laughed. "I thought you said the Relyeh conquered Earth."

"They did, but we fought back. Two ends of the galaxy, and we're at war with them in both."

"It must be hard for you. A life spent fighting, with no escape."

"It's what I signed up for. To defend what I believe in. Freedom foremost. Being a slave to a khoron isn't my definition of freedom."

"Mine either," Damian agreed. "But I gave up." His voice over the comms suggested embarrassment and regret.

"Maybe. But you're still breathing. You can still make a difference."

"I already have," he replied, voice strengthening. "I know you're tired and hungry. I don't want to keep you. Clothes should be up any moment now."

A buzz from a speaker near the door drew Caleb's attention. "They just arrived. We'll speak again soon."

"Yes, sir."

Caleb tapped the comms patch to disconnect and made his way to the door. A panel on the inside allowed him to open it. He stood on the other side, askew from the entrance and ready to act, just in case the delivery person had any ideas about becoming the next captain.

"Captain, Sarge asked me to bring these up to you."

Looking past the edge of the door, Caleb spotted a girl of no more than eleven, with short blonde hair, pale skin, and a heart-shaped face, dressed in dirty coveralls and pushing a cart stacked with clothing. He could sense Ishek's amusement, slightly embarrassed himself for setting himself to fight a little girl. Of course, Damian wouldn't send up someone he didn't trust.

*Don't feel too bad. She might still be hiding a shotgun beneath the shirts. Or a poisoned blade.*

*Shut up,* Caleb replied. He checked the pile of clothing for any hint of a weapon and looked past the girl to ensure she was alone before stepping fully into the open. "Hello," he said, offering a warm smile. "I'm Caleb. And you are?"

"Linx," she replied. "You're the new Captain, then?"

"I am."

"I heard you killed forty spacers in five minutes."

*A bit of an exaggeration, don't you think?*

"Not that many. And I didn't enjoy it."

"Why not? You're enjoying being captain now, aren't you?"

*I like her.*

"I tried to negotiate with Captain Graystone. He wasn't interested. And the ten spacers I did kill were trying to kill me. I acted in self defense."

"Uh-huh," she said, disinterested in his reasoning. "I can see why you needed new clothes. Those threads are awful."

"I didn't realize the ship had any children on it," Caleb said. "Did you talk to Graystone like that?"

Her mood darkened. "I stayed far away from Graystone." She looked up at him, teasing a hint of a smile. "Sarge says you're nothing like him. It should be a nice change."

Caleb stepped forward, putting his hand on the opposite end of the cart. "I can take things from here. Thank you for dropping this off."

"Aye, Captain," she replied. "See you around."

Lexi waved and skipped off to the right, back toward the crew lift. Caleb pulled the cart inside and closed the door. Bringing it to the bedroom, he made a face at the bed when he saw the dirty sheets stained with sweat. "I should have asked for fresh sheets, too."

*Pirates don't need clean sheets.*

"This isn't the high seas of Eighteenth Century Earth. We don't need to live like animals." He opened the door to a small closet, revealing a wardrobe half-filled with identical uniforms and underwear, all too small for him, as he expected. He collected it all and dropped it in the pile with the other dirty clothes and garbage. He took his time setting out the new clothes. Damian must have given Linx free reign on what sort of things to collect, or maybe it was all they had available in his size.

He ended up with a random assortment of shirts, pants, and coats that would have him blending in with the rest of the crew in no time. Reconsidering Graystone's uniforms, it was obvious the man wanted everyone to know he was important on sight. But this wasn't the military. On a ship like this, he wanted the crew to know he was important by his actions and the respect he showed them. Not by dressing like a snooty aristocrat.

He also found clean sheets at the bottom of the cart, and he silently thanked both Damian and Linx for their thoughtfulness.

Picking out a simple red shirt and black pants from the closet, along with ankle-high magboots and underwear, he moved to the head, kicking the towels out of the way of the door, which closed automatically behind him. The room was only large enough for a toilet and a small shower, both technologically equivalent to what he was accustomed to on ships from Earth, though he imagined all the water used was recycled in a closed loop.

He had to pick up a pair of women's underwear and an empty wine bottle from the stall before he could use it, adding that to the growing trash heap in the suite's front. His scrubs went onto the pile too. He hesitated before using the electric razor he found to shave, submitting only because it rested in a sterilizing liquid and he disliked the stubble he'd grown.

*You can take the man out of the military, but you can't take the military out of the man.*

"I'm still in the military," Caleb replied, getting dressed.

*There's no Centurion Space Force here. When they don't hear from you, they'll assume you're dead. And since there may be no way back, you're a civilian now. Dead to one side of the galaxy. Reborn in another.*

"I'm not ready to accept there's no way back," Caleb said. Returning to the front of the suite, he crouched over his combat armor, retrieving Benning's data chip. "We need to find a device that can read this."

*And someone who can decipher the math.*

"You don't think you can figure it out?"

*Perhaps, given enough time and full control of your meat sack.*

"I hate when you call it that."

*I know.*

Caleb felt what amounted to Ishek's version of a snicker. "You need to take your petty acts of rebellion where you can get them, I guess. Naya might set me up with a reader. Maybe she's good at math, too." He put the chip on the desk. He could deal with that later. His stomach needed some attention first.

Entering the galley, he found a pile of dirty dishes on the small counter and more garbage shoved into the corner by the cabinets. Checking those cabinets, he found a small stash of energy bars and little else. It wasn't the meal he'd hoped for, but he wasn't that picky. He wolfed down half of them, only to find there was nothing to wash them down with except wine or water from the sink in the head. He chose the water, retrieving a cup from the bar and filling it straight out of the tap. It tasted cleaner than he expected, and he refilled the cup a dozen times, only then realizing how parched he had become.

Finally, he retired to the bedroom, ripping off the old sheets and replacing them before falling on top of the mattress. Firm and supportive, he was out before he even tried to fall asleep.

He didn't know how much later he awoke to a loud shout in his ear. "Captain, it's Damian. I'm outside your quarters. We have a situation."

# CHAPTER 10

"What kind of situation?" Caleb asked, sliding off the bed.

"Best to bring your sidearm, and that sword of yours," Damian replied, the answer raising the hairs on Caleb's arms.

*What the hell is going on?* He questioned silently.

*It sounds like a good time. There was a reason you went to bed fully dressed.*

Caleb paused beside his armor, detaching his pistol from its magnetic hold on the thigh and picking up the overlay to withdraw Hiro's blade. He still wasn't that comfortable with the weapon despite the brute force with which he used it, but he understood it would present him as more menacing.

*How long was I asleep?*

*Four hours.*

It felt like four minutes. *It'll have to do.*

He hurried to the door, wary that Damian's emergency might be a trap. What if a group of spacers had grabbed him and forced this emergency?

He opened the door, sword ready to swing, gun at his side but in position to fire akimbo if needed. He exhaled his relief when he saw Damian was alone. The older man looked the same as the last time Caleb had seen him, only now he was carrying a gun.

"What's happening?" Caleb asked.

"There's a brawl in the crew quarters," Damian replied. "Seems two groups of idiots are fighting over which one gets to kill you and replace you with their pick."

"Are you serious? Naya said the pecking order was well-defined."

"You disrupted the pecking order by killing Graystone."

"As I recall, it was you who pulled the trigger."

Damian shrugged. "He deserved it."

"Deck Four?" Caleb asked.

"Aye."

They hurried to Caleb's personal lift. The cab was already on the deck, waiting for him. "Why didn't you stay on Four and ping me on the comms?" he asked as they stepped inside.

"I was up here, same as you," Damian replied. "About to get some shut-eye. Linx hollered at me to get down to crew berthing to put a stop to it before someone gets killed. I needed backup."

"So you picked me?"

"You're military. I can only say that about eleven other people on this ship."

"Out of how many?"

"Close to two hundred."

The lift carried them down two decks. The moment the doors opened, Caleb heard the shouted insults, the sound of flesh pounding flesh mixed with screams and the crack of furniture thrown against bulkheads.

"No gunshots," he said. "That's a good sign."

"Most of the crew isn't allowed access to guns," Damian replied. "The ones you killed were part of the boarding crews."

"Like Targan?"

"Aye. I'll bet your ass the Berserkers are one of the two groups mixing it up."

"And after I warned them, too. Did they not think I would hear about this?"

"I don't think they were planning to get into a fight with another faction over it."

*Can I please take over?*

*Why?*

*I haven't taken part in a good brawl since I became your Advocate.*

*Maybe next time.*

He could sense Ishek's disappointment.

*There won't be a next time.*

*There won't be a this time. I don't plan to join the brawl. I plan to stop it.*

*Has anyone ever told you that you're no fun?*

*Besides you? Not since my last girlfriend before I joined the Corps. She thought I was obsessed with the military.*

*You are.*

Caleb and Damian rounded the corner to the passageway leading into the crew's common area. Linx stood nearby with a pretty woman Caleb assumed was her mother, both watching the activity with obvious disdain and concern.

*How I love the smell of rioting in the morning.*

Looking down the passageway, through breaks in the crowd of looky loos, he saw enough of the melee to distinguish between the two groups of men tangled up with each other. They may not have had access to guns, but they had makeshift shivs, and beyond fists, they were swinging everything from blackjacks to hammers. Blood flew, already pooling around two men who laid on the deck, either dead or out cold. A loud shout, and another man fell out of the door to the mess, suggesting the fighting had spilled over into that compartment as well.

"Step aside," Damian growled, reaching out to part the onlookers. The initial rank-and-file pirates scrambled quickly out of their way, creating an aisle for them to pass through. Engrossed in the fight, the onlookers in the front stood their ground. "Come on." Damian shoved a couple out of his way. "Captain coming through. Move aside." Still wailing away on each other, the brawlers didn't notice Damian and Caleb even when they reached the edge of the fray.

Pinching his lips into a tight line and pressing his tongue against his teeth, Caleb let out a shrill whistle that quickly got everyone's attention. When they saw him standing there armed with a gun and of all things, a sword, they first froze in place and then broke apart to size Caleb up. Even the combatants in the mess reacted to the whistle, the sounds of fighting in there abating, a couple of men even poking their heads out of the open hatch to take stock of what was happening out in the passageway..

"Who the hell gave you permission to start a fight on my ship?" Caleb barked to the nearest fighter in his best drill instructor tone.

"N...nobody," the stunned man replied.

"Nobody what?" Caleb growled, getting in his face. "I don't know how this ship was run this morning, but this evening, it's run by a man who demands respect for himself from his crew and for each other."

"Nobody, Captain," the man restated.

Caleb turned toward the mess. "Everyone in the mess, I want you out here now!" He turned back to the others. "All of you, form into lines in front of me, six to a line. The faster you do it, the less likely I am to shoot someone. And if you don't believe I'll be happy to put a bullet in one of you idiots, go ask Targan how he's feeling. Oh, that's right, you can't, because he's dead."

The men who were with Targan when Caleb shot him moved the quickest, but the others didn't lag either. In less than thirty seconds, the brawlers had created four ragged lines, the last one with only two spacers in it.

Caleb glared at them, making sure his gaze landed on each pirate's eyes, burning there until the spacer looked away. He didn't speak until he had forced them all to silently submit.

"Sarge informs me that a disagreement over who would get to replace me once you all mutinied precipitated the cause of this pathetic scene of violent stupidity." He stepped up to the men at the end of the first row. "Is that right, spacer?"

The man hesitated, unwilling to admit their plans to the intended victim.

"I suggest you speak up," Caleb hissed, placing the blade of his sword lightly against the side of the man's neck. "I don't have all night."

"Aye, Captain," he answered. "That…that was the plan."

Caleb removed the sword and backed up a step. "And which of you sad excuses for a human being came up with this idea?" Of course, none of them confessed. Caleb didn't expect them to. He looked at the group again, locking eyes with the pirates he identified from the corridor with Targan. "I know for a fact I warned some of you about crossing me again. And I know who you are. Are you all brain damaged? Did humankind suffer a mental de-evolution that I somehow missed? Did you actually think you could get away with something so utterly uninspired? Do you even know why I'm so angry right now?"

"Be…because we were planning to kill you?" one of the female brawlers offered, licking her split lip.

"No," Caleb replied. "I've never felt a shred of concern that any of you could even get close enough to me to lay the tip of your pinkie on me without my permission. You're not even smart enough to follow one of the first rules of war. Do you know what that rule is?"

The group was silent for a few seconds until a weak voice piped up from the back. "Know your enemy, Captain?"

"Who said that?" Caleb said. "Step forward." The man moved forward from the group. The smallest of the bunch and slightly built, he already had a black eye and bloody nose. Considering the man's size, it surprised Caleb he was still alive. "What's your name?"

"Reginald Haverstrom the Second," the man answered. "My mates call me Strom."

"Well, I'm certainly never calling you Reginald Haverstrom the second, either," Caleb remarked, drawing a laugh from much of the crowd. "But you're right. Know your enemy. We have one person in this group with at least half a brain cell. Although…" He pinned Strom with a direct look. "…you knew the rule, but you didn't follow it, so maybe I'm wrong. Know your enemy!" He repeated, shaking his head. "You all know absolutely nothing about me. You don't know where I came from. You don't know why I was stranded on a damaged Nightmare. You don't even know how old I am. The one thing you know is that I climbed a grappling cable without oxygen to get on board this ship and then killed ten of you, plus Targan, plus Captain Graystone. And yet you still thought trying to kill me would be a good idea." He exhaled sharply, shaking his head again. "No, Strom. The reason I'm mad is that I already warned a handful of people in this group that if they started trouble again, it wouldn't go well for them. And now that they've started trouble again, I have no choice but to follow through with my threat. Otherwise, I look weak. And I'm anything but weak. Do you understand?"

"Aye, Captain," Strom said.

Caleb looked at the others. "Do you understand?" he shouted.

"Aye, Captain," they snapped back as one.

"That's what I call progress," Caleb said.

*Oh, this is going to be good. I wish I was less satiated.*

"If you were with Targan outside the bridge, come forward now," Caleb said.

Nobody moved.

"I know who you are. If you don't come to me, I'll come to you." He shifted his sword threateningly in his hand.

The two-time offenders moved forward, while others moved back to fill in the gaps, maintaining the six rows, though now the first row had eight and the second row, only three.

"What should I do with you?" Caleb wondered out loud as he walked the lines, challenging each of them with his gaze. "This is *my* ship. You are *my* crew. I know what I'm tempted to do." He shifted the sword again. "And I know I need to do something." He turned back to Strom. "What do you think?"

"M…me, Captain?"

"You, Strom. What should I do with this lot?"

"I…I don't know, sir."

"Strom, you can correct me if I'm wrong. But you look like the sort of person who's been bullied a lot. Pushed around. Forced into things you didn't want to do. Maybe you joined one of these groups for protection. Maybe they treat you like garbage anyway, and you secretly despise them for it. This is your chance to get even, Strom. I have to punish them. If you were captain, what would you do?"

Strom eyed the repeat offenders, his eyes betraying his emotions. A tense silence settled over the entire assembly, waiting for his reply. "I...I'm not the captain, Captain. And I don't want to be the captain."

Caleb smiled. "That's an excellent answer, from someone who knows his place in the pecking order. You know not to piss where you sleep." He turned back to the others. "You could all learn a thing or two from Reggie here. Except you don't learn, do you?"

"P...please don't kill us, Captain," a woman in the first row said. "We're sorry. I...I'm sorry."

"Please, Captain," a man in the second row said.

"Please," a third added, then a fourth, until all eleven were begging for their lives.

Caleb backed up to Damian and leaned close to his ear. "What's the cruelest thing I can do to them without killing them?" he asked softly.

*No killing?*

"Well, the waste tanks could probably use a good interior scrub," he replied, smirking, his chest shaking with silent laughter.

"Thank you," Caleb said. Turning back around to face the Errant Eleven, he slapped the flat of his sword's blade against his pant leg. "If I were Graystone," he told them, "I know all of you would already be on your way out an airlock. But I'm not Graystone. I'm Captain Caleb Card, and I believe in mutual respect, a clear chain-of-command, and that even idiots like you..." He thrust a finger at the group. "... deserve three strikes before walking the plank. Starting tomorrow, you're all on waste tank cleaning duty. That's *interior* waste tank cleaning duty."

None of them complained. In fact, they all thanked him for the privilege.

"Since I already have most of you here, I want you to know that with Graystone gone, things will be changing. In many ways for the better. From what I understand, Graystone was a smart monster, but he was still a monster. For one, my background is military, and I expect this ship to run like a well-oiled machine. Not in one night, but quickly enough. Second, this is the first and last time I'll be so magnanimous. Punishments will be harsh, because there's no room in my machine for faulty parts. Third, you'll earn bonuses based on your contributions to the machine. Fourth, as a machine, we need to work smoothly together to achieve success. If you stick with me, we'll have more success than any pirates in the history of the Spiral. That's a promise."

The statement drew surprised murmurs from the group.

"Finally, no more talk of mutiny or replacing me as Captain. I told you it wouldn't work, and you're zero for two already. Let's focus on what matters. Enriching ourselves at the expense of others."

The last comment drew a cheer from the crew. Caleb used it to offer them a wave with his sword.

"Now get back to work," he ordered, turning and heading back the way he came, Damian tight on his heels.

# CHAPTER 11

"I'm sure I don't need to tell you how well you handled them," Damian said as they boarded the lift to return to Deck Six. "But you left me very impressed."

"I've commanded Marines before. Never pirates. So you do need to tell me," Caleb replied.

"People are people. You won me over earlier, but my confidence that I made the right decision is growing."

"What was your other choice, to join one of those two groups?"

"Never. I prefer to know my enemy."

"So do I," Caleb said. "Does this ship have a conference room? Or maybe Graystone had an office?"

"There's a situation room just off the bridge."

"Let's head there. I want to talk about Crux. Is there anyone else I should include?"

"Tae, from engineering," Damian replied. "He joined Graystone a week after I did. Former Royal Navy. One of Crux's initial attacks nearly destroyed his ship, the Arrow. Coming from another branch of service and unique experience, he might have some insight I'm lacking."

Caleb nodded, tapping on his comms patch. "Tae." He

paused, waiting for a light beep signaling the open channel. "Tae, this is Captain Card. I need to speak with you. Please come to the situation room on Deck Five immediately."

"Captain," Tae replied. His groggy, hoarse voice suggested he had been asleep. "Card, did you say?"

"That's right."

"What happened to Graystone?"

Caleb raised an eyebrow. "You don't know?"

"I don't really pay attention to shipboard drama. As long as everything's purring, I'm satisfied."

"Graystone's dead. I replaced him."

"Oh. Okay." His disinterest in the change of ownership left Caleb surprised and amused. "Give me a couple of minutes to wash up and find some clean pants. I had to make some adjustments to the HVAC earlier, and it left me covered in sweat and grease." He paused. "What is this about, anyway? I don't think Graystone even knew I existed, let alone ever asked to speak to me."

"Damian tells me you were in the Royal Navy."

"Oh. Damn. Am I in trouble? Did that son of a bitch rat me out to a piece of crap Crux crony?" His tone became more agitated as he spoke. "Because if so, I'm not interested in anything you have to say."

"Relax, Tae. It's the opposite. Gorgon is a pirate ship today. I aim to turn it into a thorn in Crux's side tomorrow."

Tae's entire mood shifted. "Oh. Well, damn. In that case, I'll be there asap." He disconnected the comms, rather than waiting for Caleb to dismiss him or cut the connection.

Caleb glanced at Damian. "He's a little…touchy?"

"And his decorum is in the loo, but he's a talented engineer."

"Is there anyone else I should contact? You said there are eleven former Royal military spacers on this ship."

"I don't know all of them personally. As tactical officer,

one of my roles is head of onboard enforcement. Graystone put it on me to identify who would be most likely to cause trouble for him."

"You should have told me that earlier. Did you know Targan would go after me?"

"Not that quickly. He was on my list, just not at the top."

"How many other people are on your list?"

"Not as many as you might think. And after what you just did, that list may have shrunk. Come to think of it, there is one former RAF member you need to be aware of, though I wouldn't invite her to this meeting. Penelope Patil, commander of the Edge boarding party."

"What's an edge boarding party?"

"No, that's their unit name. The Edge. As in, they live on the edge, razor's edge—"

"I get it."

The lift arrived on Deck Five. Caleb and Damian stepped out, continuing around to the bridge doors and then back toward the area on Decks Four and Six, where the mess halls were located.

"What branch was she in?" Caleb asked as they walked.

"Special forces."

"And we don't want her at this meeting?"

"She was on my list. I'm not sure where her true loyalties lie. Maybe she was true to the Empress once, but things change when it all falls apart."

"I'll give you that. Where can I find her?"

"As a team leader, she's in the officer's quarters. I'm sure you'll cross paths, eventually. If not, her suite's in the port rear corner."

"Why didn't Graystone send her out to deal with me?"

"He probably didn't want to bother her. The group he sent should have been more than adequate to deal with one infiltrator. You just happened to be the exception to the rule."

Caleb paused in the corridor, turning to Damian. "You said that as tactical officer, you're in charge of on-ship enforcement. That means it was your job to organize the defenses."

Damian's face hardened, cheeks flushing. Was he embarrassed over his failure, or something else?

"You were hoping I would reach the bridge," Caleb accused.

The other man didn't answer right away, lips moving silently as he considered his response. Finally, he shrugged. "Guilty. I saw it two ways, Captain, assuming you made it to the bridge. One, you'd kill Graystone and take his place. There was a chance you might be worse than him, but that would be a high bar to get over. Two, you'd kill Graystone after showing yourself to be an equivalent monster, and I'd take my chances on killing you myself."

"That was risky."

"A risk I needed to take."

Caleb remembered the way Linx's face darkened when he mentioned Graystone. "Because of Linx?"

"Not only her. As much as I wanted to kill Graystone, I couldn't get close enough to him without a distraction. Like Naya told you, he was paranoid about his safety. But after watching you get into the ship up the tow cables, I saw an opportunity I couldn't pass up."

"And it worked out for you."

"I already lost my wife, my children, my career, my empress. The only thing I have left to lose are the people I care about on this ship, people like Linx and her mother. Some people don't become pirates because they want to cause chaos. Some of them are good people with no other options."

"I understand."

They continued to the situation room. Large enough to seat twenty people, it had four rows of simple metal benches in the back and a surface computer at the front. A holographic projector hung overhead. The layout was similar to the briefing rooms he'd been in on Proxima.

"I recommended we talk here because of the holotable," Damian said. "I can show you some things."

"I need you to show me a lot of things," Caleb replied. "But let's wait for Tae."

Damian nodded in agreement. "In the meantime, why don't you tell me more about the Relyeh? You said there's more than one kind?"

"That's right. All Relyeh fall under the dominion of the eldest of the Ancients, an entity known as Shub'Nigu."

"Entity? What does he look like?"

"I don't know. No human has ever seen it. Him. Whatever. Shub'Nigu has offspring. I don't think they were born. It created them and sent them out into the universe. Their entire reason for existence is to spread and conquer. To destroy or control every intelligent life form they encounter. They take the life forms whose traits they find the most promising and engineer them, twisting them to suit their purposes. Ishek, for example, once belonged to a species that had no ability or need to explore space. They knew nothing of war and lived in simple peace and harmony with their environment."

"I find that hard to believe."

*So do I.*

"But it's true. Like on this ship, the Relyeh have a pecking order, typically sorted by species. And different Ancients prefer different underlings. Each has their own methods for waging war on the rest of the galaxy."

"How many of them are there?"

"I don't know that either. At least eight. Probably a lot

more. For the most part, they each stick to their own territories, but they fight with one another from time to time."

"Which Ancient do you think is controlling the forces in the Spiral? Is it the one that killed the Empress?"

*If an Ancient had seized us, both our brains would be pudding.*

"Ishek says no. We wouldn't be able to survive an Ancient taking control. But it would take a powerful Relyeh to overpower us without a fight. It could be whoever the Ancient sent to this galaxy to claim it for them."

"Do you think Crux is that Relyeh?"

"It isn't likely. What we know is that the numbers of khoron we've encountered are too great for the Relyeh to not be creating them on a planet somewhere in the Spiral. There's a pretty good chance the Relyeh in question is there. And I'm sure you've already guessed, the only way to stop him from using us again is to find him and kill him."

"That sounds like a brilliant plan to me. He might not be Crux, but from what you're telling me, he must have been supplying khoron to Crux for a long time. If we take out this breeding ground, or whatever it is, then we can stop the Legion from receiving reinforcements. It won't turn the tide, not when there are already hundreds of thousands of Legionnaires, but it's a good place to start."

"I'm glad you agree. That's only one of my objectives. What can you tell me about Empress Lo'ane's daughter?"

Damian's brow furrowed, a confused expression forming as he shook his head. "Empress Lo'ane doesn't have any children."

# CHAPTER 12

Caleb stared at the other man, his face likely mirroring the same confused look. "I'm sorry, Damian. I know you knew the Empress much longer than me and probably much better than I did. But I'm one hundred percent certain she has a daughter. When the Legion attacked us on Galatin, Doctor Ling directly mentioned her daughter. Lo'ane didn't deny having a daughter. She said her daughter was dead to her."

"Are you certain?" Damian asked.

Caleb nodded. "Yes. That's what she said. I was standing right next to her. I heard it clearly."

"That doesn't make any sense. The entire galaxy would know if Lo'ane had been pregnant. If she had given birth. It's not something that can be kept secret."

"Lo'ane wasn't always Empress. She had multiple brothers in front of her in the line of succession. Can you say for sure she was never out of the spotlight for at least six months?"

"As the only female offspring of the Emperor, she often drew more attention from the media than her brothers. I can't claim with complete certainty that she didn't vanish for that amount of time, but it seems impossible. No one ever saw her with an infant in her arms."

"My daughter is dead to me," Caleb repeated. "Maybe she didn't mean that she had disowned her daughter out of anger. Maybe she gave the baby up for adoption?"

"Why would she do that? And how could she arrange that with no one knowing?"

"I don't know. But with Lo'ane dead, the rebels will need someone to follow. Someone to rally around. If I'm right, and the Empress has a daughter, I intend to find her."

"What if she's a drunk or a drug addict?"

"Or a pirate?" Caleb joked. "We need to find her to know what we might have in her, but even a figurehead can be useful."

*I think you're neglecting to take something into account. What if she doesn't want to be found? What if she has no interest in the Empire or in being a ruler, figurehead or not?*

Caleb was prepared to answer Ishek's concerns when the door to the room opened and Tae walked in. Dressed only in a pair of what appeared to be karate pants, his feet and chest bare, he smiled as he entered, his handsome face framed by thick black hair down to his shoulders. He walked up to Caleb and put out his hand. "Since he's not Captain Card, then you must be. I'm Tae."

"I figured," Caleb replied, shaking his offered hand. "Do you have something against clothes?"

Tae laughed. "Apologies, Captain. I couldn't find anything else that smelled presentable. I hope you don't mind."

"I've got bigger problems than your naked pecs," Caleb answered.

"Yeah, I heard you talking to Sarge about the Empress' daughter. That's wild."

"You were eavesdropping?"

"I mean, you invited me to the meeting, so no. But you didn't know I was there, so, kinda." He shrugged.

"How did you even hear us through the door?"

Tae smiled and tapped his ear. "I was born deaf. I have an adjustable implant, and I modified the max amplification settings a little. I can hear your heart beating right now. Forty-seven beats per minute. You're in great shape. You also have a second, smaller heartbeat right..about..." He stretched out his finger to where Ishek rested. "... there." He poked the symbiote. "Gross. What is that?"

*Gross?*

Ishek's tone was incredulous.

"My khoron Advocate, Ishek," Caleb answered, picking up his shirt so Tae could see.

"Oh. Cool. He's actually kind of cute."

*That's better.*

Then Tae made a face. "You said you aren't with Crux. Did you phase me?"

Caleb assumed *phase* meant *trick*. "I'm the dominant entity, not him," he said. "And if you were listening in, then you know why I was talking about Lo'ane's daughter."

"It sounded good, Captain. I didn't mean to offend you. It's just as far as I've ever seen, normal folk don't have slugs in their pits."

"I'm definitely not normal," Caleb answered. "But I am on the side of humanity, not the Relyeh, and definitely not Lord Crux."

Tae shrugged again. "Okay. So what can I do to help you?"

"You already heard some of my plan."

"I did. And I'm not sure I agree with it. Sorry."

"You don't need to apologize. But it would help for you to explain."

"Well, what if this girl, or woman, depending on her age, doesn't want to be found? Or doesn't want to be an empress? We can't just force her to help us out *for the good of the Empire*," he said the last part in a goofy foghorn-like baritone to stress its cliche nature.

*That's what I just said.*

"And like I said, we need to find her to see what we have. We can't force her to do something she doesn't want to do. But what if she would be willing? I wonder if she even knows she's Lo'ane's daughter."

"It could be pricey, gallivanting around the entire Spiral searching for one person out of billions. Even if you grease some palms, it'll probably take a lot of grease. And believe me, I'm an engineer. I know what lube costs."

"I don't expect any of this to be cheap or easy. But that ties into my next aim. I want to be Robin Hood to Crux's Prince John."

"I don't know what that means," Tae said.

"Me, either," Damian agreed.

"Your ancestors came to the Spiral on a British generation ship and you don't know the tale of Robin Hood?" Caleb shook his head, incredulous.

"What do you mean? The founders fled an adjacent galaxy where their freedoms were being repressed," Tae explained. "They were seeking a place they could settle, expand, and care for all people equally."

"How's that working out for you?" Caleb asked.

Tae shrugged. "So it didn't go the way they planned, I guess."

"The founders came from the Milky Way," Caleb explained. "I don't even know how far we are from there, but I doubt we're adjacent. They arrived through a wormhole, just like I did. And the countries they came from were mostly democracies, though by the time Pathfinder left Earth, martial law was in effect everywhere."

"Ten second history lesson. I like it. But that's not what they teach us in school."

"Yeah, I've noticed. What I haven't figured out yet is why not."

"Need to know, maybe? We don't. Nobody really even talks about the founders anymore, except that one day of one class in elementary school. Sarge, how many kids do you think even remember that much?"

"Not many," Damian answered.

"Robin Hood stole from the rich and gave to the poor. He harassed Prince John, who usurped the crown from King Richard while he was busy fighting a distant war. He became a serious thorn in John's side and was beloved and aided by all the people he helped."

"So you want to steal from Crux and give it to other people?" Tae asked. "That won't pay the bills."

"Obviously, we'll need to take some off the top for operating expenses. But if we choose the right targets, we can manage both sides."

"I'm not convinced, but it'll be fun to help you try."

"I'll take it. My last objective is a little more personal. According to the scientist who plotted the wormhole, it's a one-way trip. Once you go through, you can't go back. I need to prove her wrong."

"What, you don't like us?"

"I barely know you. I came through the wormhole with a fellow Marine. His family is on the other side. Not to mention, we're having our own troubles with the Relyeh. I'm needed there."

"Are you so special that they'll miss you that much?" Tae asked. He tacked on a non-committal "No offense."

"Ishek makes me special," Caleb replied. "I don't want to sound arrogant, but I did board your ship, reach the bridge, and kill Graystone all on my own." He glanced at Damian. "With a tiny bit of help."

"I don't get it," Tae said in response to the last part.

"You would have succeeded anyway," Damian said. "I'm convinced of that."

"There's one other goal you didn't overhear," Caleb said. "We need to find the source of the khoron Crux is using to grow his Legion, and destroy it."

"That should at least be easier than finding the Princess. Unless this source is on an unknown planet in uncharted territory."

"There's a good chance it's exactly that," Caleb replied.

"Well, darn. Maybe instead of stealing from Crux, we should just steal from whoever we can."

*I'm with Tae.*

*My vote overrides yours, remember?*

"Let's start with Crux, and see how it goes," Caleb said. "What I need from both of you is an education. I'm not from around here, and I know next to nothing about the Spiral or our enemy. I need you to get me up to speed."

Tae shrugged. "I'm sure we can do that. But it'll take a little over ten seconds."

Caleb nodded. "We have about thirty hours."

"Byron Crux," Damian said, stepping over to the holotable, "was a lesser noble, sworn to the House of Galamet. Charged with control of the planet Pillion, he ranked highly enough to be invited to the Emperor's annual assembly of the nobility, but just barely." He activated the table. "Claude, generate a three-dimensional render of Lord Byron Crux the last time he attended the assembly."

Caleb could only assume Claude was the trigger word for the AI that rendered the man in life-size above the table a few seconds later. He wasn't all that surprised by the man's appearance. Average height and build, with a friendly-yet-predatory look that suggested he was always plotting something. Salt and pepper hair. Somewhat handsome. He appeared intelligent and well-spoken. That part was unfortunate. Caleb preferred his enemies stupid and easy to outmaneuver.

"That image is from eight years ago," Tae explained.

"There's a reason I showed you this one first, Captain," Damian said. "This was two years before Crux introduced his Legion by conquering Nantes and overthrowing King Galamet. Claude, generate a three-dimensional render of Lord Crux using the latest image in our local datastore."

The old render didn't vanish. Instead, it morphed into the new one.

"Is that accurate?" Caleb asked, shocked.

"Our latest image is probably over a year old, but it should be pretty close," Damian replied. "Even I hadn't realized how much he's grown."

"Or how ugly he's gotten," Tae added.

Average height Crux had gained nearly eight inches in height and bulked up enough that he looked like a competitive bodybuilder. His handsome face was replaced by an oversized jaw and eyes too deep set, though they maintained their predatory, plotting gaze. He had traded his suit for a uniform.

*He's been Sanctified.*

*Sanctification doesn't turn a person into that.*

*That depends on who is doing the Sanctifying. They can introduce mutations. It's possible whoever did this is trying to convert humans into Relyeh.*

*To what end?*

*Most of you make decent pets.*

*I'm serious, Ish.*

*It is difficult to know for sure. Perhaps the superior Relyeh is attempting to merge human and khoron. To cut out the middleman, so to speak.*

*Could Crux be the one who overpowered us?*

*Not impossible, but also not likely. I imagine he would have wanted the Empress to know if he was the one killing her.*

"He's been Sanctified," Caleb said. "Put through a Relyeh healing process that removes impurities in the subject's DNA. It normally makes an organism genetically perfect, but Ish believes they programmed Crux with a mutation. They might be using him as a guinea pig."

"The infamous *they*," Tae said. "I hate those guys."

"I don't know anything about mutations," Damian said. "But I'm not surprised. We already know he made a deal with the devil. The changes started the year after that. I can show you the progression."

"It's unnecessary," Caleb said. "I imagine the changes began around the same time he introduced his new alloy?"

"It's almost like you were born here, Captain. That's right."

"It's obvious to me that Crux somehow made contact with the Relyeh, they came to an agreement, and things have progressed from there. The Relyeh helped him with the alloy. They provided the khoron and probably the Legion. They Sanctified him, promising him wealth and power beyond his imagination."

*That's not a very Relyeh approach to warfare.*

"Which isn't a very Relyeh approach to warfare," Caleb added. "And leads me to wonder if Benning's discovery on board Pathfinder has anything to do with it."

"Who's Benning, again?" Tae asked. "I don't think we've met this person yet."

"Charlotte Benning," Caleb explained. "She was the lead civilian engineer on Pathfinder. She uncovered some kind of conspiracy onboard the ship that led her to the discovery of the wormhole. Or rather, that the military already knew about the wormhole and planned to go through it. She said their math was wrong and would lead to the destruction of the ship. They wouldn't listen to her, so she stole a transport, escaped the ship, and set up a warning to prevent any other ships from following."

"So of course, your instinct was to follow them." Tae smiled. "I like it."

"Not initially. The Relyeh attacked us. The wormhole was our only chance to escape. Fortunately, we had Benning's correct math. Since Pathfinder made it through as well, I can only imagine the people in control of the ship listened to Benning after all."

"Narrowly avoiding disaster. I'd love to see the math."

"You will. I have Benning's data chip. What I need is something that can read it. It's old."

"There's no shortage of old equipment in the Spiral," Damian said. "If we don't have it onboard, I'm sure we can get it on Aroon. We'll be there before you know it."

"Let's get back to Crux," Caleb said. "We know where he got the recipe for the alloy and khoron for his Legion, but he still needed to build the ships. He still needed to provide the bodies."

"He made deals with two of the other Houses," Damian said. "Nobukku, a small, fledgling kingdom at the edge of the empire, and Vitali, a larger House. Nobukku is known for their shipbuilding expertise. It's claimed they have more star docks than cities. Vitali is focused on agriculture. Their three primary planets are ideal for human settlement, and they import additional laborers to work on the farms. No one noticed the uptick in people arriving in Vitali's territory."

"Or that they were leaving infected with khoron," Caleb said. "That makes sense."

"Grain ships were going out to Nobukku carrying grain and Legionnaires they delivered to the star docks where they boarded newly built warships and transports and were sent off into deep space to train. By the time anyone knew Crux was building his own military, we were already under attack."

"Something like that costs a lot of coin. Where did it come from? The Relyeh have little use for money."

"Pillion is predominantly a mining planet rich in the ore he needs for his alloy, but also in precious gems and other high-value minerals. Even skimming just a small amount off the top, less than House Galamet would notice, would be enough to bankroll his army. Once Vitali and Nobukku believed Crux might pull off his conquest, they were likely willing to invest based on promises made rather than physical value."

"And here we are," Tae said.

"What can you tell me about Crux's warships? How do you fight them?"

"The alloy is like having three extra layers of shields to punch through," Damian said. "From what I understand, we began working on weapons that would be more successful against it, but the developers didn't have time to complete anything before they were forced into hiding. They only had a limited amount of the stuff to study."

"Why didn't the Emperor give up some of the armor Crux gifted him for the effort?"

"That's where what they had came from."

"So you never defeated and captured any of Crux's ships?"

"You have to win the fight to preserve the battlefield," Damian answered simply. "The Royal Navy has destroyed a handful, but never enough to not be on the losing end."

"Understood," Caleb said. "We have a damaged but intact Nightmare in the cargo bay. I didn't realize it was such a rarity."

"That's why it's worth six million."

"I feel like it should be worth more than that. I also feel like we may need to keep it."

"That won't go over very well with the crew. They expect to be paid."

"Do you think we can contact the researchers? Find out if access to the Nightmare might help them?"

"I don't know how quickly we can make contact, but I'm sure it would help them."

"Right now, I need a crew. We'll sell the Nightmare. But one way or another, I'll get more alloy."

"Robin Hood, right?" Tae said.

"Damn right," Caleb replied. "Once we reach Aroon, we need to figure out where and how to strike first." He paused, looking both men in the eye. "I'm sure I don't need to tell you that this entire conversation is between us right now?"

"Classified," Tae said. "Understood, Captain."

"Aye, Captain," Damian said.

"Good. Tae, you're dismissed. Damian, I have a couple of additional tasks for you, and then I'll let you get some sleep."

"You know where to find me if you need me, Cap," Tae said. "Thanks for inviting me to the party. I can't wait to boogie." He offered a dip of his chin and headed for the door.

"Tae," Caleb said, pausing his exodus. "Next time, wear a shirt."

Tae laughed. "Aye, Captain."

"So, Captain," Damian said once Tae had left. "What else do you need?"

# CHAPTER 13

Heads turned, the room immediately falling silent as Caleb entered the boarding teams' training gym. His eyes swept over the assembled group of a dozen pirates, all dressed in various combinations of workout gear and military-style fatigues. They were positioned at an assortment of stations arranged across the compartment, which Damian had told him was one of the largest fully accessible spaces on the ship.

It didn't surprise Caleb to find it was very similar to gyms on Earth prior to the war. For as much as technology had changed, the human body remained the same. And while science had helped guide efficiency in maximizing the body's potential, the basic process of fitness was identical across the centuries and light-years.

*I'm not sure they know who we are.*

*Maybe you're right*, Caleb replied. "I'm—"

"Captain Card," one pirate said. A muscular man with long, dark hair, he was on his back at the bench press, head lifted to look over at Caleb. "I'd stand up and come to attention, but I don't want to."

The comment drew a laugh from a few of the others.

"Careful, Roy," one woman in the gym said. "Weren't you in the Commons last night? Captain Card smacked down the Berserkers like they were a playground of rowdy children."

"Is that right?" Roy said, releasing the bar of his dumbbells and sitting all the way up. "Maybe I *should* salute you, Captain."

"I didn't come here to have my ego stroked," Caleb replied. "I came to work out."

"With us?" A third pirate asked. "We're just the lowly grunts."

Of course, he hadn't come down to Deck Three just to work out. The officer's quarters had its own gym, smaller but with high-end equipment, not that he cared about that. He had come to see the members of the boarding crews for himself, and to meet with Fitz and Penelope if he found them here.

"And there's a few less of us grunts since you came on board, Captain," the woman added. "Neve was a friend of mine. Ashi, too. You left them in a heap on the cargo bay deck."

"It wasn't personal," Caleb replied, finally finding the woman at the free weights near the back of the room. She was heavily muscled, showing off her fitness in short shorts and a sports bra. "Graystone ordered to kill me. I fought back. Are you Edge?" Damian had shown him how to access the crew records on his terminal, so he knew this woman wasn't Penelope Pitel or anyone else whose files he had read, currently limited to the eleven former military on board.

She nodded and smiled. "I guess my reputation precedes me." She pointed to Roy. "He's Edge. too. So's Haruka there. And Fitz." She nodded at a smaller woman sitting in a painful-looking yoga pose on a mat and then a man in the back corner. Lean, with short, dark hair and a serious face, he wore full fatigues, soaked with sweat.

Fitz stared back at Caleb with a knowing gaze, as if he had innately understood that he was one of the people Caleb most wanted to meet. A former Royal Marine who had gone AWOL a year before Atlas had fallen, Damian had suggested they shouldn't bother with him. He had indicated the man wasn't a threat, but neither was he an asset. Caleb understood how Damian felt about deserters. He had dealt with his share. But he also knew that people didn't always flee the military to save their own skin, and given their situation, he couldn't afford to pass judgment.

He didn't approach Fitz right away. The man looked like he had just finished doing something exhausting, though Caleb couldn't immediately guess what it was.

"Captain," a man to his left said. Caleb glanced over, immediately recognizing one of Targan's men. A Berserker.

"Shouldn't you be scrubbing the waste tanks with the rest of your homeboys?" Caleb asked. The pirate was nearly the same height and build as he was, with a bald head and dark eyes, every inch of his bare flesh covered in bright tattoos, the ink infused with something that made the tats glitter. "Wait one." He frowned, the man's tattoos leading him to a realization. "You didn't take part in that brawl in the commons."

"No, sir," the man replied. "I followed Targan up because he said he was worried about Naya. He always had a thing for her, and I figured there was no harm in taking a walk. Anyway, I want you to know I'm sorry I even listened to him. You seem like a reasonable man. You could have tossed the others out of the airlock and nobody here would've batted an eye. It's been a while since we had a captain with a conscience."

"You can say that again, Sparkles," a different woman added. Thin and slight, she stood on the treadmill, which she had stopped when he entered. "Graystone was an a-hole."

"That's putting it mildly," Haruka said. "Right, Goldie?"

"I never had a problem with the captain," the first woman answered.

"That's because you're too butch," Roy said. "Just like Greaser's too wee to catch his eye. She's got no boobs."

"Do so," the woman on the treadmill replied. "They're just small enough not to get in the way in small spaces. Every good pirate crew needs someone like me."

"Anyway, Captain," Goldie said. "With the way you handled things last night, I wouldn't expect much more trouble from the crew. There's always an idiot who thinks replacing the Captain is a quick path to riches and glory, but the thing is, becoming captain isn't enough. You need to have the skills to keep the position. And I can tell that you do."

"What do you bench, Captain?" Roy asked, vacating the equipment. "I can spot you."

*Let's blow them away.*

*I thought I've been overusing the juice?* Caleb replied, smirking at Ishek's mischievous tone.

*What can I say, I like when we show off.*

With Ishek's help, he could press nearly a thousand pounds. On his own, he was a hair over three hundred. He had a feeling the exhibition would cement his position with the boarding crews, and considering they were the ones with the training and weapons, it didn't seem like a bad idea at all.

*Okay, hit —*

"Captain Card didn't come here to pump iron," Fitz said, his voice soft and composed. He hadn't moved from his position on the mat, remaining calm and still where he stood. "He's looking for Penn, first. Me, second." His eyes latched onto Caleb's. "Isn't that right, sir?"

"Did Tae speak to you?" Caleb replied.

Fitz shook his head. "No. Sarge didn't tell me anything, either. I made an assumption based on observation. You just confirmed it."

*A Marine, and smart to boot. He blows you out of the water.*

Caleb ignored Ishek. "How can you be sure you've read me right?"

"The posture never lies, Captain. You have Marine officer written all over you. The way you handled things in the commons fortifies that supposition. But you started out noncom. You worked your way up. You proved that by getting onto Gorgon in the first place. If I were in your shoes, the first thing I'd want to know is what I have to work with. I'd wonder how many other former military I had onboard besides Sarge." He glanced at Sparkles. "Who you can thank for getting rid of Graystone the next time you see him."

"What?" Sparkles exclaimed in surprise. The others in the gym reacted similarly.

Fitz ignored them. "And then, once I knew the names and faces, I'd pay a visit to the biggest threats to see where their loyalties lie. Maybe to drum up their support. Strength in numbers, right Cap?"

"I like the way you think, Fitz," Caleb answered.

"So why don't we haul the skeletons out of the closet? You know I'm a deserter. What you don't know is why I left the Marines. So you aren't sure what you have in me."

"You're making this all too easy for me."

Fitz grinned mischievously. "Don't celebrate yet, Captain. I want to know what we've got in you, too. No Captain will stay captain forever without the support of his crew. Graystone just proved that."

"What do you suggest?" Caleb asked. "A fight?"

"No. I abhor fighting."

"Is that why you—"

"No," Fitz replied before he could finish the question. "We have a training course on Deck One. I helped Penn design it, so it wouldn't be fair for me to race you. But if you can get through it without a scratch, you have my word that I'll go along with anything you say for as long as you're still captain of this ship. And so will the Razor's Edge."

"Wait!" Goldie said. "You can't make that promise, Fitz."

"And you want to go against someone who can run the Grinder without a scratch?" Haruka said. "I still have the scars."

"We all do," Roy said, turning to Caleb. "You can't be in Razor's Edge without completing the course. Of course, for us it doesn't matter how much damage we take, as long as we survive."

"Even if I get scratched..." Caleb stared at Fitz. "...it doesn't mean I'm going to surrender the ship."

"I wouldn't ask for that. If you get nicked, Razor's Edge gets half the coin you collect for the Nightmare."

"That's a terrible deal for me," Caleb said.

"Is it?" Fitz replied smugly. "I'm not sure you believe that."

*I think he has an inkling of your goals. Though I can't imagine how.*

*It sure seems that way,* Caleb agreed. *He's thinking like me. Which is a good sign of his true loyalties. He wouldn't be able to conceive of my desire to help the Empire unless he could consider the same.*

*If you lose, you might not be able to pay most of the crew for very long.*

*Some of them will leave anyway once they know what they're* in for. Besides, we haven't done a training course in a while. It might be fun.

If there's no fear, there's no fun.

Caleb nodded at Fitz. "You're on."

# CHAPTER 14

Beyond changing into fatigues, Caleb didn't want to waste time preparing for the training course. As difficult as the other Edge members had made it sound, he maintained a confident attitude that he would complete it. He had done so many over the years and hadn't failed one since basic training. But could he do it without taking even a single scratch? What would make the course twice as challenging was its unfamiliarity.

*I can heal any minor scratches. They don't need to know.*

*My clothes would still be torn and bloody. And you know I'm not in favor of cheating.*

*Even against pirates?*

*Let's try not to get cut.*

Even though the terms of the deal remained between him and those present in the gym, word of his imminent attempt to complete the course spread fast. Nearly two dozen other crew members, including Tae and Damian, were waiting by the time he reached the starting point near the bow. The compartment was relatively large, and judging by the matts and storage lockers, Caleb figured they also used it for melee combat training. A pair of large monitors hung at the front of the space.

Laughing and talking among themselves, most of the gathered attendees had yet to notice Caleb's arrival. Likewise, the one person Caleb still didn't see was Penelope. It surprised him she hadn't come down to observe the proceedings. He never imagined she would be so elusive. Not that he was in any position to speak to her right now, anyway.

"Hey, Cap," Tae said, approaching him with Damian. "What do you think?" He tugged on his t-shirt, which clung tight against his frame. He still wore the same black pants Caleb had seen him in hours earlier, and he had sandals on his feet rather than magboots. Hard maneuvers that would throw him off the deck weren't likely as long as they remained in the hyperspace field.

"It's a shirt," Caleb replied. "Barely."

Tae smirked. "I hope you enjoy the course. I built pretty much everything that's going to try to hurt you. So, if you get hurt, you're welcome."

"Maybe you could give me a little preview of what I'm up against."

*And you said healing you would be cheating?*

"I don't think we have time for that."

"Captain," Damian said. "You already made a statement last night. Not to mention how you got on board. You don't need to prove anything here."

"I do," Caleb replied. "I need to show them I'm not just the captain. I'm one of them."

*I recall Empress Lo'ane saying something similar, not long before she died. We wouldn't have been able to kill her if she had been on the ship with her people.*

*It's not the same*, Caleb answered.

*It's the same.*

"Fitz talked you into it, didn't he?"

"Is that the rumor?"

"No, I just saw who you came down here with. You aren't the first person he's challenged to the course. What are the terms?"

Caleb hadn't expected the wager was a regular occurrence. "I have to get through without a scratch," he said quietly enough only Damian would hear. "The details aren't important right now."

"I can't believe you agreed to that. Nobody has ever made it through without taking a hit. Greaser did the best of anyone, and she needed ten stitches in her ankle. She was practically bouncing off the walls, not able to exercise for a week while it healed."

"What about Graystone?"

Damian laughed. "He wouldn't be caught dead down here."

"Exactly. Even if I lose, it'll be worth it."

"Let's hope so."

"Sarge. Tae," Fitz said, returning to Caleb with a holstered pistol on a thigh belt in one hand and a small drone in the other. He held the gun belt out to him. "This fires energy pulses rather than live rounds. When the pulse hits the target, it'll deactivate it. I'll give you one clue about the course. The targets shoot back, formed ion blasts that can break your skin without damaging the bulkheads."

"Good to know, but not surprising." Caleb accepted the belt, wrapping it around his leg as Fitz tossed the drone into the air. It hung there for a moment while he retrieved a small tablet from his pocket and tapped on it. The drone zipped into a position over and behind Caleb's left shoulder.

"That little guy will stream the action back to the monitors over there," Tae explained, pointing to a pair of screens behind the gathered crew. "And to any screens on the ship that connect to the channel."

"I expect the entire ship is watching," Roy said. "This is a serious event."

*I hope you don't make a fool of us.*

"Great," Caleb replied. "If this is going to be livestreamed, why did so many people come down here to watch?"

"They want to see the damage when you get back. The course starts and ends here." He pointed the way they had just come. "That's the end of the course."

"I didn't notice any traps or obstacles on the way here, hidden or otherwise," Caleb remarked.

"That's what makes this one so hard," Roy agreed. "Tae did too good of a job keeping it all hidden."

Tae's only response was to shrug innocently.

"The rules are simple," Fitz said. "There are three flags positioned along the route. You start through that corridor…" He pointed to it. "… collect the flags and come back through that corridor." His finger shifted to it. "Make it without a scratch, you win. Otherwise, you lose."

"That's it?"

"That's it."

"Sounds simple enough."

"We're about to find out. Good luck, Captain."

"Thank you."

"Good luck, Cap," Roy said, patting him on the shoulder.

"You can do it," Goldie added.

Damian stepped in front of him. "Watch out for the—"

"Sarge!" Fitz interrupted. "You know better."

"So did you," he commented harshly before frowning and stepping back.

"Whenever you're ready, Captain," Fitz added,

dismissing Damien's grumbling. It was enough of a fore-warning for Caleb not to let his guard down anywhere on the course. He knew he could expect just about any challenge and that they would all be dangerous.

The compartment fell silent as Caleb crossed over to the starboard passageway. The small drone trailed behind him, remaining in a fixed position over his shoulder.

"I'm activating the course," Fitz said.

A series of thumps, pops, groans, and hisses echoed from the passageway. Caleb's heart rate jumped, natural adrenaline beginning to flow through him. He glanced over at Fitz and nodded, the assembled pirates cheering and shouting encouragement as he took his first step into the passageway.

Caleb heard the soft click despite the noise from the crew behind him. Pausing in his tracks, he leaned his upper torso back as a spinning saw blade shot across the passageway, missing him by mere centimeters before vanishing into a thin slit on the opposite bulkhead.. The shouts from the pirates grew louder, and looking back, Caleb saw the scene being replayed in slow motion on the monitors. The drone was apparently editing the stream in real time.

"Did I forget to mention that forty percent of the people who enter the course don't survive it?" Fitz asked with a sly grin.

"I'll see you soon," Caleb replied. "On that side."

He lunged forward, the same round blade shooting back in the other direction, passing harmlessly behind him. An environment as hostile as Damien's mood had forewarned, he pulled the gun from its holster and moved cautiously forward, scanning the corridor and listening for hints of what was to come. He sensed Ishek doing the same.

He didn't have to wait long.

The whirring noise of a robot rolling into the corridor

drew his attention to the starting compartment behind him. He swung his pistol around toward the tracked, trashcan-shaped bot but quickly realized it wasn't the target. The bot held a metal screen lined with blades in front of itself as it moved toward him. Caleb fired at it, but it didn't deactivate the bot. Glimpsing Tae's apologetic shrug, he realized the bot's sole goal was to keep him moving forward. He knuckled down to do just that, advancing at a speed that kept him well ahead of the bot.

A hidden compartment to his left snapped open, and another bot swung out, an ion turret mounted to its top. He shot it before it could fire, only to have a second turret drop from the ceiling, already aimed his way. Quick reflexes allowed him to duck away from its shot; good aim let him take it out.

*Eight o'clock high.*

Caleb ducked low and pivoted, firing on the turret that popped out of the wall. A soft click, and he dove forward just in time to avoid a line of blades that snapped up from the floor.

And he had only traveled a few meters.

Rolling back to his feet, he kept going, momentarily confused when an opaque curtain swung out in front of him, blocking his view ahead. He slowed, trying to make sense of the obstacle. The robot at his back forced him to keep moving. He ducked low as he thrust the left side of the curtain aside and moved past it, quickly sweeping the other side with his pistol.

There was nothing there.

Sharp hisses from both sides made him jump back and duck as gas spewed from nozzles on either side of the ceiling. A single breath of the stuff made him instantly light-headed. He shook his head to clear away his wooziness and lunged ahead to escape the fumes. Instead, he hit a solid wall, the corridor ahead duplicated by a rear projection. Holding his breath, he glanced over his shoulder. The robot sped up, a long blade swinging up in front of it. The blade swiped from side to side, making him wonder if Fitz was remotely controlling the machine.

Caleb threw himself into the fake wall. It shattered as he broke through it. The floor immediately gave way beneath him. His heart rate and Ishek's spiked as he dove and rolled forward to his feet, jumping to catch an overhead water pipe in a one-handed grab. He dangled there over a pit of lethal pointed stakes. "Shit."

*Yeah, my thought exactly.*

Caleb holstered his pistol to move hand-over-hand to the far side of the pit. Dropping to the floor, the last thing he expected was a hatch to open right beside him and a man in combat armor to burst out. Leading with his shoulder, he lifted Caleb off the floor and drove him backward toward the pit, his intention obvious.

Caleb wrapped his arms around his attacker and used his momentum to swing him around and into the pit, the man's armor preventing the spikes from piercing his flesh. Caleb landed on top of him and immediately reached for the man's helmet, unlatching it with practiced ease and yanking it off.

"Sparkles," Caleb said upon seeing the man who had attacked him.

"Captain," Sparkles replied. "First time I've had this happen. Usually the player ducks past me before I can grab them."

"Guess I was a little slow. Are you okay?"

"I'm fine."

Caleb glanced up at the robot stopped at the pit's edge, motionless rather than risk impaling Sparkles' unprotected skull.

Caleb hopped off him, using the respite to pull himself up out of the pit and make his way down the corridor. He hadn't gone far before another hatch opened, revealing the first flag stuck in a stand at the back of a compartment.

Haruka blocked his path.

# CHAPTER 15

"Let me take a quick guess." Caleb studied Haruka intently. "Fitz didn't bother telling me the course isn't entirely auto-mated, and since he doesn't like to fight, he's set up the entire Edge squad to fight for him."

"The course is a team effort," she replied, brandishing a blade resembling a short machete. "Show me what you've got, Cap."

Caleb squared off against her. He didn't know what kind of fighter she was, but remembering she had been doing yoga, he figured her for agile, especially since she wore lightweight tactical gear.

Haruka didn't disappoint, coming at him with a fast but false start, quickly shifting her weight and charging around on his left flank. She dropped into a split, thrusting the blade at his leg, just below the knee, hoping to draw first blood. She nearly succeeded. He whirled just in time to kick out with his right foot, connecting with her outstretched wrist and knocking the blade away. She rolled all the way through, coming up again, another knife miraculously appearing in her left hand. She threw it at his throat, giving him no choice but to raise Sparkles' helmet, catching the blade in the face shield. A third blade appeared in her hand, and she lunged at him. He grabbed her wrist and twisted it over just far enough to force her into dropping the blade. Spinning inside her guard, he wrapped an arm tight around her throat.

"I don't have to kill you, do I?" he asked, holding her in place.

"No. I yield." He let her go, and she respectfully bowed her head.

He turned to collect the first flag, a frayed shred of blue cloth, and returned to the passageway. Sparkles was gone, and the floor was just about done reassembling. The robot, with its panel of blades, stood ready to charge after him once the floor was back in place. While he could, Caleb hurried to put some distance between it and him.

He reached the first t-junction, slowing to peek around the corner into the open, and it nearly cost him the match, not to mention his life. He barely pulled his head back in time to avoid an ion blast from one of a handful of turrets in the adjacent passageway. Glancing behind him at the approaching robot, he had a feeling this was where Greaser had been cut and needed stitches. It would take too long to shoot out the turrets. But how could he cross before either a blast hit him or the bot let loose with its blades?

He pulled the knife from Sparkles' helmet before sliding the helmet into the junction on its flat base. Correctly assuming it would draw heavy gunfire when it stopped in the middle of the corridor, he trailed behind it, jumping onto it and then leaping off to safety on the other side of the corridor. He looked back to find the helmet melted by the ion blasts.

Caleb picked up the pace, becoming more accustomed to the simple booby-traps that lined the corridor. He paused to let a knife go past, ducked and rolled as swinging blades dropped from the ceiling, and spotted razor-wire strung almost invisibly across the passageway before he walked into it and cut himself.

He used the knife he had taken from Haruka and slipped it under the gun belt wrapped around his thigh; he slashed the wire and passed through before the blade-bot caught up to him.

Reaching the corner at the end of the passageway, he didn't slow, rolling across to the corner instead and opening fire with his pistol. Four turrets sent ion blasts where he should have been, too slow to catch up to him. He fired back in rapid successive pulses, shutting them down. Following a few more basic traps he easily negotiated, a hatch opened ahead of him, beckoning him.

Caleb entered the compartment as carefully as he could, but a sharp object like a ninja star still bounced off the bulkhead right beside his shoulder. Ducking away as a second star flew at his face, he batted the flat side of it away at the last second. Greaser, right behind the second star, leaped at him, leading with her right foot. He easily caught hold of her ankle, swinging her toward the wall. She bent toward him at an almost impossible angle, grabbing his arm and using it as a fulcrum to drop low. Blade in hand, she tried slashing his knee, but he blocked the knife with his boot, knocking it aside. Falling forward into a roll, he left her temporarily pinned beneath him before he ended up on his feet, his back to her.

*Knife!*

It was a good thing Ish could pick up details from Caleb's senses that his own brain missed. It worked as an extension of his peripheral vision, allowing Caleb to reach around and grab the knife before Greaser could sink it into his back. He still missed the handle and her hand wrapped around it, his fingers grabbing her wrist just as the knife point pricked the thickness of his fatigue shirt. Turning, he easily overpowered her, forcing the knife point up to the underside of her chin, drawing a single drop of blood.

"I yield," she said, a look of disbelief in her eyes as she released the knife, letting Caleb have it. "How the hell—"

"I've got eyes in the back of my head," Caleb replied with a grin. Greaser reached behind her, retrieving a yellow flag from her pocket and handing it to him. "I think you might actually do this," she said. "Good thing. I bet a hundred on you at twenty to one."

"Doesn't that make fighting me a conflict of interest?"

"Yeah, so? Do you think I pulled any punches?"

"Considering how close you came to cutting me, no."

"The bet isn't worth the wrath of my team if I didn't play it square."

"I've been there before," Caleb said, tucking the flag into his pocket. "Thanks for playing it square. See you at the finish line."

Once back in the corridor, he noted the blade-bot's position, well behind him now, allowing him to make it all the way across to the next corner, unscathed. Peeking out around the edge of the bulkhead, he didn't immediately spot any obvious traps. But his expert senses jangled, warning him not to trust what he couldn't see. He threw Greaser's knife forward, smirking when it sank into another projected blockade like the curtain. Only this one reminded him of ballistic gel.

Grinning, he walked up to the knife and took hold of the handle, freezing when he heard buzzing coming from the overhead vent. Small machines the size of horse flies poured from the vent, their tiny wings flapping hard as they swarmed him. Cursing, he yanked the knife down through the gel and dived through it just ahead of the tiny drones. He hurdled a blade that popped out of the bulkhead just before it could slash his thigh and slice off the fingers of his right hand.

He hustled ahead, the swarm dropping in fast behind him. Firing his pistol wildly back at them, he knocked down a wide swath of the drones with each pulse. Stragglers darted in closer, stinging him with sharp metal barbs. He swung the wide face of the knife blade at them, knocking several down at a whack. A few of them left little nicks in his fatigues, but none of them drew blood.

He breathed a heavy sigh of relief when the last one dropped. It was the closest he had come to losing, and he was near enough to the finish line to see it up ahead.

*We can do this.*

"Yes, we can," Caleb agreed, forging ahead toward the intersection where he'd started, but this time he had nothing to protect him from the turrets around the corner. *Any ideas?*

*One.*

Caleb turned around. The blade-bot trundled toward him, having closed in on him when the drones slowed him down. "That's a terrible plan."

*Then you should love it.*

Caleb turned and charged the bot, running toward the right side of the blades. His judgment had to be spot on when he hit the panel or he'd not only lose the game, he'd come away shy a few digits. Or maybe both hands.

His palms hit gaps between the spikes, pushing against the bot's forward momentum. At first, he slid backwards, his effort unrewarded. Two taps of his heels on the deck and maglock not only stopped his backsliding, it slowed the bot to a stop. Muscles flexing, he pushed against the bot, a little help from Ishek doubling his efforts. He growled, muscles straining as he shoved on the bot, its motor complaining loudly until he finally turned the thing enough for him to slip around it.

He grabbed onto it and lifted it off the deck, able to turn it sideways now that its treads were off the deck. He carried it across the intersection, blocking the turrets firing on him. On the other side, he kicked a tread off the bot, disabling its forward momentum.

A hatch a short distance ahead of him opened, the last flag within reach, with only thirty meters of passageway left to traverse.

He advanced toward it, stopping just outside the hatch. Had he been fortunate that Greaser missed him with her first star, or had she missed on purpose because she'd bet on him? He didn't know, but he didn't want to test his luck again. He moved into position at the side of the hatch, peering discreetly into the unlit compartment. The light from the corridor stretched out to the flag resting on a crate in the back. He expected Fitz to be waiting for him, but he didn't see anyone. From his perspective, the flag was wide open.

*This has to be a trick.*

Of course it was. Maybe the floor was rigged to give way. Maybe the ceiling would dump thousands of spikes on his head. The good news was disabling the blade-bot allowed him to linger while he examined the room. The bad news was that he didn't see anything out of the ordinary.

*We just need to go for it,* Caleb decided. Ish didn't have a response, but he could feel the Advocate's trepidation.

Drawing his pistol and advancing slowly, Caleb stepped over the threshold into the room, his aim directed at the crate. He couldn't rule out that someone or something waited behind or inside it. He reached the crate without an issue and grabbed the flag with his free hand, tucking it into his pocket.

"Now all you have to do is get past me."

Caleb froze facing the back wall. A woman's voice, he

didn't need to see her face to know who his third opponent was. *You could have warned me she was there.*

*I didn't sense her at all.*

Caleb turned around. "Special Officer Patil," he said. "I've been looking forward to meeting you."

# CHAPTER 16

"Well, I guess you've found me."

Penelope was average height, lean with a deep complexion, shoulder-length hair, and a pretty face highlighted by violet eyes that seemed almost luminescent. She wore an underlay beneath an armored vest, knives strapped to both thighs. Seeing him, she smiled.

"Why not knife me in the back?" Caleb asked. "Win the bet for your team?"

"That wouldn't be very sportsmanlike, would it? I prefer to fight people face to face." Taking a step forward, she pulled blades from scabbards belted to each thigh. "What did you want to talk to me about?"

"That's for your ears only," he said. "From what I understand, we have a pretty big audience." He motioned to the drone hovering just behind him.

He didn't move when Penelope hurled one of her knives toward him. Perfectly aimed, it hit the drone, knocking it down.

"Now it's just you and me," she said with a grin.

He smiled back at her. "I like your style, SO Patil."

"Everyone else calls me Penn. Not Penny. Not P. And

definitely not Penelope. I'll kill you if you call me any of those."

"Caleb." He grinned. "But I promise not to kill you if you call me Cal. However, I prefer Captain."

She chuckled. "You're obviously military. And incredibly skilled. I've been watching you run the course. Your reflexes are whiplike, your physical strength is off the charts. Your improvisation is enviable. I especially liked how you used the helmet to get past the first turret battery. Oh, and the no-look knife grab. How could I forget that?"

"Did you come here to fight me or flatter me?"

"You fascinate me, Captain. There's more to you than meets the eye."

"I'm symbiotically bonded to an Advocate," Caleb said. "An advanced form of khoron."

"But you're obviously controlling it," she replied, less surprised by the admission than he'd expected. "It isn't controlling you."

"It wishes it could," Caleb answered. "Its name is Ishek."

*You know I hate when you call me* it.

"How is that even possible?"

"It's a matter of will. Khoron rarely choose to bond to strong-minded hosts. If you've fought the Legion and they haven't tried to infect you, now you know why."

She paused, her expression becoming reflective and confirming she had been in a situation just like that before. "So they made a mistake with you?"

"In the sense that they underestimated my ability to overpower Ishek, yes. It's a long story, one I'll tell you later if you don't have your sights set on disrupting the plans I have for this ship."

"If you mean my making a run for Captain, you don't need to worry about that. I prefer a more active role. I'm curious though." She paused. "You sent out a distress signal from a Nightmare. You aren't a Legionnaire. Did Crux infect you with the Advocate?"

"No. I arrived in this galaxy with him. That's another long story. The point is, I'm loyal to humanity, which means Crux is my enemy at the most basic level. You might not have the same disdain for the Relyeh that I do, but you served the Empress once. Maybe you'd be willing to serve her again."

"So that's what this is about," Penn said. "You want to use Gorgon to harass Crux. In essence, to harass his new Empire. It's a hopeless cause."

"I don't believe that."

"You should believe it. Crux controls most of the Spiral. The people loyal to the Empress are few, and they're either in hiding or in denial. If you sting him, he'll swat you down in a hurry."

"I've been fighting the Relyeh for a long time. It won't be that easy for him to cut me off at the knees. I have a plan to eliminate the flow of new Legionnaires, but I need this ship and a loyal, capable crew to do it. And I need solid, insurgent away teams."

"You're serious," Penn said.

"Very. Tell me something, Penn. Are you a pirate by choice or by circumstance?"

"Circumstance," she admitted.

"Money doesn't motivate you. You're looking for a purpose. A reason to hope. Let my plan be your reason. We can't beat Crux on our own, but we can deal a pretty major blow to him and maybe bring some people who are still loyal to the Empress back out of hiding and denial. A snowball effect."

She stared at Caleb, considering his statement. "I think you're crazy."

"But…"

She laughed. "Maybe crazy is just what this galaxy needs right now."

*Caleb, I feel.. funny.*

"So, are you in?" Caleb asked. *Funny how?*

Penn responded by returning her knives to their sheathes and stepping aside. "You're home free, Captain."

*The pressure. It hurts.*

Caleb felt it too, a vice suddenly gripping his head.

*It's him. He's trying to get through.*

"Penn, get out of here," Caleb grunted. "Close the hatch…behind you."

"What?" she asked.

*I can't stop him.*

Caleb fell to his knees, clutching his head. He could feel his autonomy slipping away, the Relyeh breaking through Ishek's efforts to protect them and gaining control of his body.

"Penn, run," he wheezed out.

The pain vanished, but only because he had been pushed to the back of his mind, an observer as the Relyeh took over. Penn turned and lunged for the door. Too slow, the Relyeh dove and grabbed her ankle, dragging her to the deck and pulling her back toward him.

She rolled over in his grip, angry but not afraid as she stomped her other heel down on the hand holding her, breaking his grip. Hopping to her feet, she didn't retreat. Instead, she advanced on the Relyeh as he brought Caleb's body upright.

"You said you were in control," she commented.

"*I* am in control," the Relyeh replied. "This entire galaxy is mine."

She came at him, her knives slashing and cutting. The Relyeh didn't block the attacks, letting her slice Caleb's body open in multiple places as he grabbed her by the throat and squeezed. She cut him a few more times before stabbing the hand holding her, driving the blade all the way through the base of his palm and into his wrist, forcing him to let go.

*Caleb. You can help me. We can resist together.*

*How?* Caleb asked.

In answer, a dim light surrounded by pitch black replaced Caleb's vision.

*We're the light. He's the dark. We need to push him out.*

Caleb sensed the coldness of the dark, the light of a dying white dwarf in the middle of the universe, with no destiny of its own.

He refused to accept that.

Unaware of the scene outside his body, he pictured the light exploding outward, expanding, growing, and spreading to stomp out the darkness. He sensed Ishek there, pushing back with him. After his initial push, their white sphere nearly tripled in size. It was a good start. He doubled down, pressing against the cold as if he was squeezing his eyes shut tighter and tighter, all his focus on growing his sphere. It expanded again, developing tendrils that stretched out into the darkness, beginning to absorb more and more of it.

*It's working.*

He held fast, all of his energy focused on pushing out the Relyeh who had seized control. This wasn't like on Galatin, when the battle had left him and Ish exhausted. This training course had tired him some, but he still had plenty of fight left in him.

The light continued spreading; the tendrils becoming a web of cracks in the dark hold. He suddenly snapped back into his body with a ferocity that left him convulsing on the deck. Penn straddled him, holding on tight with a knife pressed against his throat, ready to end his life.

"Penn, wait," he gasped, his body going still. "It's Caleb. I'm back in control."

She looked down at him, obviously able to see the change in his eyes. "Caleb. What the hell was that?"

*We fought him off. But you've lost a lot of blood.*

Ishek's tone remained weak. Caleb's head still pounded, and he was dizzy.

"The enemy," Caleb replied. "He's afraid of me. I...I stopped him." His eyes shifted as Fitz burst into the compartment, Damian, Tae, and the other members of Razor's Edge right behind him.

"Penn, what the hell?" Fitz said as she stood up. "You just had to cut him once." He shifted his attention to Caleb. "I guess we win. He didn't even finish the course."

"Cool it, Fitz," Penn said. "He needs a doctor, not your attitude." She extended her hand to Caleb. He accepted it, letting her help him back to his feet. "I'll take him to sick bay." She slipped under Caleb's arm, keeping him upright while ignoring the blood soaking her tactical gear. "Captain Card didn't lose. We're going to honor the agreement you made."

"What?" Fitz said. "He's—"

"I said he didn't lose," she snapped. "Are you questioning my integrity?"

"N..no, Penn. Of course not. I just don't understand."

"You will soon enough."

She led Caleb past the others, out the hatch and away from the finish line, back to the lift.

"Thank you," Caleb said.

"This is crazy, you know," she replied.

"Like you said, maybe crazy is just what this galaxy needs right now."

# CHAPTER 17

"I don't need to go to sickbay," Caleb said once he and Penn were in the lift together. "Take me to my quarters. The lacerations will heal within the hour." He extricated himself from her efforts to hold him up. "I'm feeling better already."

She looked at him in disbelief. "The Advocate?"

"Yes. One benefit of carrying a slug in my armpit."

*I hate when you call me that too, meat sack.*

"That's amazing." She paused. Standing almost eye to eye with him, she looked curiously at him.

Caleb knew exactly what she wanted to know. It was the same thing on his mind. The same question. What Relyeh had such power over Ishek?

"I don't know that much," he said. "I wish I knew more. I'm sorry if I…if he hurt you."

She laughed. "Hurt me? Not a chance. I watched you against Haruka and Greaser. You're a good fighter, Caleb Card. The enemy that replaced you? He didn't know how to handle himself in a physical fight. That's how I knew you weren't yourself. And why I had a knife to your throat, instead of through it, when you regained control."

Caleb smiled back at her. "I appreciate you not killing me and getting me out of there so quickly. I just wish I knew why he would seize control of me at that moment. What did he hope to gain?"

"Maybe he wanted me to kill you."

"He could have overpowered Ish and forced us into an airlock if that's all he wanted."

*Perhaps he just wanted to know where we are. He probably knew our location when we were with the Empress. There were other Legionnaires that he could use to observe us. But with no other Relyeh around us here and now, it is easier for us to hide from him.*

"Ish suggested he was trying to locate us," Caleb explained. "I don't know if just entering our consciousness is enough to do that."

*It depends. He didn't have firm control for very long. It leads me to wonder if he isn't as strong as I first believed. We were weakened before, or simply caught by surprise. I've maintained a greater level of alertness since then.*

"At least we've learned he can't completely have his way with us. We've proven we're not as dangerous because of his power over us as we thought."

"It's weird listening to you have a conversation with your symbiote," Penn said.

"You'll get used to it," Caleb replied.

The lift arrived on Deck Six. The cab doors opened, and Caleb and Penn stepped out together. She stayed with him as he slowly made his way back to his quarters, typing in his passcode to open the hatch.

"So you don't know who this mystery puppet master is?" Penn asked, standing outside the open door.

"He's Relyeh. I know that much. But not a khoron or even an Advocate. I'll hold a briefing to go over my objectives and fill everybody in on this anonymous enemy once I've finished speaking to the other former military on the ship. I think everything will become more clear to all of us by then."

"How many Royal Armed Forces rejects do we have on this ship? I know about Fitz, Sarge, Tae, and Sparkles. I—"

"Wait. Sparkles is former military?"

"He did a tour with the Nobukkian Guard. Not the RAF, but he's still a trained fighter."

"Good to know."

"Have you met Atrice yet?"

"No. The name sounds familiar though."

"He must be on your list of former military. He used to be a starfighter pilot, but we don't have any starfighters on board, so now he's in the galley."

"He's cooking?"

"He turned his need for speed into a need to feed," she answered. "His words, not mine."

Caleb grinned. "I have eleven on my list. Seven I haven't contacted yet. I wanted to get the biggest egos out of the way first."

"I don't have an ego, Captain. Fitz's is big enough for all of us." She glanced into his quarters. "I'm sure you want to shower off the blood and get into something with fewer holes. I need to clean up too. You've earned my respect, Captain, which means you've also earned the respect of Razor's Edge. We have your back, from this moment forward."

"Thank you."

"One question before I go?"

"What is it?"

"What did you mean when you said you *arrived* in this galaxy with Ishek? Where did you come from?"

"You'll learn the answer to that question at the briefing."

"Can I have a hint?"

"What do you know about a starship named Pathfinder?"

"There are a lot of ships in the Spiral, Captain. I don't recognize the name."

"That's your hint. If you find an answer somewhere, let me know."

Penn seemed confused by his answer, but she didn't push back. "It was nice meeting you, Captain. I'll see you around?"

"It was nice meeting you too. Count on it."

She offered him the quick dip of her chin he had learned was a pirate salute before turning on her heel and heading toward her quarters. Caleb watched her for a moment before entering his suite and tapping the control to close the hatch behind him.

*You could have invited her in.*

"I didn't come here for romance, Ish. We've got a job to do."

*You didn't come here through any choice of your own. I can read your mind, remember? I know how intrigued you are by her.*

"Are you playing matchmaker now? That's the last thing on my mind."

*You can lie to yourself. You can't lie to me.*

"Did our mystery guest leave any clues as to his identity when we kicked him out?" Caleb asked, changing the subject. It didn't matter how his subconscious registered Penn's appeal. He would never mix business with pleasure. From what he had observed and even experienced first hand a couple times over the years, it never ended well.

*I was a little busy fighting to get him out of us.*

"And you pulled me into that fight. How did you do that?"

*I opened up my mind to you. If you hadn't been so focused on our attacker, you could have used the opportunity to delve deep into my psyche. I left myself very vulnerable to you. I had no other choice.*

Caleb could tell the admission made Ishek uncomfortable. "I wouldn't take advantage of you like that. But that trick might be something we can use in the future."

*How might we use it? We both need to be in my consciousness for that to happen, which leaves no one driving the meat bus.*

"That's not much better than meat sack," Caleb said while Ishek laughed. "I imagine overpowering other khoron would be easier if we were both putting our energy into it."

*Perhaps, but you would need to be sure your body remained protected while we did.*

"We made a bunch of new friends with guns today."

*Agreed. You need to hit the shower. We smell.*

Caleb entered the head, tugging off his shirt and looking at the cuts along the surface of his skin. Like the name of her boarding crew, Penn had inflicted the wounds with razor-like precision. Ishek remained amused.

*I can't wait to see what kind of trouble we can get into tomorrow.*

# CHAPTER 18

"There she is, Captain," Rufus said, enhancing the view of the distant planet in the forward viewscreen so that it became more than a blue pixel on the display. "Welcome to Aroon."

Home to nearly a million people, Caleb had learned Aroon was one of the lesser occupied planets in the Spiral. Smaller than Earth, with a faster rotation and slightly less gravity, it was the second of six rocks orbiting a yellow dwarf star the residents called Surya. Like Earth, it had a moon orbiting it, which created tidal flow for the eighty percent of the planet composed of water. Among the vast blue oceans rested a pair of large archipelagos where none of the islands measured more than a thousand square kilometers in size.

From what Sasha had told Caleb, the islands didn't all have names, and most remained uninhabited. At least when it came to paying taxes to the Empire. One small group of islands at the northern tip of the eastern archipelago was, by all accounts, uninhabited when in truth it was home to one of the largest black markets within a thousand light years. It was run by a consortium of underground cartels who could only get along because of the amount of coin involved. They were apparently as much a myth as Pathfinder, a place most people in the Spiral knew next to nothing about. They would never truly understand or experience it for themselves.

Damian had told him that even Lo'ane had heard of the Sunshine Isles, but since the cartels' side hustle wasn't causing trouble for the Empire, the Empire had deigned not to kick the hornet's nest. Besides, the Royal spy network had operatives in the Isles, the success of the illicit trade markets making it easier for them to track.

*It's about time.*

Caleb ignored Ishek. The symbiote had been in a sour mood in the sixteen hours since the enemy Relyeh had overpowered him. After the initial shock had worn off, Ish had lamented allowing Caleb into his senses, despite the benefits the newfound capability might prove to offer. He'd tried to ease his bonded companion's concerns, but for Ish, it was more about giving away some kind of secret than it was a fear of Caleb misusing the ability. Ish just needed to come to terms with the issue on his own. The more Caleb thought about the symbiote's response, the more hypocritical it seemed, which wasn't altogether unexpected, considering Ish was Relyeh. And it wasn't as though Caleb didn't understand his misgivings. Being forced upon each other had been a mutual violation, fostering a vulnerability neither one had ever experienced before, and neither would want to go through it again.

*Sometimes I wish you could keep your thoughts to yourself.*

*Ditto*, Caleb replied. "How long before we reach orbit?"

"Not long," Rufus replied. "We can keep coming in fairly hot. It'll give Orbital Defense fits, but we have the credentials to keep them from going on the offensive."

"What credentials?"

"The Aroon government controls OD, at least on paper," Damian said. "In reality…"

"The cartels run OD," Caleb finished. "So we'll have to bribe them."

"They don't call it a bribe," Naya said. "They call it a tourism fee."

Caleb laughed. "Of course they do. How much?"

"A hundred thousand," Damian said.

"That's steep."

"That's just to prove you're a serious buyer needing to get a ship to the surface. The Consortium claims ten percent of every sale."

"Damn. Can we land Gorgon down there?"

"No. You'll take the transport down and meet with a broker. We have a drone on board that meets intergalactic trade requirements for accurate holographic depictions of the merchandise. We'll broadcast everything to prospective buyers to bid on."

"Bid? I thought we could do a straight up sale?"

"We'll set a decent minimum. But this is all illegal cargo, Captain. None of it has a sticker price."

"Okay, but if we have a drone to broadcast a depiction of the goods, why are we paying a hundred thousand to go down to the surface?"

"Collateral. You're it."

"And you're sure the Berserkers won't leave me stranded down there?" Caleb asked only half-jokingly.

After cleaning up from running the training course, Caleb had sought the other former military on board. Only Hank, the ship's head of logistics, had been ambivalent about his overall ideas for Gorgon's future. He enjoyed life on the pirate ship, along with his duties but didn't care a whit for politics, claiming the galaxy at large was a steaming turd badly in need of a supermassive black hole. The other former members of the Royal Armed Forces were all in. With Penn and Razor's Edge on his side, he wasn't nearly as concerned now about the potential for mutiny.

"I think the Berserkers believe if they try their luck again, you'll hunt them down across the entire Spiral," Damian replied with a chuckle.

"That isn't too far from the truth. I'm sure Penn would be happy to help me find them."

"You could always lock out the helm and arm the self-destruct. That's how Graystone handled away trips."

"I'd prefer not to be so drastic. I'd like to trust them."

"Captain, we're being hailed by Orbital Defense," Sasha announced.

"Open the channel," Caleb replied.

"Channel open, Captain."

"Incoming starship, we're tracking you on a high-velocity ingress. Our orbital batteries are calculating firing solutions as we speak. Identify yourself and your intentions immediately, or we will open fire."

Caleb glanced at Rufus. He had said their speed would upset Orbital Defense, not that they would reply immediately with threats. The pilot smirked, glancing back at him. He was playing games and enjoying it.

"Orbital Defense, this is Captain Card of the starship Gorgon," Caleb said. "We're transmitting identifiers now." Caleb nodded to Naya, who transferred the coin. "We're here for some rest and relaxation on the Summer Isles."

"Identification approved," the controller responded a few seconds later. "Orbital batteries are standing down. You should be more careful in the future, Captain Card. The wrong controller might shoot first and ask questions later."

"And risk losing a good chunk of coin by blasting a trading partner?" Caleb replied. "I doubt that would end well for the controller."

The man on the other side of the comms laughed. "A fair assessment. I'm setting a marker in geosynchronous orbit for your primary to occupy during your stay. You'll have thirty minutes once you reach the mark to depart for the Summer Isles. Failure to comply will result in termination of your landing permit and orbital rights. Do you understand?"

"Perfectly," Caleb replied.

"In that case, enjoy your vacation, Captain."

"Transmission ended," Sasha announced.

"That was easy," Caleb remarked.

"Not as easy as you might think," Naya said. "We just burned eighty percent of our local funds for the honor. As of right now, we don't have enough coin left to pay the entire crew."

"Can we keep that quiet for now?" Caleb asked. "We should be replenished within the next few hours."

"Aye, Captain."

"Since you mentioned it, are you any closer to accessing Graystone's accounts?"

"Not yet, Captain. We needed to be out of hyperspace for me to attack the problem from a cooperative angle."

"What does that mean?"

"I either need to be highly confident of Graystone's passcodes or I need to convince someone at his institution to let me change those passcodes."

"The latter sounds harder than the former."

"They'll have verbal codes we'll need to talk our way around."

"And you think you can do that?"

"Not me. Sasha. She's more of the fast-talking, social engineering type."

"And she's getting a percentage from your take?"

"I thought we could split it."

Caleb looked at Sasha. "How much?"

"Ten percent," she replied.

Caleb stifled a groan. "We're all on the same team here, aren't we?"

"We're pirates, Captain," Sasha said in reply.

"Fine. Naya, you get thirty-two percent. Sasha, you get ten."

"Nice doing business with you, Captain," Sasha said.

"Yeah, right," Caleb groused.

*You should have haggled. You're being taken for a ride.*

*Efficiency is more important to me right now. You heard Naya. We can't pay our bills.*

*Whatever.*

"I'm going to get ready for my little excursion and head down to the cargo bay," Caleb said. "Damian, you have the bridge."

"Aye, Captain," Damian replied. "I have the bridge. But why are you going to the cargo bay?"

"I saw the transport there when I came on board."

Damian laughed. "Do you think Graystone would let anyone see him in a ride like that? The hangar bay is on Decks Three and Four, halfway between amidships and the stern on the port side. Your away team will wait for you there."

"I didn't realize this ship had a hangar. Atrice said we don't have any starfighters."

"We don't, but we have space for them if we ever have enough coin to pick up a few."

"Our transport's the next best thing," Rufus said.

"What do you mean?" Caleb asked.

"You'll see when you get there. Enjoy your vacay, Cap."

# CHAPTER 19

Caleb entered his passcode into the control pad next to the twin blast doors leading into the hangar, the pocket doors promptly sliding open. A secured area, the laser sensor over the door was there to scan crew members before entry, but for now he chose not to feed any more of his information into the ship's systems than was absolutely necessary.

*You're being paranoid.*

Caleb ignored Ishek's grousing as he advanced into the hangar. He had returned to his quarters before heading to the hangar, having swapped out his basic utilities for a more fashionable outfit befitting a pirate captain. Black pants, ankle-high magboots, and a red shirt covered by a long coat with the appearance of leather. It was much lighter however, offering a modicum of protection from various offensive threats. Of course, he had his underlay on beneath the street clothes to further protect him from any potential attack. He also had an ion blaster strapped to his thigh. It felt like overkill considering how organized the black market operation already appeared to be, but he'd decided not to take any chances. Not when he knew the Relyeh were already aware of him. And there was always an outside chance they had guessed where he was headed.

Occupying nearly the entire port side of two decks, the hangar was large, open, and relatively empty. On one side, a dozen or so pallets were secured to the bulkhead and deck with cables. A grated metal staircase and simple lift were attached to the opposite bulkhead. Glancing up to the top of the stairs, he found a small transparency where the hangar boss was standing with his arms folded across his chest, looking back at Caleb. He offered an exaggerated nod, which Caleb returned.

The deck had only four ships arranged across its over-sized expanse. Three of them were identical. He had wondered how boarding crews crossed over from Gorgon to target vessels, and he felt pretty sure these three ships answered that question. Small and sleek, they reminded Caleb of cruise missiles, only instead of fins, they had a handful of vectoring thrusters jutting out from all sides and a large ion thruster in the rear, all of which promised incredible maneuverability.

The ships had no armaments that he could see, and assuming the rear two-thirds of the craft housed the engines, they could carry six people. Each craft rested on small skids, with a rounded rectangular extension hanging almost low enough from their bellies to scrape the deck. It stood to reason they were interlocks, allowing the ships to dock with airlocks and external hatches in a variety of shapes and sizes.

The process of elimination meant the fourth ship had to be the transport, though it didn't look like any transport Caleb had ever seen. Rufus hadn't been kidding when he said the vessel was the next best thing to a starfighter. Designed for both space and atmosphere, it was relatively flat, with an aggressive-looking hybrid wing design. A pair of ion thrusters at each end of the wing offered increased maneuverability, while a larger block occupied the craft's slightly rounded rear. While the flight deck wasn't visible from outside, the weapons systems were currently on full display, which Caleb assumed was for his benefit.

Two weapons bays hung open beneath each of the wings, the paired modules matched on the top side. One bay held tubes for small rockets, or maybe even something akin to the tacks Spirit had carried. The other one appeared to be a wide-barreled ion cannon or beam weapon, the barrel telescoped out to clear the fuselage. The guns were fixed forward, which he didn't love, but by the way the bays extended from the wings he had a sense the armaments were intended to be a guarded secret. He wondered if Orbital Defense even let them into the atmosphere if they knew the ship was carrying so much ordnance.

The entry to the transport was through an open hatch that descended as a ramp on the starboard side. Caleb expected his away team would wait for him there, but it appeared they had already boarded.

"Captain, we've just arrived at our assigned orbital coordinates," Rufus announced through the comms patch behind his ear. "You have thirty minutes before departure."

"I'm in the hangar," Caleb replied. "We'll be ready for departure in a few minutes."

"Aye, Captain."

He hurried to the transport, reaching up to touch the ship's exterior. Rather than cold, hard metal, it looked and felt rubbery, not unlike his combat armor. It was definitely a strange material for a starship. He had never seen anything like it before.

*You haven't seen that many starships, and certainly not from this galaxy. Yet you think as if the material is odd when it may be relatively standard here.*

*Do you have to be so touchy about everything right now? It's already gotten tiresome.*

*I'm simply making an observation.*

*I know that you're upset, but what's done is done. And it may be a good thing in the end.*

*I still don't see how.*

*I need you to knuckle up, Ish. Put your issues and your attitude on the back burner until we're done with this business.*

Ishek didn't answer, which Caleb took as a good sign. He'd rather the symbiote kept his thoughts to himself than be distracted by his bad mood. Ascending the ramp, he found himself in a small, empty compartment just ahead of the reinforced cocoon of the flight deck. Unlike the drab, bare metal of a military craft, the walls here were painted over in soft tones, the deck covered in a rich red and gold carpet, illuminated with warm overhead lights.

Following a passageway behind the flight deck, he stepped through an open hatch to find a half dozen plush seats arranged in the center of the rear cabin. The frontmost pair faced forward. The rear four were on swivels. While there were no transparencies in the fuselage, external cameras provided an outside view on internal displays that ran the length of each bulkhead. A full bar occupied the area behind the seats. Linx's mother waited there, in a stewardess outfit Graystone had undoubtedly ordered her to wear. The short skirt, high boots, and low-cut blouse didn't fit his vision of an away team in the slightest.

She smiled at him when his eyes landed on her, and he noticed her mouth quivering slightly at the corners as she fought to hold a seductive smile when she wasn't happy providing it. Caleb could taste her discomfort and fear through Ishek, who enjoyed it as a matter of his nature. Even though Damian had likely told her he wasn't like Graystone, the apparent trauma of the past wasn't so easily overcome.

"I'm sorry," Caleb said. "We haven't been formally introduced. I'm—"

"Captain Card," she said nervously. "I...I saw you in the commons. And my daughter, Linx. She...she met you earlier. She says you're the nicest man, aside from Sarge, that she's ever met. I...I'm Lucinda. Lucy. Can I get you something to drink?"

"No, thank you, Lucy. I appreciate the offer, but I won't be needing your service on this trip. You're free to go."

She seemed more upset than relieved by the statement. "Captain, will you still pay me?"

Caleb nodded. "Of course."

She relaxed immediately. "Thank you, Captain. Thank you." She offered him a series of nods as she left her station near the bar and moved to pass him to the exit.

"Lucy, one thing," he said, pausing her in the corridor just past him. She turned around.

"Aye, Captain?"

"Why are you here?"

"I don't understand, sir."

"Linx is so young. Why are you working on a pirate vessel?"

She seemed taken aback by the question. "No one's ever asked me that before. I...uh...I got into some trouble, back home. Coin has always been tight, and I needed to take care of my daughter. Here we get room and board, and I can send money to repay my debts. One day we'll be square, and we can go back to Persephon without worrying about the law arresting me." She had tears in her eyes by the time she finished explaining. "Linx will finally have the normal life I've deprived her of."

Caleb remembered what Damian had told him about the crew. They didn't all want to be thieves. Some just had no other choice. Clearly, Lucy had done something her planet considered illegal at some point. Just as clearly, she regretted it and was trying to make amends. "I understand. Thank you."

She nodded again before hurrying from the ship. Penn stepped through the flight deck hatch right after she left.

"Captain Card," she said, looking him over. "Welcome aboard Medusa. Nice get-up."

Caleb looked back at her. Damian hadn't told him who would be part of the away team, but he wasn't completely surprised to see her. He was glad to see they shared a similar style. He didn't want to stand out. "Special Off… Penn," he corrected, almost too late. "You, too. I was wondering where my crew was hiding. Who else do you have in there?"

"Only Atrice, Captain. He'll fly us down."

"Just the two of us? I expected a full complement."

"Sarge felt it would draw too much attention. I agreed. This kind of operation isn't my typical MO, but it's not totally out of line with my training. You?"

"My specialty is search and rescue," Caleb replied. "Recovering people from difficult situations."

She grinned in response to the statement. "So your *save the Empire* objective is right in your wheelhouse."

"I wouldn't go that far."

"Billions of people are in a difficult situation. It seems appropriate to me."

"I'm referring to individuals, small groups at most. And normally, I'm helping them escape a threat. But right now there is no escape."

"I'm sure you'll adapt. You already have in fact."

"I appreciate the vote of confidence."

"You convinced me with your briefing. I'm excited to get started."

"Medusa, huh?" he asked regarding the transport's name.

She shrugged. "Graystone never named her. It seemed fitting."

"I'm surprised you're familiar with Greek mythology, considering Earth is a myth here."

"I don't know what Greek is. I am familiar with Medusa. Snakes for hair, turned anyone who looked upon her into stone."

"I guess it's all Greek to you," Caleb quipped with a smile.

*That was bad. Even for you. Or perhaps especially for you.*

*Your mood seems slightly improved.*

*A tasty snack does that.*

Caleb leaned his head past her, looking into the flight deck. There was only a single pilot station in the center, outfitted with standard flight controls, a pair of touchscreens, a projected HUD, and a large forward viewscreen. Atrice sat in the pilot seat, strangely wearing his chef's apron over his flight suit.

"Cookie, are we prepped for launch?" he asked, deciding not to ask about the apron.

"Aye, Captain," he replied, glancing over. "I just need to tuck up the merrymakers." He tapped one of the touchscreens. Caleb felt a soft vibration as the weapons pods sealed shut. "That'll do it. Buckle up in the rear cabin and we're good to go. It's a half hour drop to Summer Isles spaceport."

"Copy that," Caleb said, turning back to Penn. "Shall we?"

She smiled, motioning to his blaster. "You'll want to lose that before we disembark. Carrying weapons onto the Isles is grounds for immediate expulsion and a hefty fine."

"Good to know. So everyone down there who isn't a guard is unarmed?"

Her grin turned more sly. "Don't be ridiculous. You just have to be a little more subtle about it. I came prepared, Captain."

"I figured you would." He returned to the rear cabin,

leaving through the outer hatch to strip off his gun belt and leave it with a deckhand with instructions to give it to Damien for safekeeping before getting back onboard. "Cookie, you can close the loading ramp."

"Aye, Captain."

Choosing the forward-facing seat beside Penn, Caleb sat down and strapped in.

"This should be interesting," she said.

"Hopefully not too interesting," Caleb replied, sitting back in his seat, relatively calm. "Cookie, we're all set."

"Aye, Captain," Atrice answered.

Red lights flashed outside the transport, warning anyone in the hangar that a ship was about to launch. Caleb couldn't see or hear the bay doors opening directly in front of them but he knew it was happening as the ship gently vibrated, the thrusters powering up. The magnetic clamps holding the skids to the deck released, inertia shoving Caleb further back in the seat as the ship rocketed across the bay and out into space.

Immediately, Caleb noticed the other two dozen starships parked in geosynchronous orbit over the Summer Isles. A variety of shapes and sizes, most were smaller than Gorgon, more scuffed and worn, blocky and ugly, with few visible gun batteries. While none of them had painted a jolly roger anywhere on their exterior, their size and condition made it painfully obvious they were pirates or scavengers. It was much easier to identify the cartel ships and traders. The large rectangular freighters and cargo haulers stretched across space, their exteriors smooth save for sensor whips and the bulbous exhausts of powerful ion thrusters at their sterns. Those ships were in pristine shape, practically sparkling, with registry names and numbers printed along their sides, sometimes with the name of the company they belonged to. He wasn't at all surprised to find a Star Line Transport Company freighter hanging in a nearby orbit.

"Have you ever seen so many starships in one place?" Penn asked, obviously recalling what he had told them about his origins during the briefing.

"No, never," Caleb replied, head on a swivel while he gawked at both sides. "Proxima only has about twenty larger spacecraft right now. Earth has a pair of starhoppers and nothing else."

"You should see Atlas. The only time I've ever seen less than a few hundred ships in orbit was when Crux launched his attack."

"You were there?" Caleb asked, surprised.

"I was nearby, with too little to offer, too late. When Atlas fell, I made my way out here with the three operatives under my command. We sold our ship, divvied up the profits, and I swore to myself that I no longer cared what happened to me or the Empire," She sighed heavily, glancing over at him. "Then you came along and screwed it all up."

Caleb smirked. "Sorry about that."

"It's not a good feeling, coming back here. It just reminds me that I'm a coward at heart."

"If that were true, you wouldn't be here now. I told Damian the same thing."

"I hope you're right," Penn said, the two of them falling silent as the transport pushed into the atmosphere.

# CHAPTER 20

"It's amazing," Caleb commented, looking down on the surface of Aroon. Although it was currently daytime, the islands of the archipelagos remained illuminated because of the planet's accelerated rotation. Millions of pinpoints of light rose from thousands of land masses, most of them between ten and fifteen square kilometers in size. They were connected by bridges that created a pattern from the air which reminded him of a circuit board.

"Those are the Sunshine Isles, there," Penn replied, pointing out the viewscreen to the northern edge of the islands, where the illumination became more sparse. A transport was on its way back to orbit from the area, launching in a vector that would cut through the center of their looping descent. While the land masses further south were speckled with a mix of architecture that ran the gamut from tall glass skyscrapers to cabana-laden beachfront resorts, their destination appeared to be home only to a group of old structures that could easily have been abandoned. The area was supported by a tiny spaceport that appeared, at least from their current position, as if it hadn't been used in over a hundred years. It was an illusion, of course.

As Medusa continued the descent, the truth of the Sunshine Isles became more apparent. The spaceport was like a smaller scale, two-dimensional facsimile of the scene in Aroon's orbit, and clearly active. Dozens of small transports were either parked, taking off, or about to land in individual spots. Each was enveloped by a square of light sized to the particular dimensions of the ship parked or about to land there. Caleb couldn't help but notice that their designated parking for Medusa spot was one of the largest.

"Do you have any idea where Graystone got this ship?" Caleb asked, glancing over at Penn.

"He already had it when I joined the crew," she replied. "Rumor is he won it in a card game from Jake Leighton."

"Should I know who that is?"

"No, I guess you wouldn't. Jake Leighton is the pirate king. He started with a single ship, and now has a network of forty crews running all sorts of scams, interdictions, and illicit cargo hauling operations."

"And this all happens outside of the cartels?"

"He's a member of the Consortium."

"So he probably knows Medusa is hiding weapons pods in her wings."

"I'm sure, but he would never say anything to anyone else. It would be unsportsmanlike conduct."

"Pirates have rules of conduct?"

"Only a few. That's one of them."

"How did you wind up joining Graystone aboard Gorgon? It sounds like there are quite a few pirate ships out there."

"Not as many as you might think when you consider the size of the galaxy and the number of planets involved. Leighton's network has half the entire pirate fleet, give or take."

"What about the ships in orbit? I thought those were pirates."

"Mostly salvage crews and scavengers. They're still picking up the pieces left behind by the war. As for how I found Graystone, it was just a matter of coincidence. He was in the right place at the right time, and I didn't know enough about the pirate life to be picky. That's the same reason most former RAF ended up under his command. There are others scattered everywhere, from pirate ships to mercenary crews, to localized orbital and planetary defense contractors and corporate militias. We had to go somewhere that wasn't under Crux. Your origin story is a lot more exciting."

"You haven't heard half of it."

Atrice guided Medusa to its spot on the tarmac, touching down gently in the designated landing zone. Penn was on her feet the moment the ship gently bounced on its skids, Caleb right behind her. She paused ahead of the hatch, which was already descending to let them out.

"Cookie," Caleb said through his comms patch. "Keep the ship ready for a quick departure."

"Aye, Captain," he replied. "Are we expecting trouble?"

"No, but it's always better to be prepared." He disconnected and followed Penn to the tarmac, glancing at the two ships in the adjacent spots. Neither had the same dark, rubbery outer layer as Medusa. *Still haven't seen any other ships with the same coating,* he mentioned to Ishek.

*Small sample size.*

Caleb smirked, about to ask Penn if they had to walk from the landing zone to the spaceport proper, nearly a kilometer away when he noticed a hovercraft racing toward them. Large enough to seat eight passengers, the driverless vehicle pulled to a stop in front of them, waiting while they climbed in. Always the gentleman, he guided Penn to a seat with a hand at her back. The moment Caleb's butt hit the seat beside her, the hovercraft started moving again, winding its way around the other transports to a second ship that must have landed right behind them. Small and rusted, it was in such poor shape Caleb wondered if it would make it back to orbit.

The hatch opened as the automated taxi came to a stop beside the ship, the mechanism sticking a few times before a slender, pale hand grabbed the bottom and lifted it the rest of the way. Caleb stared as a slim humanoid covered in a layer of short, light-brown fur and dressed in a dark flight suit stepped out of the transport. It had a wide face and wide, narrow eyes, a flat nose and a slightly protruding jaw leading to a smaller, thin-lipped mouth. A pair of small, catlike ears rose from the sides of its head, split in the middle by a line of black fur. Its hands were composed of three fingers and a thumb, its bare feet more like stretched out paws. It regarded Caleb confidently.

"A Jiba-ki," Penn whispered somewhat excitedly.

Caleb continued to stare, not because he was looking at an intelligent non-human life form. He had encountered other non-humans before, starting with Ishek. But they were all Relyeh. This was the first alien he had seen that hadn't been subjected to their will. Ishek confirmed his thought.

*I've never seen or heard of a Jiba-ki before.*

It approached the transport, its eyes locked on Caleb. He knew he was staring, but he'd been looking for long enough that turning away now would be worse than keeping his gaze on the creature. The taxi got underway as the Jiba-ki settled in the seat directly behind them, mouth opening to emit a series of low growling tones and vibrations. A small pendant around its neck translated the sounds to English after a short delay.

"You have never seen a Jiba-ki before, have you, human?" he asked in a baritone male voice.

"No," Caleb replied. "First time. I'm sorry to stare."

"It is a common reaction. I am not offended. Do you think I am beautiful? It is true."

The question caught Caleb off-guard, as did the alien answering his own question. He wondered if the soft growling sigh the Jiba-ki ended his sentences with was throwing off the translation pendant around his neck.

"I do," Penn replied.

The Jiba-ki purred softly, the sound translated to, "Thank you." Caleb thought that would be the end of the pleasantries, but the alien spoke up again a moment later. "I have come to the Isles in search of work. It is true."

"What kind of work do you do?" Caleb asked.

"I am a hunter."

"A bounty hunter?"

"I hunt in exchange for coin. It is true. I have heard there is a Dark Exchange here. I will locate a new hunt."

Caleb had heard of the Dark Exchange. A black market for services rather than items. From what Tae had told him, there was a hefty fee to join an exchange, as well as an annual cost to maintain membership. As a job board, businesses would post contracts, professionals would bid on them, and everything would be done without anyone ever knowing the identities of the parties involved. That detail meant a lot of business that flowed through an exchange was based on reputation, and of course the higher the reputation, the higher the bid, and often the more difficult or dangerous the job. Damian had told him it was entirely possible Crux had used the Dark Exchange to buy the murder of Lo'ane's father before he had assassinated him with the help of a khoron.

That the Jiba-ki was already a member of the exchange said a lot about him, though it didn't reveal the type of jobs he took or how unsavory they might be. He would certainly never reveal his identity to them. For all Caleb knew, he was talking to the greatest bounty hunter in the Spiral.

*Judging by his ship, perhaps not.*

*Don't you always tell me that looks can be deceiving.*

*Not* that *deceiving.*

It was a good sign that Ishek was trying to be funny again. His mood was headed in the right direction.

"Are you also a hunter?" the Jiba-ki asked Caleb. "You have the look of a hunter. It is true."

"Yes, and no. I'm definitely hunting for things, but right now I'm a starship captain."

The Jiba-ki let out a high-pitched whine that served as a laugh. "Right now? Do you change your profession as you change your pants?"

"I hear when you return to your homeworld, your kind don't wear pants," Penn said.

He continued laughing, tugging at his shirt. "It is very confining. It pulls at my fur. It is true."

"My job has changed a few times in the last few days," Caleb agreed.

"I will ask. What brings you to Aroon?"

"Selling some surplus. Nothing too exciting."

"Of course. It is true."

The hovercraft pulled to a stop in front of a single-story, white stone building open to the elements, though Caleb doubted that was ever a problem here. Three guards were stationed just inside the open front door, armed and armored, their faces shrouded by opaque visors.

"Line up," one of them grunted, pointing to a spot on the floor just inside the building. Caleb could see the other end of the structure was open as well, the water lapping at the shore only a few meters past it. This island was barely large enough for the tiny spaceport, and he didn't see any boats. He glanced at Penn, who stepped into line beside him, seemingly unconcerned.

One guard approached her with a wand, running it down one side of her body and up the other, back and front, and between her legs. It didn't make any unexpected sounds, so Caleb assumed that meant it had registered her as unarmed. The wand had to be more than just a metal detector. Didn't it?

He stepped forward next. The guard repeated the process, again finding nothing of note and allowing him to pass. "Where do we go from here?" he asked, looking around the small building. He felt like he was on vacation in Tonga, not preparing to visit one of the busiest black markets in a galaxy billions of light years from the small island nation.

"We process visitors in groups," she replied. "Hold tight."

They waited while the guard checked the Jiba-ki. While the wand didn't go off, they didn't immediately let him through.

"Let me see your claws," one of them said.

He held up his hands, extending four-inch razors from them. His feet reacted similarly.

"You aren't clipped."

"They are within acceptable limits. It is true."

Caleb watched in surprise as one guard used a laser device to measure the claws on both hands and feet.

"Ten millimeters. Within regulations," he said, straightening up. "Go ahead."

The Jiba-ki retracted his claws, walking over to Caleb and Penn. "I am versed in this game."

Two of the guards moved to the front of the building facing the tarmac. The other approached the wall on the far side of the building. He did something that caused the wall to sink into the floor, revealing a ramp behind it.

"Welcome to the Sunshine Isles," he said. "Enjoy your stay."

# CHAPTER 21

Caleb and Penn started down the ramp. The Jiba-ki quickly fell in step beside them, apparently pleased not to be alone. "Today, I will be called Gontar," he announced. "What will you be called? It is true."

"Athena," Penn decided, sticking with Greek mythology, even if she couldn't identify it as Greek.

"Well met, Athena," Gontar said, bowing his head before looking at Caleb. "And you?"

"Caleb," he replied, drawing a momentary look of shock from Penn and a full-on complaint from Ishek.

*You're supposed to use an alias, dummy.*

*When everyone else is using a pseudonym, the real name becomes the alias*, he replied.

He sensed Ishek's switch from annoyance to amusement. *Why did I never think of that?*

*Maybe I should have told him my name was Ishek.*

"Well met, Cayheb," he said, unable to vocalize his name. "Is this the first time you have come to Aroon? It is true."

Caleb almost affirmed the question, but a look from

Penn suggested he should be more coy. "Perhaps," he replied. "And you?"

"Perhaps," Gontar said, laughing. They both knew he had already confirmed it was his first time on the planet.

They reached the bottom of the ramp, having descended nearly twenty meters and exiting into a large, open space.

"Oh," Caleb said, looking to his left. "Wow."

The entire wall was transparent, revealing the ocean and its inhabitants just beyond. Myriad aquatic life forms gathered around vibrant coral, some drifting, some darting around and through the reef's nooks and crannies, the sunlight passing through the water reflecting off iridescent scales. A creature resembling a turtle floated overhead, its hardened carapace coated in a thick layer of algae that smaller fish swarmed around, feeding on. Closer to the bottom, a large eel slithered between the coral and the glass, its large eye regarding Caleb with a look of curiosity. When a smaller crustacean swam too close, its tongue lashed out like it was a frog, catching the creature and pulling it into a toothy maw.

"Now I know this is your first time on Aroon as well," Gontar said, apparently unimpressed with the display. Caleb tore his gaze from the undersea entertainment, following him to a small, pill-shaped pod resting on the far side of the room. A transparent tunnel extended away from the island in both directions.

*I'll remind you to be more careful about accidentally giving away information better kept private.*

"Don't these islands have bridges?" Caleb remarked, confused by the underwater transit.

"These islands are rumored to be uninhabited," Penn reminded him. "The real secret of the Sunshine Isles is that it technically isn't a rumor."

"What do you mean?"

"You'll see."

A pod floated nearly silently into the room, stopping a short distance behind the already present tram. A hatch slid open, a ramp extended, and a heavily tattooed man in a dark orange vest and black pants stepped out. He barely looked at Caleb, his gaze lingering on Gontar as he rushed past.

"It is a common reaction. It is true."

The hatch to the front pod opened at their approach, revealing a warm blue interior and four seats. Once again, Caleb and Penn sat in front, with Gontar behind them.

"Destination?" an ephemeral voice asked.

"Recreation," Gontar replied.

"Auctions," Penn said.

"You will arrive at Auctions in three minutes. You will arrive at Recreation in three minutes and thirty-seven seconds." The hatch closed and the pod slowly sped up into the tunnel, its interior walls becoming a full surround view of the ocean on the other side. Caleb continued gawking at it, unable to help himself. He had always loved the ocean, and had once considered the Navy hoping to become a SEAL before settling on the Marines. He didn't regret the career path, but he regretted that he never had the chance to dive as much as he might have wanted.

"Looking at these creatures, I am hungry," Gontar admitted, continuing to make small talk. He pointed to a larger, fast moving fish with flickering iridescent scales. "I would like to eat that one. It is true."

"He's pretty fast," Caleb said. "Do you think you could catch him?"

"In trees, yes. On plains, yes. In mountains, yes. Underwater, no." He laughed.

"It is true," Caleb added.

Gontar's head tilted to the side, more like a dog than a cat. "I do not understand." The reaction drew a laugh from Penn, which prompted Gontar to laugh. He looked out into the water, spotting a smaller fish than the one Gontar had pointed out. "I bet that one tastes pretty good."

Gontar growled softly before speaking. "I would also eat that one," he agreed.

They continued the game for another minute before the next underwater station came into view. Already, Caleb could see multiple tunnels leading into the cavern, and dozens of people inside, entering and exiting trams that soon zipped off into their transparent tubes. Following them away from the station, he spotted four more destinations carved out beneath individual surrounding islands. They reached their stop soon after, the pod slowing as it navigated traffic with the other trams.

"It is decided," Gontar said. "If you intend to spend any additional time in the Sunshine Isles, I would like to purchase a drink for you both. Often, I am stared at but not spoken to. I am honored by your attention. It is true."

"I would think someone in your line of work would prefer not to draw attention," Caleb said.

Gontar's face stiffened, suddenly becoming serious. "When I am working, none will see me if I do not want it."

Caleb smiled. "I believe that. I'm not sure what our itinerary looks like, but if we don't cross paths again, it was fun riding down here with you."

"And you, Athena and Cayheb. It is true." He put out his hand, and Caleb took it to shake, noticing how soft his fur was. Gontar laughed. "I have always enjoyed this custom. Farewell."

The pod came to a stop. Caleb and Penn stepped out. He turned back to offer Gontar a wave before the hatch closed and the pod continued on to Recreation wherever that was.

"This isn't bad, so far," he said to Penn as they crossed the station. Like the spaceport, this area wasn't very busy, with only a pair of women in casual dress passing them before they reached the far side. Unlike the spaceport, there was no ramp. Instead, a pair of lifts waited to carry them deeper beneath the surface.

"We're here to make a simple business transaction," Penn replied. "Let's hope it stays that way."

# CHAPTER 22

Caleb's perception of the lift's speed as it descended led him to believe they must have traveled nearly two kilometers below the surface by the time the cab came to a stop. Waiting for the doors to open, he expected to find himself in a corridor similar to the passageways on Gorgon, or maybe even the smaller passages of Glory. He figured they would be painted in brighter colors to match the coral reefs, especially since the cab was well lit and colorful, its entire back wall a feed from somewhere in the water outside.

His assumption left him disappointed as the area beyond the lift revealed a roomful of computer terminals, most of which were currently unoccupied. He'd wrongly imagined that becoming living collateral for illicit pirate booty would have an air of danger and intrigue to it. That Damian had sent Penn down with him had only bolstered that opinion since she was the most well-trained fighter among the crew and had smuggled a hidden weapon past the spaceport guards. Now, considering the roomful of innocuous computers, he couldn't guess why she thought they might have needed the armament.

At each computer in use, what looked to be a pirate,

salvager or trader stood with a seated drone pilot and a Consortium representative, all of them watching on screen camera feeds. Each rep wore a comms patch, while the pilots paused the drones at selected crates for crew on board each ship to open a crate for viewing. Each crew member seemed to describe a crate's contents and perhaps answering any questions the Consortium reps asked for buyers on the other end of their respective comms. It all seemed overly tedious, and not very high-tech.

*I think we might die of boredom.*

It wasn't the first time Caleb had noticed that the Spiral had a shortfall of advanced technology, especially considering how much time had passed since Pathfinder had arrived. He could only wonder why that was and who might be responsible for the deficiencies.

"Captain Card." A tall, slender man in a tuxedo approached, offering a warm smile. His voice was soft, his entire demeanor peaceful. "My name is Okambe. I will be your concierge during the auction."

"Nice to meet you, Okambe. This is my companion, Athena."

"My lady," Okambe said, respectfully bowing his head to Penn. "If you'll follow me. Your operator, Christopher, is at station seven."

"You seem to have a lot of stations for the small number of auctions occurring right now," Caleb said.

"A keen observation, Captain," Okambe replied, though there wasn't really anything keen about it. The lack of action was plain as day. "Auctions have slowed as the situation in the Spiral has stabilized. War salvage is getting harder to collect, and there is a rumor that Lord Crux does not see the Sunshine Isles in the same neutral light as his predecessors."

"Does that mean there's less supply and greater demand?" Penn asked.

Okambe chuckled. "As always, that depends on what you have to sell."

He led them to the first terminal in the second row of workstations. A shorter, heavier man sat there, a gesture-controlled interface in front of him and a joystick on his right side. A large, curved monitor allowed easy viewing of the feed from the drone, once it was established.

"Christopher, this is Captain Card and his companion Athena," Okambe introduced.

"Hey," Christopher replied, glancing back at them. "According to your ship's identifier, this is your third visit to Aroon for auction, so you already know what to expect."

"It's actually my first visit," Caleb said. "I recently took over for Captain Graystone."

Christopher made a face, as if he had been hoping not to have to explain anything. "Right. I should have realized that from the name change. The process is simple. I'll guide the drone through your cargo hold, take a look at anything you want to sell. There are buyers linked into the feed both locally and remotely. They have ten seconds to bid on each item. The highest bid wins. That's it."

"No questions asked?"

"Our entire operation runs on no questions asked. Nobody here cares what you acquired or how you acquired it, only if they can profit from it."

"There is one more thing," Okambe said. "Once we've completed the bidding, half the funds will be delivered to your account. You and your companion will be sequestered on the Isles until the transfer of goods is finished, to ensure both the quality and quantity of the lots and that you won't flee with both your goods and the down payment. After everything is settled, you'll be free to leave."

"How long will the transfer take?"

"That depends on how much you are selling, but typically less than twenty-four hours."

"Understood."

"Are you ready to start?" Christopher asked.

"Let's do it."

The operator gestured with his left hand. The screen turned on, revealing Gorgon's small cargo bay. Bones stood in front of the drone, only his upper half visible in the feed. "Buyers are ready to start the bidding," Christopher announced.

Bones pointed to the left and led the drone to the crates on the outside of the bay. Caleb cringed when he saw how some of them were damaged from his earlier firefight with the pirates. Bones opened a crate to reveal a single vase. It appeared to be hand painted.

"We have fifty of these," Bones said.

"Bids are in. Next," Christopher replied.

Bones brought the drone to another group of crates, which contained fancy china dishes.

*Graystone must have held up a luxury yacht,* Caleb commented silently to Ishek.

*I doubt this material will be worth much.*

Bones went around the cargo hold, purposely staying off to the side so the drone camera wouldn't capture their pièce de résistance. They had a few crates of perfume that Caleb assumed would go for a higher bid than the china, as well as one crate of plasma rifles. Christopher laughed when Bones pointed out the large golden dragon before announcing there were no bids on it. At least that meant all the other items had sold, even if their overall take was still a mystery.

The bidding took nearly two hours, leaving Caleb so thirsty and bored the only things he wanted was water and a nap. He could tell Penn felt equally fed up, while Okambe's placid demeanor made sense to him now. Someone would need a good grip on their alertness to withstand these auctions day after day, hour after hour. At least the buyers got to calculate value and place bids. There was a competitive nature to that side of the job that kept their minds at least somewhat active.

As Bones finally directed the feed to the center of the cargo bay, it all became worth the wait.

Both Christopher and Okambe gasped as the Nightmare came into view. Even Caleb was surprised. He hadn't expected their techs to repair the forward transparency he had shattered. The ship actually looked like it was back in operating condition.

The atmosphere in the room changed in an instant. Shock and awe gave way to sudden, heavy tension. Okambe glanced sideways at Caleb. The feed suddenly went dark.

*They are very nervous. It is tasty, but I'm not in approval of our positioning here.*

"What's going on?" Penn asked. "Did you finish the bidding?"

"Captain Card," Okambe said, his serenity giving way to fear. "You should have informed us beforehand that you have Legion contraband in your possession."

"What are you talking about?" Caleb asked. "You just said nobody cares what we acquire or how we acquire it."

Okambe swallowed hard. "That is correct, Captain. But we had no idea..." He trailed off, glancing at Christopher. "Are you wiping the data?"

"Working on it," Christopher replied.

"So you won't bid on the ship?" Caleb asked. "I got it—"

"Please, Captain. We don't need or want to know how you came into possession of the ship. I'm sorry, we can't honor the auction."

"None of it?" Caleb growled, becoming angry.

"Please understand, Captain. We are in a difficult position. I—"

"You're in a difficult position? I need the coin that ship is worth. Since when does a group of criminals give in to the decrees of a false Emperor?"

Okambe reacted like Caleb had punched him. "Captain, it's in everyone's best interests if you walk away quietly. We can both forget this ever happened."

"Captain," Penn said, taking his arm. "He's right. We should go."

A hidden door opened in the room's front. A handful of armed guards entered, surrounding a well-dressed, square-jawed man with salt and pepper hair. He approached them in a hurry, initially ignoring Caleb. "Christopher, did you wipe everything?" he asked the operator.

"Yes, sir," Christopher replied. "And I killed the feed as quickly as I could."

"What the hell is going on here?" Caleb asked.

The man turned to him. "Captain Card. You need to go. Now."

"I came here to sell that ship. I was told it would fetch a good price. Enough to keep my crew happy for a few months."

"Two weeks ago, that would be true. But things have changed." He leaned in close, lowering his voice. "Lord Crux's spies are everywhere, and I believe they've infiltrated the Consortium. These are dangerous times, Captain. For all of us. We can't afford the risk. Even if we left that ship on screen, no one would bid on it. However, there's a good chance someone is already looking to profit off the knowledge it's been offered for sale. If you don't already have a target on your head, you will soon."

"I'm used to that," Caleb replied. "But why are you telling me this, instead of just kicking us out?"

"Kicking you out would be suspicious. You're free to remain in the Sunshine Isles for as long as you want. But the Consortium can't purchase anything you're selling. The transfers can be traced from the inside, and with a rogue element infiltrating our systems, we have to be more careful than ever."

"That still doesn't explain why you're giving me so much information."

The man smiled. "Because I recognized my ship when it landed, and I'm sure it's still armed to the teeth. You also aren't the man I lost it to. He was an asshole. You somehow acquired an intact Nightmare, and anyone who can do that has already earned my respect."

"You're Jack Leighton?" Caleb asked.

He nodded. "Between captains, you should leave Aroon as quickly as you can. There are others who would buy the Nightmare from you, but not here. There's too much at stake. I'm sorry, Captain Card."

*Even he's frightened of Crux and the Legion.*

"Yeah. I'm sorry too," Caleb replied. "Athena, we're leaving." He locked eyes with Leighton. "The less you resist, the more he'll take, until you have nothing left. And I mean nothing, including your lives." He slipped past the man and his guards, heading for the lifts with Penn right behind him.

Caleb turned around after boarding the cab. Leighton had turned to watch him leave. The so-called pirate king's expression was stiff, perhaps feeling the sting of his last words.

*The Hunger are winning this galaxy. It is only a matter of time before fear permeates every corner of every world.*

*Not if I can help it.*

# CHAPTER 23

"I guess that's it," Penn said as the cab ascended from the depths of the island. "We'd better hope Naya can crack Graystone's bank accounts or we're going to be in big trouble."

"Mutiny?" Caleb asked.

"More like desertion. Although it sounds like the pirate way of life is becoming even harder to sustain."

"I'm not exactly in favor of piracy, but I imagine there are a good number of people like Lucy and Linx out there."

"Too many. The war allowed the most unsavory of people to take advantage in so many horrible ways. But there isn't much we can do about that."

"We don't quit until we're dead," Caleb answered. "How many do you think will leave?"

"Most. I'm not sure we'll have enough crew left to operate the ship."

"We need money from somewhere. I'm not giving up."

"What are you thinking?"

"Plan B."

*Not this again.*

"Which is what?"

"Leighton said there are spies in the Sunshine Isles. He can't easily identify them. Ish and I can."

*This is a bad idea. We're liable to open ourselves up to too much attention.*

"We've already drawn their attention. If you can get into the minds of one of these spies, you might extract valuable intel."

*It is risky, and there are no guarantees any khoron we locate will know anything useful.*

"It's possible. Maybe even likely. But we need to take the risk. We're dead in space right now."

"You're right," Penn said. "I am getting used to you talking to yourself."

*Give me a moment.*

The lift reached the station. As Caleb stepped out of the cab, a sharp pain knifed through his head. Initially, he froze in place and then he stumbled to his knees, his clawed fingers grasping at his forehead.

*Ish?* The pain vanished as quickly as it had come, leaving a pulsing throb in its wake.

"Captain, what's wrong?" Penn asked, dropping to one knee beside him and gripping his shoulders.

*There are four khoron nearby, as well as an Advocate. When I tried to reach out to the lessers, he attacked. I cannot attack and defend simultaneously. He knows we are here, and what we are trying to do. No doubt, he will alert his superiors.*

"Nothing ventured, nothing gained," Caleb groaned out, getting back to his feet. "I'm okay," he told Penn, shaking off the dull ache. "My plan didn't work out the way I'd hoped."

"Does that mean we're leaving?" she asked.

*We placed our bets and lost. We need to go. Now.*

"No," Caleb replied stubbornly. "I told you, I'm not giving up until I'm dead. Ish, what if you let me in, and I help defend while you attack?"

*I'd rather not.*

"Ish, I need you to back me on this one."

*You don't like to allow me to control your body, or enter too deeply into your mind. And yet you ask me to do the same.*

"This is important."

*But only when it is something you want.*

*Fine, the next time you ask, I'll let you take control.*

*Only once?*

*I'd be more open to it if you weren't always such a pain in the ass about giving me my body back.*

He and Penn reached the far end of the station, coming to a stop in front of the waiting pods.

"Captain," Penn said. "We've got company."

Caleb looked back over his shoulder. Jack Leighton was stepping off the other lift, still flanked by his guards. He had a nervous, greedy look in his eyes, though he walked toward Caleb rather than rushing him, or worse, opening fire.

"I have a feeling he'll either arrest us or force us to leave," she continued.

*Ish, are you in? I can't do this without you, and you can't do this without me.*

*Very well. The very unfortunate nature of our relationship. But you will not have awareness beyond the Collective. Penelope will need to defend our helpless meat sack.*

"Cap, are we going?" Penn pressed. "We need to decide."

Caleb motioned to the forward most pod facing the spaceport. "We're leaving." He turned back to Leighton, halfway between them and the lifts. "We're leaving!" he shouted.

Leighton put up his hand, bringing his entourage to a halt. Nodding to Caleb, he waited while they boarded the pod.

"Destination?" the pod's AI asked.

"Spaceport," Caleb replied.

"You will arrive at the spaceport in three minutes." The hatch slid closed and the pod sped up out of the station.

"Penn, I'm going to work with Ish to find and interrogate the enemy. Don't let anything happen to me while I'm unresponsive."

"Copy that," she replied, lifting her magboot. She reached under it with one hand, pressing in on the sole with the other. A small ion blaster dropped from the middle of the boot.

"Clever," Caleb remarked.

"I told you I came prepared."

"You didn't bring one for me."

She grinned. "You don't need one."

*Let us get this over with.*

Caleb closed his eyes, immediately greeted by the bright white light that served as home base for the collux. Knowing from helping Ishek with the Empress' assassin that he would need to fight back against any black that tried to worm its way in, he kept close attention on the light. A strand of black had already crept into the top corner. With only a little effort, he pushed it away. Another strand tried to push in from the side, and a third from the bottom. He easily eradicated them as well. Six more tendrils appeared all at once, but again he rejected their attack.

*This is easy,* he thought to Ishek.

*I haven't done anything yet. Those are random attempts to sync across the Collective, which I deflect all day, every day, subconsciously. These are your training wheels.*

*Are you serious?*

*Do I not feel serious? You need to build up to what is to come or I will need to aid your defense, preventing us from achieving our goal.*

*We only have three minutes.*

Caleb continued beating away minor strands, unaware

of the passage of time. It didn't take long before he began deflecting the meager attempts to connect with no effort at all, keeping his white light completely clean.

*You are prepared. I am reaching out to the khoron now.*

Caleb maintained his focus and attention on the light, ready to pounce if any new tendrils appeared. It didn't take long, and when it came, it came quickly, out of nowhere, like a xaxkluth with nearly a dozen thick tentacles stretching into the light. Despite Caleb's preparation, the fury of the assault nearly caught him off-guard. One tentacle reached nearly all the way to the center before he mentally shoved it back. Another darted in, and he fought that one off too.

Immediately on his metaphysical back foot, he didn't want Ishek to have to come to his rescue. The thing they needed most was information, and this was the easiest way to get it. Or at least, it had seemed like the easiest way before the Advocate's arrival.

The tendrils kept coming, the darkness gaining sway over the fringes of the light and closing in as they stretched toward him. He continued pushing back, remembering the effort he had made recently against the Relyeh assassin. Gaining confidence as he successfully knocked the tendrils away with increasing ease, he built a wall around the center of the light. The Advocate tried but failed to breach it.

Caleb didn't know how much time passed or whether Ishek was having any success questioning the khorons. If he tried to think of anything other than defending the light, the tendrils regained their momentum, threatening to over-power him. Instead, he kept all of his energy on the wall, which he continually expanded, fighting back against the Advocate's attack.

Soon enough, he realized he was winning. The tendrils pressed hard against his wall to no avail, struggling to maintain their ground. He held his mind firm, letting them batter against his defenses with growing confidence that Ishek was successfully picking the minds of the khoron he had found in the Sunshine Isles.

The attack ended suddenly, the darkness not so much retreating as vanishing, conquered by the light. The Advocate had given up, leaving Caleb ecstatic in his victory.

It was short-lived.

His eyes snapped open, his consciousness fully back in his body. The pod slowed as it neared the spaceport.

Ishek's distressed tone flowed through his mind.

*We have a problem.*

# CHAPTER 24

"What kind of problem?" Caleb asked. "Everything seemed good to me."

*Which is precisely the problem. Everything went too well. The Advocate gave up the attack against me and assaulted the khoron instead.*

"Wait. What?" Caleb expected bad news. He didn't expect that.

*He killed them, rather than let me break into their minds. They are all dead, save for him.*

"What's going on?" Penn asked as the pod pulled into the spaceport station, coming to a stop. The hatch slid open

"We need to go after the Advocate. He can't kill himself, can he?"

*Not like that. But I'm not strong enough to overpower him.*

"I can help you."

*It doesn't work that way. Defense is much easier than offense, and you have no experience reaching out across the Collective. It may be too much for your puny human mind to handle.*

"Please disembark," the pod's AI requested.

"Captain, are we going?" Penn asked.

"Then we hunt him down the old-fashioned way," Caleb said. "Do you have his position?"

*A general location, but he is on the move.*

"Does he know we're headed to the spaceport?"

*Possibly.*

"Good, then he most likely won't come this way."

"Please disembark," the pod's AI repeated.

"Penn, you're free to get off and wait for us with Atrice on Medusa. Ish and I are going hunting."

Penn didn't miss a beat. "And miss all the fun? Forget it. I'm staying with you, Cap. You may need me."

"Ish, can you ping him again as we get closer?"

*Not without him knowing.*

"We'll have to risk it. Can you estimate a distance?"

*Between six and ten kilometers.*

"Penn, what part of the Isles is between six and ten kilometers from here?" Caleb asked.

She considered the question. "I would guess…Recreation."

"Please disembark," the pod's AI said a third time. "You have ten seconds to comply, or I will notify the authorities."

"We need to go back," Caleb announced, hoping the AI would understand. "Our destination is Recreation."

"It looks like we're taking too long for Leighton's comfort," Penn said, pointing out the door. His three guards from the upper part of the spaceport were running down the ramp toward them.

"Recreation," Caleb repeated. "Now."

The hatch remained open. Caleb opened his mouth to try again, only to have the door slide closed.

"You will arrive at Recreation in four minutes."

The pod continued through the tunnel, heading out the way it had come, looping back around the outside of the spaceport station.

"Can you explain why we aren't leaving yet?" Penn asked.

"Ishek tried to grab intel from the khoron on the planet. Only there's an Advocate on the planet as well. When he realized what we were doing, he killed the khoron to keep them silent."

Penn stared at him. "I'm not sure how I feel about that."

"The Guardians with the Empress killed themselves and one another so they couldn't become hosts to a khoron. Against this kind of opposition, drastic measures make sense. On both sides."

"I suppose you're right."

"The Advocate is the only Relyeh still on the planet. If we don't want to leave here completely empty-handed, we need to catch him before he can elude us."

"Why not just remote into his mind?"

"Apparently, we aren't strong enough. It's something I intend to work on." He turned his conversation inward. *You're going to teach me how to reach over the Collective.*

*Do not be too hasty. Remarks about your lack of brain capacity aside, there is a real risk to such an endeavor. One that could leave you paralyzed and drooling.*

"First things first," Caleb said. "We'll try to get close before Ish attempts to locate him again. Once we're close, it's likely he'll make a run for it."

"Do you have any idea what the host looks like?" Penn asked.

"He could be anyone," Caleb replied.

*Not anyone. An Advocate would not choose a weak host. And Leighton's willingness to capitulate to Crux's interests may be a clue.*

"Ishek thinks the Advocate may be bonded to someone Leighton cares about. Does he have a wife? Children?"

"He has a son. Nineteen years old."

"Do you know what he looks like?"

Penn reached into the inner pocket of her coat, retrieving a personal assistance device and tapping the screen to activate it. Caleb was pleased to watch her enter a passcode instead of relying on biometrics to get into the device.

"Do you mind if I link your comms patch with the pad?" she asked.

"Not at all," Caleb replied.

"Mink, link Captain Card in my comms list to your audio output."

"Task complete," a young female voice said through Caleb's patch.

"Mink, I need the name and an image of the pirate Jack Leighton's son," she said. "The more recent the better."

Looking over her shoulder, Caleb saw a progress bar advancing across the otherwise blank screen. It was only half finished when it faded away, replaced with a three-dimensional image of a young man projected slightly above the screen.

"The feeds and images on the hypernet are of substandard quality," Mink said. "I've constructed a composite based on a collection of images from different angles. His name is also Jack."

"I bet he hates to be called Junior," Caleb said, examining the image. The kid had a mop of dark brown hair over a square jaw and light eyes that matched Leighton's. The thought of an Advocate gaining control of him made Caleb sick.

*I don't know if that should offend me.*

*You're definitely an acquired taste. And that kid's a prisoner to the Relyeh.*

"At least we have some idea of who we're looking for," Penn said.

"If Ish's hunch is right. It's the best lead we have."

Penn used hand gestures to spin the three-dimensional

image, getting a full look at Jack Jr. from all sides. "Mink, put him in some different styles of clothing common on Aroon."

"I've selected the top ten most common male styles found on Aroon," Mink replied. "Tap to switch styles."

The first style was similar to what Caleb wore, leaving him feeling good about his wardrobe selection. Penn cycled through the others, spinning the composite around each time so they could hopefully recognize him more easily in a crowd.

"Mink," Caleb said. "How many people typically occupy Recreation in the Sunshine Isles?"

"I'm sorry, Captain Card. The Sunshine Isles are uninhabited."

Caleb glanced at Penn, who smiled back at him. "That's not something the Aroonian government allows to reach the hypernet," she said. "At least in any official capacity that the AI can interpret. But I know there's pod access from Gita, the northernmost city. I'd expect a few thousand, at least."

"That'll make Junior harder to find."

"It'll also make it easier for us to blend in. Jack Senior still wants us off the planet. And I doubt the Consortium will hesitate to kill us if we refuse to comply. Which we already have, by the way."

"Good point," Caleb said. Looking past Penn, he gawked as Recreation came into view.

He had expected another station carved out beneath one to the archipelago's many islands. Instead, the most popular attraction in the Sunshine Isles appeared to be set in a transparent dome sticking out of the side of a trench, nearly two hundred meters deeper than their current position. Only visible because of the colorful light emanating from the artistic structures inside, the place made Vegas seem like a cemetery. Wondering how the light wouldn't be visible from the surface, Caleb glanced up, immediately spotting a huge cover suspended in the water, blotting it out.

"I didn't expect that," he said, grinning in awe despite himself.

*I hate it.*

*I know,* Caleb replied.

The pod descended toward the outer edge of the dome, where the clear tunnel vanished into the side of the trench's rocky face. Caleb craned his neck from one side of the pod to the other to keep the small city in view. He remained mesmerized until they plunged into the darkness.

"We won't be able to see the station until we're in it," Penn said. "We may need to force our way past whatever guards Leighton's sent to escort us back to the spaceport."

"I assume you don't plan to kill any of them," Caleb replied. "We don't need to make a bad situation worse."

"I'll try not to, but I'm not letting them arrest me. They aren't official law enforcement, and we're pirates. It won't end well for us."

The comment returned Caleb's focus to the task at hand. "Right. Ish, once we're out of the station, you'll need to ping the Advocate and try to get us a better estimate of his location."

*Are you certain you want to reveal us so soon?*

"With the guards on our tails, we won't have much time. Mink, can you provide us with a map of Recreation?"

"This is an unofficial rendering of Recreation," Mink replied as a simple map of the city's layout appeared on the pad's screen, "produced to show what the area might look like, if the area existed."

"Of course," Caleb said. The top-down display showed a method to the madness of the architecture, with winding streets creating a grid pattern throughout the city. "Once Ish has an estimate, I'll point it out. Our target's going to run once he knows we're looking for him. Where's the pod station for Gita?"

"If there is a pod station for Gita, it might be found here," Mink said, a red mark appearing on the right side of the map.

"And the pod station leading to the spaceport?" Caleb asked.

"If there is a—"

"Yes, we know. The Sunshine Isles are uninhabited. Skip the prefacing."

"The pod station to the spaceport is here," Mink said, a green dot appearing on the bottom edge of the map.

"If he's anywhere between those two dots, we should be able to cut him off," Penn said.

"If he isn't, he'll still need to go for one or the other to escape."

"The wild card is Jack Senior. Who knows what he'll do if he figures out we're chasing his son."

"We aren't chasing the kid, per se. We're chasing the Advocate."

"But will he understand that? Will he realize we're trying to help? Maybe. Maybe not."

The pod slowed as it approached the station. Caleb leaned back in his seat to calm himself and focus. He had a lot more experience on a battlefield than he did in the middle of a civilian city's downtown, but he was determined to catch his prey.

Caleb and Penn both stood before the pod came to a complete stop, silently positioning themselves on either side of the hatch before it opened. A unit of guards stood at the front of the station, one facing inward to manage crowd control. The other four had rifles drawn, monitoring the arrivals.

He glanced across at Penn, using hand gestures to signal her to take the two on the left, while he dealt with the two on the right. Whoever eliminated their two guards first would be responsible for the last one. She nodded her agreement, waiting for him to make the first move.

*Ish* —he started.

*Boost you. I know. Already done.*

The familiar warmth flooded into him, lending him unnatural strength. The sensation reminded him that Jack Jr. could be similarly enhanced. He would need to make sure Penn didn't try to physically block the kid when the time came.

One last inhale just as the hatch opened, and he exploded out into the station.

# CHAPTER 25

Caleb came out of the pod like a lightning bolt, launching himself at the pair of guards apparently waiting for them. Failing miserably to get their rifles up, they never knew what hit them. Caleb's hard right hook crashed into one man's helmet, the force enough to drop him. Landing on his left leg, he thrust his right foot into the second guard's chest. The strength of the blow cracked the thin plate of his light armor and doubled him over, the man's breath exploding from his lungs.

Caleb rushed the next two, both still in the process of turning toward him. He caught one by the throat, grabbed his arm, and swept his legs out from under him. Driving him to the floor, he slammed his man's helmet against the hard surface, knocking him out. The other guard brought the butt of his rifle up to crack Caleb in the jaw. Blocking it, he jerked the rifle out of the guard's hands and rammed the butt into the man's gut, quickly bringing it up into the chin of his helmet. The guard went down hard and stayed there.

Glancing back at Penn, he saw her level her ion blaster at the last two guards still standing, firing twice to disable their weapons. Her eyes met Caleb's, a sly smile gripping the corner of her mouth. He didn't need to guess her plan. From behind, he wrapped an arm around their throats and squeezed, cutting off their air long enough with his enhanced strength to daze them. He threw one into the side of the pod. The other stumbled, splaying out across the front seats. Penn sprinted past him toward the exit. Caleb took off after her, the surrounding crowd too stunned to challenge either of them.

Gaining on Penn at a full run, Caleb wondered if the pair of large doors at the end of the space would automatically open for them, or if the guards could lock them down, trapping them inside the station. If they could escape into the chaos of the city beyond, they might have a chance to disappear in the crowd.

He had his answer a few seconds later. The doors opened, matching their velocity with the speed of Penn's approach. Immediately, bright light beamed in through the open space, nearly blinding Caleb. Doing his best to ignore the surreal effect of sea life swimming through water high above his head, he gradually adjusted to the sudden bustle of the domed city while evading the sizzling rain of rifle fire flashing past him. Fortunately, the gunfire stopped as Recreation came into full view; the guards losing their clear line of fire.

Caleb and Penn cut to the right, running onto a wide walkway; Angling around a few pedestrians, they slowed to a normal walk, quickly losing themselves in the crowd.

"That was easy," Penn commented, smirking as she glanced at him.

"You didn't do much."

"Work smarter, not harder, Captain."

Ishek's laughter filled Caleb's head.

*She has you there.*

Caleb ignored Ishek's remark, taking a moment to acclimate to their new surroundings. He had thought Recreation resembled a sunken Las Vegas when they approached from the outside. Now, being in the middle of the city, his view only cemented that opinion.

The eclectic architecture crossed the spectrum, from a twisting, snakelike building to a structure that reminded Caleb of a gothic cathedral. There were banners, billboards, holograms, and lights everywhere, flickering and flashing from the face of every building. The dazzling lights cast the streets in a constant daylight glow. It even permeated the dome's transparency, highlighting the sea life swimming overhead and around the outer perimeter.

In their immediate surroundings, dozens of civilians moved along the twisting grid of streets, ducking in and out of shops, bars, and clubs. All of them were human, most around Caleb's age or younger, dressed primarily in the styles in which Mink had showcased Jack Jr. They all seemed to be having a good time, so much so that Caleb quickly wondered how many of them knew who controlled this city and what kind of business was conducted in the shadows. For that matter, if they did know, would they even care?

*Ish, we're clear of the station. Find the Advocate.*

*Are you sure you're ready?*

*As ready as I'll ever be.*

Caleb tapped Penn on the shoulder. "On your toes. We're going to break in whichever direction Ishek pinpoints the Advocate. She nodded. *Do it, Ish.*

Only moments passed before Ishek replied.

*I have it. I need control to mark it on the map.*

*Okay, but don't make me fight you for my body. Remember, trust goes both ways.*

*Yes, yes. Hurry. He knows I pinged him. He's ready to bolt.*

Caleb ceded control of his body to Ishek, his consciousness sinking into the background. "Let me see the map," Ishek said, speaking through him. As Penn held the pad out to him, he tapped on a group of buildings on the other side of the dome. "The Advocate is there, within a street or two." he stipulated, the location closer to the Gita exit than to that of the spaceport.

"A street or two?" Penn replied, frowning. "I thought you'd have better accuracy."

"That's because you don't know the complexity involved," Ishek snapped. "I'd try to explain, but your puny human mind would never grasp the concept."

"What?" Penn gasped, flinching at Ishek's outburst.

*Ish!* Caleb barked. *Give me back control. Now.*

He expected Ishek to argue. Thankfully, the symbiote honored their agreement.

*Trust.*

"Sorry," Caleb said. "Ish doesn't like his abilities being questioned."

"I figured. He's a little touchy, isn't he?"

"You could say that. He's used that puny human mind line on me so many times it doesn't bother me anymore."

*Ish, keep your mind on the target. Don't let him disappear.*

*He won't get away from us.*

Caleb and Penn picked up the pace, walking as quickly as they could without drawing too much attention to themselves. Reaching an intersection, they passed a pair of guards leisurely holding rifles across their chests. Yet, their heads were on the swivel, monitoring the surrounding activity. Glancing back at them, Caleb noticed one watched their progress down the street.

*He's headed for the Gita station. We must move faster or we'll lose him.*

Suddenly laughing, Caleb grabbed Penn's hand and broke into a jog. She caught on, giggling loudly as she scampered off with him. Caleb gave the guards a second surreptitious look-back as they neared the other side of the street, confirming the interested guard was now looking back the other way, having dismissed them as merely a young couple horsing around. He and Penn continued down the street, slowing a few steps before he playfully snatched the pad from her hands and sped up again.

*Left!*

Ishek's direction sent them careening around the corner into a narrow side street, nearly colliding with a bruiser of a man. Caleb heard the man cuss him out, Penn apologizing as they continued running along the street. More people crowded in ahead of them, forcing him to push and shove his way through. He hated barreling through the pedestrians, but he had no choice. Throwing his shoulder into a man blocking his path, he cast him out of the way, doing the same to a woman who stepped into his way. She cried out when she knocked into a bench along the street. Behind them, Penn apologized profusely to her. Her laughter became less forced as her enjoyment of the mad dash increased.

*Go right!*

Caleb cut the next corner, entering onto an even more crowded street. Ignoring more angry cursing from the people he shoved out of the way, he heard Penn's breathing begin to labor as she fought to keep up with his enhanced speed. Glancing back to check on her, he didn't see the guard who stepped out of a small pastry store in front of them. Helmet in hand while he ate his confection, the man took the full brunt of Caleb's impact, both of them grunting as they collapsed together in the middle of the street. Caleb released his grip on Penn's hand just in time to keep her from stepping into the guard's dropped pastry and tripping over the top of them. She bent over, bracing her hands on her knees to catch her breath as the guard's rifle and helmet clattering to the street, along with the pad from Caleb's hand.

*We don't have time to stop.*

Caleb locked eyes with the guard as the man's helmet rolled a short distance away, its inner speakers crackling to life.

"Attention all units. Attention all units. Two persons of interest have entered Recreation. Apprehend immediately. Use caution. They are considered armed and extremely dangerous."

Caleb glanced at the helmet as tiny images of himself and Penn in Auctions appeared on the helmet's HUD.

The stunned guard noticed them too. Turning his narrowed eyes on Caleb, his muscles tensed as he got up. Caleb didn't give him the chance to get an advantage, cracking him across the temple with his fist before he could get both feet under him.

"We have to go," Penn said, scooping the pad off the pavement and grabbing Caleb's hand, pulling him up.

*That's what I said. The Advocate is only two blocks from Gita station.*

"How far is he ahead of us?" Caleb asked, picking up the guard's rifle.

*Nearly four blocks.*

"Damn." He fired the rifle into the pavement, the clear gel round splattering against the street. A small pill in the center unleashed a powerful discharge. "Stunners," he said. "Let's go!""

He and Penn broke into a fresh run, sticking close together as they navigated their way through the side street into a wider thoroughfare. Humming overhead drew Caleb's attention. He cursed, spotting a group of drones spreading out across the dome and descending toward the streets, no doubt dispatched to look for them. A drone streaked over them before spinning around to sweep back down over them.

"Facial recognition," Penn said, maintaining her pace. "We need to get clear of it."

"There," Caleb said, using the map to trace an alternate route to the pod station.

They swung around the corner only a few seconds before the drone reached them, hopefully escaping its facial recognition scan. Their luck held when Caleb realized they had ducked into an alley, not a street. Instead of crowds of people, there were only pristine dumpsters, the chutes dropping garbage into them sealed off to prevent refuse from spilling onto the pavement and the smell from wafting into the city.

The entire exterior of the building on their left had a single gigantic video screen on it, currently displaying a colorful liquid metal animation that reminded Caleb of a lava lamp. The building on the other side was covered in thousands of large white feathers, each the size of his torso. It rose almost all the way to the top of the dome in a twisting wavelike pattern, leaving him to wonder why anyone would want to cover a building in feathers.

He didn't have time to ponder it as they raced down the center of the alley. They were halfway to the next intersection when Ishek screamed so loudly in Caleb's head he thought his brain might explode.

*Incoming!*

# CHAPTER 26

Caleb didn't have time to look up for whatever was coming at him. Only Ishek's senses allowed him the milliseconds advance notice he needed to dive sideways before a familiar dark form landed in a hunched crouch, claws extended, right where he'd been standing.

"Gonthar?" Caleb said, surprised by the sudden appearance of the Jiba-ki. "What the—"

The alien didn't speak. Recovering from his missed strike, he lunged at Caleb, who set himself just in time to grab the Jiba-ki's wrists. Falling backward, he pulled Gonthar over his head, throwing him back into the feathered wall. At least, that was his intent. Gonthar twisted in the air like a cat, both hands and feet finding purchase beneath the feathers, the white down puffing out around him. He clung there as Caleb pushed himself back to his feet and faced him. "Nice seeing you again, Gonthar."

Gonthar snarled and sprang from the wall, leading with his claws. A fist to the Jiba-ki's throat dropped him at Caleb's feet, momentarily stunning him.

"Captain?" Penn cried. She was too far down the alley to help him.

"Go to the station!" he shouted. "Find Junior. I'll catch up."

She didn't hesitate, nodding before she sprinted around the corner, vanishing from sight.

*She'll never make it in time.*

*You need to slow the Advocate down,* Caleb replied.

*How?*

*If you're attacking him through the Collective, he won't be able to move as fast.*

*That's not a guarantee.*

*We have to try.*

*What about you and the big fur-ball?*

*I can take care of myself.*

Caleb's boot caught Gonthar under his chin, sending the cat-like assassin tumbling away. Rolling onto his feet, he charged Caleb, veering side to side to avoid the stun charges from Caleb's rifle. The rounds flashed as they hit the pavement behind him. Spinning and ducking, Caleb avoided all but the slash of Gonthar's claws to the tail of his coat, the lethal talons sliding harmlessly off the armored material.

Gonthar turned and plowed into him, knocking him down on his back, a move Caleb morphed into a backward roll. Jumping to his feet, he was ready for the Jiba-ki as he followed up with a pair of swift claw swipes. Caleb jerked back to avoid them, whirling and bringing the rifle around to crack Gonthar across the face, sending him flailing backward.

Ready to pounce, Caleb grimaced as a sudden pain knifed through his head, slowing him as if he were slogging through thick mud. Gonthar rushed him a fourth time, his right arm swinging toward him, claws aimed for his face.

He blocked them with the rifle, hooking the curved nails around the gun as he was pushed backward into the other building's swirling video screen. Diodes blew, interrupting the picture as Gonthar held Caleb there, the rifle pinned across his chest. Face to face, they were so close Caleb could feel the warmth of the assassin's breath.

"I take it you found a contract on the exchange," Caleb gritted, his muscles flexing to hold Gonthar back.

"A good sum of coin and no travel involved. Easy profit. It is true."

*Ish, any luck?*

The symbiote didn't respond, still locked in his fight with the enemy Advocate. If he had Ishek to boost him, he could have ended the fight right here and now. Instead, he was gradually losing to Gonthar, who had nearly shoved the rifle up into his throat. A few more seconds and he knew the weapon would cut off his air supply. He was strong, but the Jiba-ki was stronger. Still, he wasn't about to give in.

"Not so easy after all, am I?" Caleb replied. "How's your jaw?"

Gonthar growled in amusement. "Painful. You are faster than any human I've hunted before. I knew you were also a hunter. You have not disappointed."

"Has Crux's war reached your planet yet?" Caleb asked.

"Jibasoon is near the new territories, far from Atlas. Yet a war such as the one Crux has waged reaches even there. The Emperor has decreed no more Jiba-ki may leave their homeworld. He says it is unsafe for us. He says we are hated by humans. They do not know the truth, so they do not resist. It is true. They believe the word of the Emperor, and they have no desire to leave."

As expected, the rifle pressed into Caleb's throat, limiting his breathing. He used his last full breath to speak. "How does that make you feel?"

The question surprised Gonthar, and the pressure

against Caleb's throat eased. It was enough of an opening to shove Gonthar off-balance and drive a knee solidly into his groin. Gonthar cried out, his grip on the rifle weakening. Caleb eagerly took advantage of the moment, jamming his foot to the alien's gut and throwing him over his shoulder to the pavement. He dropped him, wrapping his legs around his throat in a scissoring chokehold. Gonthar flailed and clawed at him, unable to break the hold.

"How does that make you feel?" he asked again, grabbing the Jiba-ki's wrists.

"Sadness for my species. Anger at the Emperor," Gonthar grunted out, the voice from the translation pendant he wore muffled by Caleb's leg. His deep mewling growls grew weaker as he struggled for air. "Humans do not...hate us. They just...do not...know us."

Caleb let go of Gonthar, rolling off him and back to his feet. Gonthar remained on the pavement, catching his breath as he looked up at Caleb, obviously confused by his mercy.

"The kill is yours," Gonthar said. "You have earned it."

"I have another idea," Caleb replied. "Crux is an imposter. Your emperor's decree to keep you and your kind on your planet today will become a decree to make slaves of you tomorrow. Killing you won't help me prevent that."

Gonthar chuckled. "I believe I know what you would suggest, but you do not understand. The contract is signed. The deal is made. I may take no other jobs until it is fulfilled, and if I walk away, I am banished from the exchange. It is true."

Caleb offered Gonthar a half-smile. "So maybe you can kill me later. Once we're finished with Crux. Assuming you agree to help me and we both live that long."

Gonthar's expression changed. "Perhaps that is acceptable. There is no time limit in the contract." He rolled onto all fours before rising to his feet. "As you have spared my life, so I shall spare yours. For now," he hissed. "But one day, I will kill you."

Caleb grinned. "Deal. We need to—"

"Caleb!" Penn's strained voice sounded through his comms patch. "Help me!"

# CHAPTER 27

Caleb broke into a run, passing Gonthar, who quickly caught up to him in an all out race along the alley. They maintained their speed as they reached the next intersection, the Jiba-ki digging his claws in to tear cleanly around the corner. Caleb chose not to slow, swinging wide into the turn and falling a few steps behind Gonthar.

"Penn, what's your status?" Caleb snapped into the comms as they dodged pedestrians on the street. She didn't answer, but she didn't need to. He spotted a pair of drones in formation up ahead, chasing her around a large building shaped like a giant robot head. From the look of the people entering and exiting the building, it had to be a nightclub and a popular one, judging by the number of people in line at the front doors..

*Ish, if you can hear me, I need a sitrep.*

Ishek didn't respond either, but Caleb's sense of his growing fatigue was again all the answer he needed. The symbiote continued wrestling with the Advocate across the Collective, stealing its attention and slowing its exit from the city. Ishek's interference was undoubtedly the only reason the Relyeh hadn't already escaped with Junior.

Still hot on Gonthar's heels, Caleb realized they were nearing the east side of Recreation at the outer edge of Gita station. The descending curve of the dome limited the height of the buildings up ahead. The sea life on the other side of the thick transparency was so close he could make out the shapes of individual fishes swimming in schools around the huge girders stretching up from the ocean depths to support the pod tunnels connected to the dome.

Slowing to a stop when he reached the next corner, he found the street leading to the station nearly deserted. Or rather, the pedestrians who had been on it had cleared out to avoid the mess he found up ahead. The drones had all gathered in one spot, along with two full units of guards. They stood near the closed doors leading to Gita station, surrounding Penn, who had Junior clutched in her arms, her ion blaster held threateningly against the side of his head.

He understood immediately why Penn needed help, and why Ish remained in remote conflict with the Advocate. The Relyeh would likely risk being shot to overpower its captor, and the guards would no doubt focus all of their attention on Penn while leaving Junior to escape, if he could. It was a lousy situation, and more drones and another unit of guards only made it worse.

"Athena is in trouble," Gonthar said, as Caleb moved in beside him. "But why does she hold that man captive? It is true."

"He's infected with a powerful khoron. Like a Legionnaire, but more dangerous. We need to interrogate the khoron to get information."

"There are many guards."

"Yeah. I can shoot some of them, but once I do, those drones will be all over us. I don't think they're vulnerable to stunner rounds."

"You may be surprised. No weapons are allowed here, and all defenses are designed with this rule in mind."

Caleb nodded. "If I deal with the drones, can you take out the guards, preferably without hurting them?"

"That is not the way I hunt. Perhaps I should just kill you now." Caleb started swinging his rifle toward the Jibaki, who wheezed with laughter. "Am I not amusing? I will do what I can. Your hand should have already ended my life, so every moment from here to eternity is one I have borrowed from the stars. I am ready. It is true."

"Penn," Caleb said softly, activating his comms patch. "I'm here. Get ready."

She didn't reply, but she didn't need to. "Go," he said to Gonthar, just before moving out into the open.

Gonthar dropped to all fours, racing along the street alongside the buildings while Caleb sighted the nearest guards facing away from him. Assuming a single round wouldn't be enough to down a man in light armor, he fired three shots, rapidly switched targets, and unleashed three more rounds. He repeated, a third guard shuddering before he collapsed, probably before he knew what had hit him.

As expected, the drones immediately spun away from the scene and zipped up the street toward him. Most of the guards turned his way as well, but none of them noticed Gonthar streaking along the side of the lane until he broke toward them, a black blur moving too quickly to get a bead on.

Caleb opened fire on the drones, blasting them with stunner rounds. The jolt of electricity obviously short-circuited their controls, all of them careening wildly into the buildings or down to the pavement. Meanwhile, Gonthar hit the guards like a bowling ball, knocking them down like pins, his claws slashing across their faceplates, distracting or blinding them with the wide scratches to their visors. Within seconds, Caleb and Gonthar had the attention of all the units on them, leaving Penn free to finish subduing Junior. If she could.

It was all going as planned until Caleb felt the return of Ishek's exhausted consciousness. *I'm spent,* he relayed with barely enough energy to be heard, a wave of debilitating weariness washing through Caleb and siphoning away his strength. His next few rounds went well wide of the four remaining drones.

Leaning his shoulder into the corner of a building, Caleb watched Junior elbow Penn in the gut, sending her stumbling backward. The kid sprinted away, desperate to escape. Penn aimed her blaster at his back, pulling the gun up before Caleb could comm her to hold fire, knowing she couldn't afford to kill either the Advocate or Leighton's son. She chased after him instead, tailing him as he ran toward the closest alley.

Two of the drones followed her, the rest firing on Caleb. He turned away, lifting his coat to shield his face as the ion blasts slammed into the protective fabric, a little more of it burning away with each hit. As nearby buzzing drew his attention, he spotted more drones arriving from the other side of the city. He had nothing left until Ishek could recoup his energy. His shoulders drooped, and he dropped his chin to his chest, and stumbled to a stop. Tossing his rifle to the street, he raised his hands, hoping Leighton would call off the attack.

The drones stopped shooting, buzzing like bees as they quickly surrounded him. Close to the station, he saw Gonthar grab Junior, and from the positioning of his claws near the kid's armpit, he knew Penn must have told him where the Advocate would be. Around him, some guards he and Penn had taken down were getting back on their feet and moving to surround the trio.

"Leighton, can you hear me?" Caleb shouted, looking up at a drone. "The other spies in the Isles are dead. Only one remains, and I know you know which one I mean. I under-stand if you're afraid for your son. But of all the people in the galaxy, I can help him. I need the Advocate that stole him from you alive, which means I need Junior alive. If you ever want to see or speak to your son again, you'll tell your guards and drones to stand down so we can both get what we want."

A response wasn't immediate, leaving Caleb to wonder what Leighton was thinking. The man was a member of the Consortium, not the representative of the entire Consortium. Maybe he had to discuss the situation with the other cartels. Either way, the scene remained static while Caleb waited for a reply.

*Ish, are you hurt?*

*My pride is more than bruised. That Advocate is stronger than me, and I dislike it. I had no choice but to retreat.*

*You slowed him down long enough for Penn to reach him. You did well.*

*I failed.*

*So did I. But we don't quit—*

*Until we're dead. Yes, I know. I see you found Gonthar.*

*He found us, and tried to kill us.*

*And you defeated him without me?*

*I was a Marine Ranger long before I got stuck with you. I still remember how to fight without being boosted.*

*So you tricked him?*

*Sort of.*

Finally, after waiting for over two minutes while Leghton decided, the drones retracted their weapons. Further afield, the guards lowered their weapons. One of them offered Penn what appeared to be restraints, while another jogged down the street to his position.

"Captain Card," the woman said. "Executive Leighton has requested your peaceful return to Auctions to discuss the terms of his son's release into your care."

"Terms?" Caleb replied. "This isn't a negotiation."

The woman laughed. "You're a pirate, Captain. You should know that everything is a negotiation."

Caleb smiled back at her. "Right. Tell Executive Jack that I accept his invitation."

"Of course. It will be our pleasure to escort you back to the station. We hope you've enjoyed your visit."

"I have, mostly. Have you enjoyed hosting us?"

"My ribs say, not so much," she replied. "But it's the first genuine excitement we've had here in a long time." She paused, lowering her voice. "I heard about Galatin and the Empress."

The comment surprised him. "How much have you heard?" he replied quietly. "And from who?"

"I used to be a member of the Royal Navy. I still have connections."

"Are you still loyal to the Empire?"

She nodded. "I heard you helped the Empress' ship escape the Legion, but the Empress was killed in the fighting. May the stars guide her to her next life. If Leighton lets you off Aroon, I'd like to come with you."

"Do you know any other loyalists who feel the same?" Caleb asked.

"We don't talk about our pasts here. If there are, I wouldn't know them. But if they have a chance, they might approach you as well. I'm Commander Elena Shirin."

"Commander Shirin," Caleb said. "We surrender to your custody."

# CHAPTER 28

Rather than stopping in the auction room, Commander Shirin led Caleb, Penn, Gondar, and Jack Jr. past the rows of terminals, now fully unoccupied, to the hidden door that led to Auction's back rooms and offices. Restrained by a pair of electromagnetic cuffs that even the Advocate's enhanced strength would have no chance at breaking, Junior followed placidly along thanks to Gonthar's claws placed near the enemy slug. None of the other guards who had escorted them followed Shirin through the door, though Leighton's personal retinue picked up where they left off, marching on either side of the group as they made their way through long, brightly lit corridors to a glossy wooden door deep inside the facility. Surprisingly, it bore the jolly roger Caleb had yet to see anywhere else.

One of Leighton's guards opened the door. Caleb expected the former pirate king to be on the other side. He didn't expect the entire Consortium to be in the room with him.

*Ish, can you block the Advocate from sending any of what he sees back through the Collective?*

*I'm too tired.*

*So is he, I'm sure.*

*You owe me.*

*Yes, I do.*

Ishek's consciousness faded as he resumed his attack on the Advocate, keeping him from communicating through the Collective. Otherwise, the creature could easily pass along the identities of the Consortium members to Crux and his allies. Maybe they already knew who every member of the group was.

Or maybe they didn't.

The eight members of the Consortium's leadership ranged in age from a man who appeared to be at least ninety to a teenage girl, who rightly or not, Caleb assumed had inherited her illicit cabal. They were mostly dressed as the executives they fancied themselves to be, in crisp suits of varying styles, or in the young girl's case, a fitted red dress with a black sash around her forehead. They stared at Caleb as he entered the room first, gasping when a Jiba-ki led Leighton's son into the room at clawpoint.

"Jack, you said this was an emergency," the woman in red said. "What the hell is this?'

"Rita, you already know my son, Jack," Leighton replied. "I'd like to introduce you to Captain Caleb Card, the man who replaced Deven Graystone, and his companions, Athena and…I'm sorry, I don't know your name."

"Gonthar. It is true."

"I doubt that," Rita quipped.

"Why is Gonthar holding your son hostage?" the eldest Consortium member said.

"That's why I called you all here, Oslo. I told you how Crux's spies had infiltrated our upper echelons. That they've been working to subvert us from the inside. You told me I was crazy. Gonthar, please lift his shirt."

"Stay away from me," Junior whined as Gonthar

grabbed the bottom of his shirt and pulled it up. "Father, help me."

"You aren't my son," Jack replied, paling as the Advocate came into view. Caleb shuddered too. This one was larger and thicker than Ishek, with dark green skin and a slimy sheen. A mutated version of Ishek's kind.

The Consortium members gasped. One of them, a middle-aged woman laden with tattoos, groaned audibly. "Your son is one of them?"

"Lord Crux has threatened our establishment, and our livelihoods if we continue to resist him," Leighton said. "He's used my son to bind my hands and force my cooperation. Captain Card has put a stop to that."

"How?" Rita asked.

"There were five Relyeh in the Sunshine Isles," Caleb said. "Now there's one." He pointed to Junior's symbiote. "There are thousands of Relyeh like this who form Lord Crux's Legion. If I have my way, there will be none soon enough."

"You want to go to war against Crux?" Oslo snapped indignantly. "Good luck, kid. The entire Royal Navy couldn't stop him, but you think you can?"

"Ridiculous," one of the other Consortium members agreed.

"But what if I can?" Caleb asked. "Which side would you choose?"

"Not yours," Rita replied. "Jack, your son being one of them changes nothing. Neither does Captain Card's ability to kill the spies. Crux will send more spies, he'll infect my sister, or Oslo's granddaughter. If he's that serious about shutting us down, then we need to play along or he will shut us down."

"Maybe if it were your sister, you wouldn't be so easily swayed," Leighton snapped.

"Rita's right," Oslo said. "One man isn't enough to

change the outcome of a war that the Empress has already lost."

"I heard the Empress is dead," Rita said. "Killed by the Legion after they found her secret base."

The Consortium grew tensely silent at the news, which most of them apparently had yet to hear.

"Then all is truly lost," the tattooed woman said.

"That's right," Junior said, speaking up. "You might as well let me go. You can't defeat the Relyeh. This meat sack is only the beginning. Do you have a sister? We'll control her too. A granddaughter? I bet she'll make an excellent host. Or maybe we can come right to the source." He looked at Rita. "You might—"

Leighton stepped forward, slapping Junior in the face. "You shut your mouth, or I'll ask Gonthar to run you through with his fingernail."

The Advocate laughed. "You wouldn't dare. Captain Card and his pathetic excuse of a khoron need me."

A collective gasp went up from the Consortium. "What?" Tattoo said. "You're a Relyeh too?"

"No," Caleb shot back. "I carry a symbiote. He's not in control. I am. And I plan to help Jack's son overcome his khoron as well."

The Advocate laughed harder. "Good luck, Card. The boy is nowhere near strong enough."

"We should just kill it," Rita said, reaching for a blaster on her hip through a high slit in her dress.

"If you kill it, you kill Junior," Caleb warned.

"Not much of a loss, if you ask me," Oslo chirped.

"And if you kill it, then I lose an opportunity to hit Crux where it hurts."

"Which is the heart of the matter," Leighton said. "We've done our best to stay out of the affairs of the Empire. Through years of war, we remained in the shadows, going about our business and making good profits from the conflict. We've all become wealthier than we ever imagined. We may not want to be involved, but Crux already made that decision for us. He wants to own and control everything, and to destroy anything he can't. We can either let that happen, or we can do something about it."

"How?" Oslo said. "By backing some upstart pirate?"

"Card's not just a pirate. He's like Legion, but not Legion. He did more to help us deal with Crux in two hours than we've done in two years. And you saw his drone feed. He captured a Nightmare intact."

"After sixteen years, I'm tired of war."

"But war isn't tired of you, old fool," Leighton replied.

"Aren't you even listening to your enemy?" Caleb snapped, interrupting. "Do you think Crux will be satisfied with your bent knee? You're thieves and pirates. He won't trust you, which means he needs to keep you close. Junior won't be the last to serve a khoron master, and when you lose everything you've worked so hard to gain, you'll think back to the moment I stood here in front of you, telling you I can kick that son of a bitch where it hurts, and you laughed at me like I was crazy. I'm not."

"It's nothing personal," Rita said. "You've got a lot of heart and courage. But neither of those things will penetrate the armor of Crux's ships. And if you can't defeat his ships, you can defeat him."

"That's not true. Crux needs more than ships. He needs spacers to fly them, and boots on the ground to keep the civilians in line. He needs the Legion. But I have a plan to cut the Legion down to size. That'll be the beginning of the end."

"Hell, I'm open to backing you just to see you try," Tattoo said.

"You aren't out much if I fail," Caleb said. "All I need is an interest free loan. Coin to pay my crew for the next three months. Anything more would be too suspicious. Let me prove myself, and then we'll see who's laughing, and who's crazy."

"I'm in," Tattoo repeated.

"Me too," Leighton said, winking at Caleb.

"Sure, why not?" Rita added. "You're cute enough to take a flyer on."

The other four members of the Consortium who hadn't spoken nodded their heads in agreement.

"Oslo?" Leighton said.

"I still say no, but I'm clearly outvoted," Oslo replied, looking at Caleb. "You're going to get yourself killed."

"Maybe. If I go down fighting, then I'll die with my values intact."

"You really are a joke, aren't you, Card? *I'll die with my values intact,*" Junior mocked him.. "Please."

"Jack, I need to bring your son with me," Caleb said, ignoring the Advocate.

"I know. I hope you can bring him back as himself. But if you can't, I won't hold it against you."

"Commander Shirin has also asked about joining my crew," Caleb said. "I think she might be an asset to me."

"You've got the hots for the slug, Elena?" Rita said.

"I like what Captain Card is fighting for, Executive Rita," Shirin replied. "It's rare for anyone to be so noble anymore."

"I think you've forgotten who you're speaking to," Tattoo said with a smile. "All of us have made our fortunes in a variety of unsavory ways. Noble it isn't, but I don't regret it."

The other members of the Consortium murmured their agreement. They played the role of business executives so well, Caleb had almost forgotten how awful most of them probably were behind the scenes. The outward appearances of their posturing, not to mention the Sunshine Isles, were definitely deceiving.

"She's a free woman," Leighton said. "She doesn't need to ask, and neither do you."

Caleb nodded. "If there's nothing else, I'd like to return to my ship. I have a lot of work to do."

"I'll have the funds you need transferred to your auction account immediately. You're free to go, Captain."

# CHAPTER 29

Caleb waited at Medusa's entrance hatch while the others filed past. Penn led the still-restrained and bitching Jack Jr., with Elena bringing up the rear, a large duffel stuffed with her gear slung over her shoulder, a blaster pointed at Junior's armpit. Gonthar had split from them, returning to his own ship. At first, Caleb had thought the rust bucket the Jiba-ki had landed in was his transport vessel, only to learn that the ship was the only ship Gonthar possessed. His new ally had agreed to follow their lander back to Gorgon.

None of the members of the Consortium came to the spaceport to see them off, which didn't surprise Caleb. He knew he had been right to have Ishek block off the other Advocate's ability to communicate through the Collective, though the effort had taken a toll on his symbiote. And him. His body felt weak, his mind foggy, and despite the fear Ishek had fed on recently, he had used enough of his strength that even Caleb sensed the hunger's pull in the corner of his mind. It hadn't been a problem before, when he had synthetic replacement to keep Ishek satiated. But he had lost all the vials on Spirit. He knew from experience he would grow continually weaker until he found an alternate source. Failing that, he had about a month before both he and Ishek would starve.

He could worry about that later. He had enough to occupy his mind right now.

Trailing Elena into the ship, he closed the hatch behind him. He remained in the narrow aisle between the bulkhead and the flight deck while Elena quickly stowed her gear in a storage compartment before helping Penn put Jack in his seat. The Advocate hadn't stopped jabbering since they'd left the meeting with the Consortium, his constant flow of insults and taunts now filling the cabin with constant noise. Caleb had no problem ignoring him.

*I really wish he would shut the hell up.*

*We'll be able to silence him once we return to the Gorgon,* Caleb replied. *Let him wear himself out in the meantime.*

*That one won't tire of being an annoyance for the sake of it. I didn't realize right away, but when I saw the look of that Advocate…* Caleb felt the chill that ran through Ishek. *I believe it has been Sanctified, though it's also possible they genetically mutated it before creation.*

*He wasn't lying about being stronger than you?*

*No, and yes. He is definitely stronger, but I am more agile.*

*Float like a butterfly, sting like a bee.*

*I don't understand that comment.*

Caleb brought to mind historical videos he had seen of boxing champion Muhammed Ali to show Ishek what he meant.

*Yes. It is an apt analogy.*

With Jack strapped in, Caleb entered the passcode to the flight deck and stepped inside the compartment, pressing the door control to keep it open behind him. He wanted to hear if Junior caused any trouble. Atrice remained in the pilot seat, though he had removed the chef's apron while he waited.

"Are we clear to launch?" Caleb asked.

"Aye, Captain. As soon as you're buckled in," the pilot replied. "How'd it go?"

"Worse than I expected, and better than I'd hoped."

"That sounds like it might be good news," Atrice said, confused by the statement.

"The bottom line is that we captured an Advocate and have fresh funding to pay everyone."

"That's definitely good news."

Caleb remained on the flight deck, strapping into the co-pilot seat. "I'm ready when you are."

"Aye, Captain." Atrice tapped on the comms controls. "Aroon Ground Control, this is the transport Medusa, requesting permission for immediate liftoff and egress to orbit."

"Medusa, this is Ground Control," a man's voice answered. "Permission granted. You are clear for liftoff. Thank you for visiting the beautiful Sunshine Isles. We hope you enjoyed your stay."

"Copy that, Control," Atrice said. "We enjoyed it just fine. Medusa out."

He disconnected the comms, continuing to tap on the control screen, starting the reactor and running basic flight checks. Less than a minute later, the thrusters came to life with a soft whine and subtle vibrations of the deck's anti-gravity plates. The transport lifted off the tarmac, rising to a dozen meters before Atrice pushed the throttle open. The starship jolted forward at an increasingly steep angle, until they were rocketing upward and continuing to gain speed.

"Captain, it looks like we have a tail," he said half a minute later.

"That's Gonthar," Caleb replied. "He's with us."

Atrice opened a rear view on the main surround, zooming in on Gonthar's ship. "Is that a Falcon Twelve?" he said. "Those things went out of production when my grandpa was a baby."

"It looks even worse up close," Caleb answered. "But it flies. We can't all have the Pirate King's former lander in our possession."

"I'm just glad we didn't need to use the guns."

"Agreed. I'm not itching to get into any fights right now."

"It's not that, Captain. I didn't want to tell you before, but the energy weapons are all disconnected, and the rockets in the launchers are duds."

"What?" Caleb said, craning his neck to look at the pilot.

"Graystone stripped the ion cannons and sold the converters. He also pawned off the real rockets and replaced them with pretty fakes."

Caleb couldn't believe it. If they had needed to fight their way off Aroon, they wouldn't have stood a chance. "We'll need to undo that short-sighted stupidity as soon as we can."

"Aye, Captain," Atrice replied.

"And next time, don't wait to tell me something that you think I might need to know."

"Aye, Captain."

Medusa reached Gorgon fifteen minutes later, touching down smoothly in the hangar bay. Damian was already there to meet them, flanked by Goldie and Roy in two suits of well-worn combat armor. As Caleb had requested, a fourth person stood a short distance behind them. Doctor Jane Haverblaad was a tall, middle-aged blonde the crew had affectionately nicknamed Butcher. From what Caleb had been told, she'd received the moniker because she'd caught her husband cheating on her and had cut him up like stew meat before becoming a pirate.

Already alerted to their special passenger and newest recruits, neither Damian nor the others batted an eye when Gonthar's battered ship entered the hangar close behind Medusa and landed beside the transport.

Caleb moved out into the passageway, checking on Penn, Elena, and Jack Jr. The Advocate was still mouthing off, having devolved into shouting out curses and vulgarities. Seeing they still had the prisoner under control, Caleb opened the hatch and exited the transport.

"Captain," Damian greeted him, nodding at the others.

"Damian. Doctor Haverblaad," Caleb acknowledged. "Did you bring the sedative?"

"Every drop we had," she replied. "Are you sure a dose like that won't kill him?"

"Positive. The Advocate will filter toxins quickly. Even the amount you brought will give us ten minutes to get him into the brig for safekeeping. Now that he's here, he's going to be more desperate to free himself, and if he gets loose… Let's just say we can't afford to have him run amok through the ship. Keep him restrained until Doctor Haverblaad tranqs him."

"Aye, Captain." Roy nodded. "We'll keep him in line," he said, leading Goldie and the doctor into the transport.

"It sounds like you had quite an adventure down there, Captain," Damian said.

"One that didn't work out the way I'd planned, but it still worked out better than I could have asked. I'm confident I can get *something* out of the Advocate. Whether its useful is a different story. I'm hoping to keep Jack Jr. alive, and we should have the funds to keep the crew happy for a few months."

"I'm sure they'll be pleased to hear that." Damian frowned at Caleb, something about his expression obviously bothering him. "What is it, Captain?"

"Lucy was on board Medusa before we launched. I asked her about why she was here with Linx."

"She told you about her troubles on Persephon?"

"Yes. How many other crew members do we have that

are here because they're in such dire straits? How many children?"

"I'd need to review the records, Captain. Lucy and Linx aren't the only ones."

"I don't want them here, Sarge. Where we're going is no place for kids, especially with what we're planning."

"I agree, but what—" He froze as Jack began screaming inside the transport. Elena, Roy and Goldie started shouting, their words garbled as their strident voices rose over each other. Then Jack appeared at the transport's hatch without his escort. Hands still bound and his eyes wild, he jumped out, making a break for it.

He didn't make it far. Gonthar raced around his ship's bow and grabbed the teen off his feet, his claws wrapping around the meaty Advocate in his armpit.

"You just settle down there, worm," he said.

Haverblaad was next off the transport, her eye already swelling shut. "Bastard head butted me," she hissed, rushing over to Jack Jr. She doubled up her fist and punched him in the face. "How do you like it?" Another punch. "And another one for good measure." She drew her fist back again.

"That's enough, Doctor," Caleb said.

She glared back at him, but begrudgingly dropped her arm. "Aye, Captain." She pulled her injection gun out of her coat pocket and shoved it against Jack's neck.

"You told me you made a new friend," Damian said, his eyes on Gonthar. "You omitted the part about him being a Jiba-ki."

"Is that a problem?" Caleb asked.

"No, Captain. I think it's pretty fascinating, to be honest."

"Our apologies, Captain," Penn said, emerging from the transport. "He was faster than I expected. It won't happen again."

"Is that a Jiba-Ki?" Roy asked, following her out, Elena right behind him.

As Jack's head dropped to his chest and he stopped thrashing, Gonthar took him in a one-handed hold by the back of his collar, let him drop to his knees, and turned to face Caleb and the others. With his free hand, he offered a slightly self-conscious wave. "Greetings. I am Orin. Do you think I am beautiful?"

Caleb raised an eyebrow at the name change before realizing his new ally had dropped the pseudonym.

"You are beautiful," Roy said confidently.

"Thank you. It is true."

Caleb grinned. "Penn, I need Jack in the brig before he wakes up. Goldie, Roy, accompany them."

"Yes, Sir! We're on it," Roy snapped, he and Goldie rushing toward Orin and Jack, Penn right behind them.

"Orin," Caleb said. "Do you mind giving them a hand?"

"I am yours to command, Captain Card," he replied.

Penn led the way, with Orin right behind her, dragging Jack Jr. by the scruff of his neck. Shrugging when the Jiba-Ki apparently didn't need their help, Roy and Goldie followed along at the tail end of the procession leaving the hangar.

Atrice finally disembarked Medusa. "Sarge, I told Cap about the weapon modules."

"We need to fix those cannons and pick up fresh rockets," Caleb said.

"We couldn't before. If you have coin, we can now. I'll have Hank contact a trade ship that can deliver the ordnance."

"It's that easy?" Caleb asked.

"Only because we're already orbiting Aroon."

"Atrice, excellent work today. You're dismissed."

"Thank you, Captain." Atrice said. "My shift in the galley starts in an hour. That'll give me just enough time to grab a bite before I cook for everyone else. Should I have some chow sent to your quarters?"

"No, thank you."

"Doctor Haverblaad, you're dismissed as well. Thank you for your help. I hope your eye will be okay."

"It's nothing I can't fix," Haverblaad said, nodding before hurrying away in Atrice's wake.

"Sarge, I want you to meet Elena Shirin," Caleb said, turning his attention to the newest member of the crew. "She was Royal Navy and has contacts with ties to the resistance."

"Elena, this is our Tactical Officer, Damian…"

"Just Damian," he replied. "But the crew calls me Sarge. Welcome aboard."

"Thank you, Sarge."

"If you have contacts with the resistance, then—"

"I know the Empress is dead," she finished for him. "I also know Captain Card aims to give Lord Crux all kinds of trouble. That's why I'm here."

Damian smiled. "You and I should get along just fine."

"Sarge, I want Elena to take over leadership of the Berserkers."

"The who?" Elena asked.

"Captain, are you sure that's a good idea?" Damian responded.

"Why, are they still causing trouble?"

"No, but Granger inserted himself as their de facto head. He won't take well to being displaced."

"He'll get over it."

"That's not how things work here," Damian insisted. "Remember?"

"Does Granger have experience leading a unit?" Caleb asked.

"No, but—"

"I run the show now. Things work how I say they work,

not by some unwritten pirate rules. I need experienced commanders running the boarding crews."

"Captain Card, if I could say something," Elena said.

"Go ahead," he replied.

"If you want to change the hierarchy without ruffling feathers, you'll need to disband the Berserkers and reform the underperformers into a crew of their own and perhaps give them a different job, with this Granger guy at their head."

"This isn't your first rodeo, is it?" Caleb said with a sheepish grin.

"I don't know what a rodeo is," she replied. "But I've served on ships like this before. I know how to play the game."

"Captain, it may be better if Elena takes on a different role," Damian said. "Considering our future endeavors, it wouldn't hurt for me to have a backup."

Caleb wasn't sure. *Ish, what do you think?*

*I don't care. Let me rest.*

"See Elena to a berth in officer's quarters. I'll think about it."

"Of course, Captain."

They started for the hangar exit together. "Sarge, as I was saying earlier, I don't want any children on my ship."

"I understand. But most of them have nowhere else to go."

"Because of their circumstances. I know Lucy has debts to pay. We should pay them. If any of the other families are in a similar situation, we should help them, too."

"That could get expensive, Captain."

"I don't care. I'd rather get the kids offloaded than arm the transport."

"It's an honorable desire, Captain. But—"

"No buts," Caleb interrupted. "Assemble a team if you need to, but I want to know how many children we have on board and how we can put them in a better position off this ship."

"Aye, Captain."

"Contact me as soon as that's done. I'm going to check on Jack and help see that Orin gets settled."

"Aye, Captain."

They exited the hangar bay, splitting in different directions. Finally alone, Caleb reached out to Ishek again.

"Are you okay, Ish?"

*No, and not just because I'm exhausted. Junior's Advocate is unnatural, as are the mutations to Crux. I'm concerned about the way the Relyeh are using the Sanctification process, and I cannot help thinking Pathfinder is related to all of this.*

"I left the data chip with Tae. We can see what he's come up with after we pay Junior a visit."

*Very well. And if you could badly frighten someone while you're at it, I would be grateful.*

Caleb smiled through his concern about keeping Ishek fed. "I'll see what I can do."

# CHAPTER 30

"Oh, look who's here," Jack sneered as Caleb entered the brig. Penn and Orin immediately silenced a conversation they were having and turned in his direction. Penn offered him a nod, while Orin bared his teeth at Jack, showing off his sharp incisors while straightening his posture. "And look how the little slaves jump to attention."

Positioned in the lowest deck of Gorgon's bow, the brig was a long way from any of the occupied areas of the starship, and it had taken nearly ten minutes just to make the trip from the hangar at the opposite end of the vessel. That Penn and her team, plus the Jiba-ki, had gotten Jack here before he awoke, or even more dangerously, after he had woken, left Caleb impressed.

"As you were," Caleb said to them, allowing them to relax their posture as he looked past them to survey the brig's layout.

The compartment wasn't large. Only four cells positioned behind electrified wire mesh lined the room from left to right, each one similar in size to the smallest individual crew berths on the lower decks, and in some respects they were better outfitted. Every cell had its own head positioned behind a privacy screen, which offered only a silhou-ette of the prisoner whenever they had to take care of business. Opposite the toilet, thin mattresses covered two bunks beside a desk with a built-in network terminal and a padded stool. None of the furniture looked like anyone had ever used it before, which reminded Caleb that Graystone never imprisoned his pirates. From what Damian had told him, Gorgon's former captain liked to airlock first and ask questions later.

"I am impressed though, Card," Jack continued. "After the beating I gave poor Ishek, I would have thought you would be too weak to stand."

*I would hardly call his resistance to my inception a beating.*

"Maybe you aren't half as strong as you think you are," Caleb replied, smirking at Junior. He glanced at Penn. "Did you get him down here before he woke up?"

"Almost, but not quite," she replied. "It helps to have a friend with sharp fingernails and quick reflexes."

Orin laughed. "It is my pleasure, Penelope."

Caleb grimaced, glancing at Penn while waiting for her reaction to Orin using her full name. Rather than become upset, she smiled and returned Caleb's look. "When he tried to say Penn, his pendant translated it as something else." She made a face. "Think male anatomy."

Caleb chuckled. "That's as good a reason as I can think of to give someone permission to use your full name," he replied before returning his attention to Jack. "I know you think you're in control, Jackie boy. That ended the moment you stepped off Medusa and onto my ship."

The Advocate laughed. "That isn't how I see things from this side of the mesh. You need everything from me. I need nothing from you. I'm willing to endure whatever tortures you can imagine to remain silent. I'm willing to give my life and especially this pathetic human's to defend Lord Crux. Do you know what that means, Card? It means you have no leverage. There's nothing you can do to break me."

"We'll see about that," Caleb said. "Penn, show Orin to quarters in officer's berthing."

"Captain, I believe the quarters on the officer level are full."

"Then choose someone he can replace."

"Replace, Captain?" Penn replied. "You want me to kick someone out of officer's berthing?"

"I understand that isn't how things normally work, but Orin is a special guest. Perhaps you can assign double occupancy to two lower-ranking officers so Orin can have private quarters."

"Aye, Captain," Penn said.

"Also, I want him on your boarding team."

"Gladly," Penn replied. "Thank you, Captain."

Once they were gone, Caleb retrieved a simple metal chair from the watch desk in the corner, placing it in front of Jack's cell. He seated himself on it and stared silently at the kid.

"Well now, it's just you and me," the Advocate said. "I suppose this is the part where you make a feeble attempt to intimidate me."

"Not at all," Caleb answered. "In fact, I'm just going to sit here."

Jack's brow wrinkled in confusion. "Why?"

Caleb didn't answer him. *Ish, I need you to give me my first lesson in reaching out through the Collective.*

*We are not strong right now. This is a bad idea.*

*You always say my ideas are bad ideas.*

*Because they are.*

*We need intel from this Advocate. You aren't strong enough to overpower him yourself, but the two of us can do it together.*

*I already told you, it's not that simple. And I wasn't joking that your mind might not be able to handle it.*

*Try me.*

*This isn't the time for your Marine bravado. If you fail, we may both die.*

*I already have experience coordinating thoughts through Spirit's interface. How hard or different can the Collective be? This is our edge, Ish. The thing that gives us an advantage humankind hasn't had before. We need to pursue it. You have to teach me.*

*I told you I would teach you, and if this were a normal Advocate I would be less hesitant, though it would be better to start with a basic khoron.*

"Are you really just going to sit there and stare at me all day?" the Advocate asked. "I'm sure you have better things to pretend to be good at."

*Come on, Ish. If we walk away now, it's going to make things harder every time we deal with him. And I promised Leighton I would help his son regain control. I intend to keep that promise.*

*It was a stupid promise to make. You have a strong will. Not always the sharpest mind, but you're possibly of average intelligence. I doubt Junior can say the same. At least Leighton told you he would understand if his son didn't survive.*

*I'm not giving up on him that easily.*

*I hunger, Cal. This will make it worse.*

*We don't have any synthetic. The only way you feed again is when we find a target of Crux's to hit. Junior might lead us to that target.*

*Not true. You could sneak up on a crew member and assault them. You don't need to hurt them, only make them think you will for a few minutes.*

*I know you're okay with that, but I'm not.*

*It doesn't have to be someone you like. A Berserker, maybe?*

*No. This is how we get it done. Teach me.*

Ishek didn't answer right away. Before Caleb could prod the symbiote, his vision failed, replaced with an infinite blackness. Sudden pressure stabbed at his ears, the sounds of a billion screaming voices piercing them like pins and needles. Every nerve in his body seemed to fire at once.

It went away as quickly as it came, leaving Caleb with his hands clenching the sides of his chair and the Advocate laughing on the other side of the cell mesh.

*What the hell was that?* Caleb asked.

"You're trying to reach me through the Collective, aren't you?" the Advocate asked. "I give you credit for trying, Card. But your brain will explode long before you ever get across the collux, nevermind into my head."

*Ish?*

*I opened your mind to the Collective. Only for an instant, as though you were blinking. Do you feel so confident now?*

Caleb stared at Jack. The Advocate was more than a little amused.

*I've experienced worse. Hit me again.*

# CHAPTER 31

Caleb's vision faded, introducing the pitch dark of the Collective. As with every other time, his first sense was that he was completely alone in a vast universe, while simultaneously overwhelmed by the sheer volume of consciousnesses, as numerous as the stars, surrounding him. And each was like a star in this place. A black pinpoint deeper than the backdrop, creating splotches where they were most dense.

Immediately, the dark points closest to him tried to break into his mind, using Ishek's collux as a route to connect with him. To know everything he knew, the way he was trying to learn to do the same. With Ishek backing him up, the curious Relyeh couldn't pierce his defenses. They sensed a Relyeh stronger than they were and quickly retreated, lest it punish them for their insolence.

Further afield, Caleb could see a distant, larger black spot. Ishek had already explained that it belonged to an Ancient, the most powerful and senior of the Relyeh. While the symbiote didn't know which Ancient, the important thing was that it was distant—not in the sense of measurements of length or gaps between two objects.

Everything was technically adjacent on the Collective. Instead, it was a metaphysical representation of how much attention the Ancient was currently giving to the Relyeh in their part of the universe. Like the Eye of Sauron, they didn't want to draw its gaze. According to Ishek, the black spot could crush his mind instantly if it took notice of him.

He turned his attention away from it as the Collective drew into sharper focus. He sensed the dull beginnings of what would become the sharp stabs against his nervous system, caused by his mind struggling to adapt to this strange reality. After three hours of practice he had learned to slow the advance, but had yet to conquer it completely.

Back in Gorgon's brig, his body was coated in a sheen of sweat. His muscles were fatigued, his brain tired in a way he had never known possible. The Advocate had grown tired of laughing at him and had settled on the mattress, leaning against the wall and watching him with a bored expression on his face. He showed no concern that Caleb might eventually find him on the Collective, much less break through his defenses. If he was impressed by the hours of effort, he was smart enough not to let it show.

Caleb's perspective shifted on the Collective, rotating in place as he sought the Advocate. He had lost track of how many times he had already searched for the Relyeh, forced to abandon the quest by the constantly increasing pain that would spread throughout his body. Ishek had already told him to call it a day more than once. He refused to give up. He just wasn't made that way.

Finding a specific Relyeh was like echolocation, combined with elimination and guesswork. He had learned to break apart the cacophony that had greeted him during his first forced foray into the Collective, separating the sounds into groups of tones which were stronger or weaker, depending on relative distance. By projecting himself toward the tones, he could further separate the dark blobs, until they became individual points of nothingness.

From there, he picked out the sounds by a hard to describe sense of attraction he called the Relyeh's charisma. The combination of all these things helped him push aside the hundreds of Legionnaires within a few hundred light years, whittling the potentials to a handful considerably closer. Within a dozen light years or less, Ishek could get even nearer, within a few meters, but the symbiote said that would take him years to master.

He didn't need to get that close. The Advocate's charisma stood out from the others, leaving him sure of the black spot's identity without needing to ping him to confirm. So far, he had stopped short of actually contacting the Advocate, who had yet to react to his presence on the Collective. He was certain the Advocate knew he was there. Either he didn't see him as a threat, or his charisma was reading a lot stronger than he had guessed it might.

*The former is much more likely.*

*Thanks for the vote of confidence,* he replied.

*How is your burn?*

Caleb took stock of the stinging across his body. *Manageable.*

*Then you are prepared to make contact. Consider yourself a spermatozoon, hoping to fertilize an egg.*

*I'd really rather not.*

*You need to push hard to bypass the defenses. You must expend great energy to get inside.*

*Can we do this without the reproductive similes? Besides, aren't I more like a Trojan horse?*

*Horses aren't part of this equation.*

*Nevermind. Attacking isn't much different than defending, is it?*

*The general concept is the same. Defending is easier.*

*Which is why we settled on trickery.*

*It is the only way you will get the information you seek within a reasonable amount of time. And the only way we will get the nutrients we need to survive. Unless you've reconsidered my suggestion.*

*I haven't.*

*Are you prepared?*

Caleb's senses locked on the Advocate's place in the Collective. *Yeah, I'm ready.*

*Then do it.*

With a thought, Caleb projected himself toward the Advocate, launching like a missile at the darkness. He immediately understood what Ishek meant by attacking being more difficult when he slammed into the Advocate's defenses. Instead of being able to estimate his progress as black tendrils against white light, his darkness mingled with the Advocate's, making it nearly impossible for him to tell how deeply he had pierced it, or if he had even punched into the Relyeh at all.

That lack of feedback might have caused most to pause or pull back. Failure meant the Advocate would have an opportunity to turn the tables, and if he got into Caleb, he could capture nearly all of his memories, his entire life, in less than a minute. Conceivably, he could also gain control of his body the way the assassin had, and even force his heart to stop if he was so inclined.

And Caleb was sure the creature would be so inclined.

He didn't hesitate to keep plowing forward, pushing his consciousness into the Advocate's, fighting to bore his way through. He could tell he was losing when the stabbing in his body spiked suddenly, sending waves of pain rippling through his Collective senses. The shock nearly made him falter. Only his determination kept him from failing catastrophically. He held on, forcing his way forward, forging ahead in small steps that spent nearly all his effort.

He could only hope he was making some progress and that Ishek could finish what he had started.

The Trojan horse. Their secret weapon. The Advocate believed Ishek was back on defense when he had actually come along for the ride, hiding his charisma inside of Caleb's, a true Relyeh assassin. All Caleb had to do was get the weakened symbiote most of the way through the Advocate's defenses. If he succeeded, then all Ishek had to do was pull memories from the creature's consciousness. They could see what their expedition recovered once they were both safely out of the Collective.

First, he had to make it deep enough. He kept pushing. He kept fighting, even as the stinging in his body increased. Even as a sense of the agony found its way into the Collective. He was nearly out of gas, but he wasn't dead. He refused to quit.

There was no sense of time in the Collective. He didn't know how long he continued fighting. One moment, he felt like he was on fire. The next, he had gone completely numb. At first he believed the Advocate might have overpowered him, but then he realized he was no longer pushing into the Relyeh's collux. Free floating in the Collective once more, he stared at the Advocate's dark spot, confused.

*I have it. Bring us home.*

*When did—*

*Don't delay. Get us out of here.*

It only took a thought, and he was back in the brig. Of course, his body still suffered the effects of the attack against him, and his consciousness immediately became aware of his convulsions, the pain rippling through his body like a maelstrom. He had already fallen off his seat, shaking on the floor while Jack stood at the front of his cell, staring down at him.

"I hope you die, you son of a bitch," the Advocate

cursed. "But not before you suffer the worst pain any organism can suffer. You think you put yourself on equal footing to a Relyeh? To an Advocate? Your pain amuses me, Card. It brings me great joy."

The stinging faded as Ishek released an abundance of chemicals into his system to combat the effects. The effort would weaken the already exhausted symbiote but now that they had captured some part of what the Advocate knew, they were that much closer to taking action.

The Advocate continued taunting him as his body finally relaxed, his pounding heart slowing, his tense muscles releasing. He remained on the deck for another minute, collecting his strength before sitting up and locking eyes with Junior. The Advocate's satisfied smirk slowly faded as he realized Caleb wouldn't die. A different sense rolled through Caleb at the moment the enemy Relyeh realized Ishek had snuck in like a thief in the night.

*This is an unexpected relief. I huuuunnnnggeeeerrr.*

Caleb's smirk replaced Jack's, the influx of pheromones from the Advocate's human host flooding the room and helping to refuel Ishek, and by extension to him. He practically jumped to his feet as Junior retreated from the mesh, returning to the mattress with a dejected look on his face.

"Your fear amuses me, Gareshk," Caleb said, picking up the Advocate's name from the memories Ishek had collected. "It brings me great joy. Let's do this again some-time. Soon."

He mocked Gareshk with a nod before leaving the prisoner alone in the brig.

# CHAPTER 32

*Someone's at the door.*

Caleb's eyes snapped open, his initial effort to jump out of bed failing. More stiff and sore than he would have expected, he tried again, more slowly this time, as someone began pounding continuously on his sealed hatch.

"Nearly everyone on board has a comms patch," he groused, still half awake, his head pounding. "Who's knocking?"

*Unfortunately, neither of us has x-ray vision.*

"How long was I asleep?"

*Nine hours.*

"It felt like ten minutes."

*Your mind was especially weakened from your foray onto the Collective. It might be damaged, but it will be difficult to notice any change if that's the case.*

"I have to admit, you're getting more refined in your snark."

*I believe it's improved from reviewing Gareshk's memories.*

"Just be you, Ish. The last thing we need is another Gareshk." He paused excitedly. "Did we get anything useful?"

*Yes, I believe so.*

"Incredible! What?" The pounding again rattled the door to his quarters.

*Perhaps we should answer the door first.*

Caleb diverted to pick up his blaster, which he had apparently left on the desk next to his terminal. He realized he had no memory of returning to his quarters from the brig, but somehow he had showered and changed his clothes.

*It's an aftereffect of Gareshk's defenses.*

"Did you take control of my body?"

*Yes. And I saved our lives by doing so. You made it out of the brig and another dozen steps before you staggered into the bulkhead and I caught you before you collapsed. Now you have a Collective-induced hangover.*

"But you gave me back control without making me work for it. I like how we're building trust, Ish."

*Do not be so appreciative; I did it for selfish reasons.*

Caleb reached the door and opened it, leading with his blaster. Lucy was on the other side, her fist raised to hit the door again, tear trails glistening on her cheeks. Linx stood beside her, her smile huge. The next thing he knew, Lucy rushed headlong at him, hitting him so hard in his groggy condition she knocked him back a step. Her arms went around him, and he wrapped an arm around her, more to maintain his balance than to hug her back. Following her mother's lead, Linx wrapped her arms around his waist and beamed up at him.

"Captain Card," Lucy sobbed. "Oh, thank you, thank you, thank you. You don't know what you've done for Linx and me."

"You're just the best captain ever!" Linx exclaimed, squeezing him as hard as she could.

"Hey, you two." He looked down at Linx, laying his other hand on her back before returning his attention to

Lucy. "I'm still half asleep here," he told her, confused. "You're right. I don't know. What is it you're thanking me for?"

"The severance coin," she replied. "It's enough to pay off all of my debts and take Linx back to Persephon. It'll even pay for the transport tickets to get us there. You're our savior, Captain Card." She stood on her tiptoes and kissed Caleb on the cheek. "Thank you, Captain."

Caleb's confusion turned into a smile. Obviously, Damian had finished going through the crew records and identifying the needs of the people onboard with their children. He hadn't waited for Caleb's permission before taking care of Lucy and Linx, at least. "You're welcome. I've ordered everyone with children off Gorgon. It's too dangerous for you here now."

*I feel strange.*

*It's called tenderness with a large dose of compassion.*

"We're not afraid of danger," Linx said. "We're pirates."

Caleb backed up from Lucy and knelt in front of the girl. "No, not anymore you're not. You're going to go home and be a happy little girl." He looked up at Lucy. "We're done hijacking ships and stealing cargo. We're going to war."

Her expression turned serious. "Against Lord Crux. Sarge told me. I hope you'll be careful, Captain."

"I don't want you to get hurt, Captain," Linx added. "You're too nice to get hurt."

Caleb smiled at them both. "Maybe it will work out for me," he said. "I've made it this far. I don't expect Crux to stop me." He centered his attention on Lucy. "When do you leave?"

"In a few hours. Sarge is still informing some of the other crew of their release, and the transfer ship won't be here for another hour or two."

"I'm glad he could book passage for you from here. "

"From what he says, we have you to thank for that as

well. He told me you befriended the pirate king, Jack Leighton."

"I wouldn't call it a friendship. More like we have a shared goal."

"Whatever happens, Linxie and I will always be grateful to you. If you're ever on Persephon, please look us up. I'd like to offer whatever hospitality I can."

"I absolutely will. I hope everything works out for you both."

Linx wrapped her arms around his neck and pulled him down into a bigger hug. When she let go, he stood up, his eyes again meeting Lucy's. It was a surprising struggle to say goodbye. "You have a safe trip home."

"I hope I'll see you again."

"I hope so, too. I'm sorry we didn't have time to get to know one another better."

"Linxie, come on. I'm sure Captain Card is very busy."

"Goodbye, Captain." She threw Caleb a kiss and continued waving as Lucy led her down the corridor toward the lift.

"Goodbye, Linx." A little quieter, he said,"Goodbye, Lucy."

He waited until they disappeared around the corner before shutting his door. He tapped on his comm patch. "Damian," he said, pausing while the comms system connected them.

"Captain," Damian said. "I was beginning to worry about you, especially after the way you brushed me off earlier."

*We needed to rest.*

Caleb sighed in response to Ishek's excuse. "That wasn't me, it was Ish. We spent hours with the prisoner, but I think we got what we needed."

"That's excellent news."

"Lucy and Linx just left my quarters. They were unexpectedly animated." Caleb left it at that, waiting for Damian's reaction.

"Knowing Lucy, I'm sure she wanted to express her gratitude for the severance stipend," he said. "I thought you wanted the issue with members of the crew having children on board settled as soon as possible. I spent all day working with Hank and Sasha to identify them and prepare packages that would allow them fresh starts away from pirate life. If that was wrong, I apologize. But I stand behind my decision to take action."

"No, it wasn't wrong of you. I want my top leadership to think for themselves and take the initiative when it's needed. If you had waited on me, we would just be starting the process now. How many crew members did you identify?"

"Twenty-six adults and thirty-one children," he replied. "The payouts burned half our loan."

Caleb grimaced at the news. It was more than he had wanted to spend, but he didn't regret it. Especially knowing that Lucy and Linx were on their way to begin a new, safer and hopefully happier life. "What about the replacement munitions for Medusa?"

"Hank took care of it. We already made the exchange. Yamato and O'Shea are taking care of the repair and replacement as we speak."

"You've been busy."

"Aye, Captain. We also resupplied our overall ammunition, parts, and sundries. Oh, and we picked up some parts for Orin's starjumper. Another two million all in. Gorgon has some armor damage from our earlier scrape that'll need some attention once we reach a stardock, but it's nothing we can't live with for now."

Caleb did the quick math. They had started with just a little over six million in coin and were already down to less than two. "How long can we afford to pay the remaining crew?"

"Three weeks."

"That's tight. I should have asked Leighton for more coin."

"We'll be fine as long as we even up before we return to anywhere the coin can be spent. Pirates are accustomed to going short for a few weeks now and then. If things get really bad, that's when you need to worry about mutiny or desertion."

"Lucy mentioned there are transfer ships coming to dock with Gorgon. How long before we're clear to get back underway?"

"The transfers should be completed within the next four hours. Do you have a destination in mind?"

"Not yet. I need to work through what Ish and I picked from Gareshk, the Advocate's, mind. Have you spoken to Naya?"

"About Graystone's accounts?" Damian replied. "Not recently. No news is good news, I suppose."

"No news is no news. I had hoped she'd have some kind of resolution before we went back into hyperspace."

"She still has a few hours. Should I check with her?"

"No, I'll take care of it when I get to that part of my to-do list. Thank you, Damian."

"Of course, Captain. Is there anything else?"

"Just make sure Gorgon is ready for action as soon as the last transfer ship separates."

"Aye, Captain. She will be. You have my word."

"Thank you. Card out." He tapped the patch to disconnect, returning his blaster to the desk before heading for his closet and a fresh change of suitable clothes. His stomach rumbled.

*Mess?*

"To start. And I want to catch up with Tae, to see how his review of Benning's datachip is coming."

*I'm also quite interested in his findings.*

When Caleb stepped out into the passageway and closed his door, he immediately saw a group of crew members coming his way.

*This can't be another mutiny.*

He turned to face them, standing his ground. "We're about to find out."

# CHAPTER 33

Caleb didn't recognize any of the crew members approaching him, leaving him certain he hadn't crossed paths with most of them before. Unarmed and wearing a mixture of work utilities, coveralls, and civilian clothing, they didn't appear threatening, but that didn't mean they weren't.

"Is there a problem here?" someone asked from behind him.

Caleb glanced over his shoulder as Fitz and Greaser appeared around the opposite corner, wearing protective underlays with blasters strapped to their legs. He doubted their perfectly timed arrival was a coincidence, but who had directed them here, and how had they known about the approaching group?

The two Edgers moved in front of Caleb, blocking him from the other crew members, who pulled to a stop a few meters away.

"We didn't come to cause trouble," the man at the front of the group said, putting his hands up. "We don't want a fight."

"What do you want?" Fitz asked.

"Fitz, Greaser, stand down," Caleb said. "I'll do the talking."

"Aye, Captain," they replied, backing off to let Caleb step between them.

"Apologies for the interruption, Captain," the man continued. "It's just, well, we heard from some of the other crew that you're offering payouts to folks who want to leave the ship. We wanted to find out straight from your mouth what the story is."

Caleb stared at the group. Knowing why they had come, he could see now how they didn't carry themselves the way other members of the crew like Fitz, Greaser, Sasha, Rufus, or even Bones did. They looked more downtrodden. Less comfortable. These had to be some people who had joined the crew because they had run out of choices, not because they saw *pirate* or *rebel outlaw* as a viable career path.

"I offered payouts to crew members with children on board," he said. "My intention is to increase our per interaction profits by an order of magnitude, and that approach means taking on significantly greater risk. Gorgon will be in harm's way, and I don't want children to be in the line of fire."

A few of the crew members grumbled behind their spokesman, but Caleb couldn't make out what they were saying.

"That's a compassionate perspective, Captain. No doubt about it. But some of us, we stuck with Graystone even though he was a tyrant primarily because he didn't seek conflict. He operated on scams and traps, and chose targets that were more likely to pay ransom rather than fight back. We're not Edgers like your bodyguards. We're just trying to survive, which doesn't mean getting dragged into a battle as our primary means of earning a living. That might work for you, but it doesn't work for us."

"I already told you and everyone else that you're free to leave at your own discretion."

"I know, sir. But that's the thing. We can't just leave. Where are we going to go? How are we going to cover transfer costs to another planet? Maybe some of us can latch onto another pirate ship, or a salvager or scavenger vessel, but not all of us, I'm sure. There's a real risk that we might end up stranded."

"Didn't Graystone pay you?" Greaser asked.

"Of course, but we have expenses."

"Drinking, gambling, and paying for prostitutes doesn't count," Fitz quipped.

"Molly there spends most of her coin on medication," the man said, pointing to one of the women. "I have three kids and a wife I chose not to put into harm's way, just like you want, Captain. But if I had brought them on board, I'd be getting a nice payout right now. It ain't fair. I'd like to get home to them."

*If existence were fair, I wouldn't be stuck in your armpit.*

*Agreed*, Caleb replied silently. *Although I don't want a group of unhappy crew members threatening morale for the rest of the voyage.*

*You can't let them dictate your actions.*

*I have no intention of doing that.* He locked eyes with the group's spokesman. "To be honest, I'd gladly give severance to any member of the crew who doesn't want to follow where I'm leading, but we only have three weeks worth of funds as it is. Whatever choices you made are the reason you're here, and I'm not responsible for those choices, even when it means that one crew member might benefit more than another. As my grandfather used to say, them's the breaks, kid. What I can offer you is free passage to wherever you want to go, nothing more. And if you don't like it and start causing trouble, I have no qualms about removing you by force, no matter how many children you might have at home. Spread the word to the rest of the crew. Anyone who wants a free ticket off this ride has one hour to speak to Sarge or forever hold their peace. Understood?"

"Aye, Captain," the group's leader said. He wasn't happy with the outcome, but he wasn't about to argue too much with Fitz and Greaser there, hands close to their sidearms. "I'll let the others know. Thank you for hearing us out."

The group turned and headed back toward the crew elevator, while Fitz and Greaser turned around to face Caleb. "Well, that went better than I expected," Fitz said.

"How did you two know to come up here?" Caleb asked. "And did you use my personal lift?"

"Sarge gave us access to the lift," Greaser replied.

"He also asked Penn to assign a couple of Edge to keep an eye on you after what happened last night," Fitz added.

"What happened last night?" Caleb asked.

"Sarge said you were acting strange. Anyway, we just happened to be the lucky pair. Sarge told us to come up as soon as he knew you were awake."

"I wasn't acting strange. That was Ishek. I guess it's a good thing you were around."

"It doesn't seem like they would have challenged you. They're lower deckers. They keep the ship clean, but not much else."

"You may say that now. Wait until you have to clean up after yourselves."

Fitz made a face. "Maybe we can convince them to stay."

"I'm heading down to the mess. I appreciate your concern, but I'm fine without you."

"We haven't eaten yet," Greaser said. "We'll join you."

"Do you eat?" Caleb asked, eyeing her slender frame.

"You wouldn't believe how much she eats," Fitz said. "I don't know how she stays so thin."

"Hypermetabolism," Greaser explained.

"You're welcome to join me, then."

They made the short walk from his quarters and then down the central passageway to the officer's mess. There were only a few spacers eating there when they entered, but Penn and Orin were two of them. Seated together, the Jiba-ki had an enormous pile of raw meat on his plate, while Penn had a bowl of stew sitting in front of her.

"Cayheb," Orin growled before looking up, apparently having smelled him first. "Good morning, Captain."

"Good morning, Cap," Penn said, looking at him over her shoulder. She seemed pleased to see Fitz and Greaser with him.

"Pull up a seat, Captain," Orin said, tapping the empty chair beside him. "It is true."

"Is that raw meat?" Fitz asked, noticing Orin's plate.

"Delicious, is it not?"

"Not. Definitely not."

"I'm just going to grab some chow," Caleb said, approaching the line and picking up a tray and a plate. Atrice stood behind the counter and offered Caleb a nod when their eyes made contact.

"Good morning, Captain."

"Good morning, Atrice." Caleb eyed the chow. "What kind of meat is in the stew?" he asked. The stew's gravy was thick and brown, with chunks of red and purple vegetables sunk into it with squares of almost black meat. It smelled good, at least.

"That's grovish," Atrice said. "It's one of the most common livestock in the Spiral."

"What does it look like?"

"It's a giant insect," Fitz explained. "About three meters long and two meters high, with a tough exoskeleton. The dark meat comes from the body. The light meat, from the pincers and legs. It's an expensive delicacy."

Caleb stared at the meat, trying to get the image of a giant scorpion out of his head. He had eaten crickets before, not to mention lobsters, crabs and crayfish. This wasn't much different. "What about that mashed potato stuff?" he asked, pointing to a tray of greenish mush.

"Mashed lhurn. It's the pulp of a small tree. It has a smokey, fruity taste and goes great with the stew. Trust me."

Caleb scooped some onto the plate before ladling two helpings of stew on top of it. After eating MREs for months, the alien concoction could probably taste like vomit and he would still eat it. He grabbed a fork and brought his meal back to where Penn and Orin sat, joining them there.

"How did it go with Junior?" Penn asked.

"Ish and I had a breakthrough," he replied. "We'll be ready to make a move by the time we're done offloading the children."

"And the lower deckers who want to leave," Greaser added, returning to the table with an overloaded plate of food. "A group of them showed up at Cap's quarters to bitch about fairness."

"I offered them free passage wherever they want to go," Caleb added.

"I don't know if that was a great idea," Penn said. "It could get pretty pricey, depending on where they choose."

"How bad could it get?" Caleb asked, taking his first bite of food. It was tangier than he expected, with a kick of spiciness as he chewed and swallowed. Not as good as Thanksgiving Dinner, but he could eat it.

"From here to Atlas is probably twenty thousand coin," Penn said.

"Minimum," Fitz agreed. "More like forty, if the transports are filling up."

"How many lower deckers are there?" Caleb asked.

"About a hundred."

"I can't imagine they'll all leave."

"No. But figure maybe two hundred thousand coin to get them where they want to go."

"If we don't replace them, we'll make that up in time."

"Assuming you don't get us killed," Fitz said.

The comment could have been a buzzkill, but Caleb soothed it before it could seize the momentum. "I'm not claiming there's no risk. But I've been in the military for close to three hundred years, and I'm still here."

The others around the table laughed, having already heard more of Caleb's story. Orin was the exception.

"I do not understand," he said. "Humans do not live more than one hundred years or so, at most. And Jiba-ki live only sixty. How have you survived so long? It is true."

The others helped provide Orin with Caleb's backstory while he downed his meal, feeling a lot better by the time he was done. It was nothing against Ham or Jii, but he had missed the camaraderie of a larger crew. He had just stood to drop his scraps into the trash and return his tray when Tae hurried into the mess, his expression intense. Seeing Caleb, he thrust a finger toward him.

"Just the Captain I've been looking for," he said. "Sir, you have got to see this."

# CHAPTER 34

Concerned about what Tae wanted him to see, Caleb followed him from the mess to the briefing room, Damian, Elena, Penn, and Orin right behind them. He almost laughed out loud as they gathered around the holotable at the back of the room and Tae stuck Benning's tiny datachip into a small drawer in the center of the cumbersome computer connected to it. Battered and smudged, the thing looked like a refugee from twentieth-century NASA. Caleb squinted suspiciously at it, expecting it to go up in sparks any second.

"I had to cook up something to interface with the chip," Tae explained in defense. "They don't make readers for this kind of device anymore, and it's not like we have every part imaginable to work with. It's actually a minor miracle I could read the thing at all, especially within a couple of days."

"I didn't say anything," Caleb replied.

"You didn't need to. I could tell by the look on your face."

"I'm just pleased you discovered something."

"Yeah, I'm pretty stoked about it."

"We're ready when you are."

Tae's expression stiffened as all eyes in the room turned to him. "Right. I'm not good at being the center of attention."

"And yet you walk around shirtless most of the time," Caleb said.

"That's for admiration from afar," Tae answered.

"Are we permitted to discard our clothing, Captain?" Orin asked. "It is not comfortable."

"I prefer you continue wearing pants, at least," Caleb replied.

"Very well."

"Carry on," Caleb said, attention returning to Tae.

"Right. So, a little background for the people...uh...can I say people? I've never been in mixed company like this before."

Orin laughed. "I am comfortable being regarded as a person. It is true."

"Great," Tae said. "Yeah, so a little background. Charlotte Benning was a lead civilian engineer on the starship Pathfinder. By the way, I pulled some archival footage of the wreckage on Atlas, and ran it through the engineering AI to compare the reconstruction models with the schematics I found on the datachip. Assuming the chip is authentic, and this isn't some weird hoax, I'm confident Caleb is correct. The founder's ship is Pathfinder, and Pathfinder is the ship sitting on Atlas."

"I figured you were telling the truth, Cap," Damian said. "But it's still chilling to hear Tae confirm it."

"I don't understand," Penn said. "Why doesn't the historical record corroborate this? Why is there no mention of the name Pathfinder, or that it came from Earth? Or that Earth is real, for that matter?"

"Someone deliberately erased the truth," Caleb said. "For reasons unknown."

"Maybe not fully unknown," Tae said. "That's why I came looking for you." His nervousness faded, replaced with his excitement over his discovery. "There's more on this chip, Captain, than just Benning's diary after she escaped Pathfinder. There's more than the algorithms that describe the nature of the wormhole and how to traverse it. Needing to reverse-engineer the chip to build the reader, I came upon a hidden encrypted partition on the chip. Video recordings that will leave you speechless. This is all so wild, I still haven't completely wrapped my head around it."

"Before we get to that," Caleb said. "What about the algorithms? Have you made any progress on those?"

Tae looked confused. "Sir, I just told you I'm about to blow your mind, and you're asking about the wormhole?"

"That research is my potential ticket home. And my friend Ham's ticket home to his family. It's incredibly important to me."

"I'm sorry, Cap. I haven't had time to work on it yet. It took days to build the reader, and hours to brute force the passcode to decrypt the hidden partition. I'll get on that next."

"Right now, to me, the future is more important than the past. The future, we can change."

"And the past, we can learn from," Damian said. "And allow it to help direct us going forward."

"At the very least, I think it'll answer some questions about the coverup," Tae said. "And to be honest, opening up this can of worms was a lot more exciting than poring over advanced physics calculations. I can work out the math, but I don't really want to. And it's not magic. It'll take some time."

"Understood," Caleb said. "What did you find?"

"Oh, so let me back up here. Where was I?"

"Benning," Orin said. "Lead civilian engineer on Pathfinder. It is true."

"Right. From what she said, she worked in Metro, which was the city inside the starship where all the civilians lived. They were locked in while the military had the run of things outside."

"Locked in to keep them out of trouble," Caleb said. "The military on board were all supposed to enter stasis. The Guardians were military volunteers who took shifts coming out of stasis to ensure everything ran smoothly during the trip. Anyway, the civilians didn't need to go beyond Metro. There was nothing out there for them but a maze of passageways to become lost in."

"You don't need to defend the decision to me, Cap," Tae said. "Anyway, it's literally ancient history. Benning's job was to manage the lower level techs in charge of keeping the city running. Not only life support, but simple stuff like the lifts in the apartment blocks, the comms terminals, even the cooktops in the restaurants."

"The city had restaurants?" Damian asked, surprised.

"That's what Benning said," Tae answered.

"It ran like any other city," Caleb explained. "They gave people an allotment of chits of different kinds every month. They could spend them on whatever they wanted. The only difference is that they also gave business owners an allotment. They had to turn in the rest of their profits for redistribution. Since it was all a closed loop, they could have hoarded all the chits otherwise."

*You should stop explaining, or we'll never get to the good part.*

"I'll shut up now," Caleb added. "Carry on."

"Benning discovered that one of the exit doors in Metro wasn't properly sealed, and the sensors that would have alerted engineering to the problem were disabled. She later figured out that someone had been entering or leaving the city when they shouldn't have."

"Do you know who?" Caleb asked.

"Which brings us to the video I found," Tae replied. He used the touch surface to navigate a list of files, opening one labeled *BENNING_LAW_CAM4*. It played on the tabletop screen, revealing Charlotte Benning handcuffed to a table in an interrogation room. Metro's apparent sheriff sat across from her.

"Why did you do it, Charlie?" he asked. "Mayor Pine was a fine man. Loved in the community. Respected. He never did a thing to you or yours. In fact, he promoted you to Lead Engineer."

"It was a lie," Benning replied in a low growl that sounded almost feral. "All of it, a lie. You're still lying. Covering your tracks."

"You mean we're lying about you killing Mayor Pine?"

"Don't be stupid," she said, glaring up at him. "You know exactly what I mean, because you're one of them."

"One of who?"

"Not who. What. I've seen it, sheriff. The files on the servers hidden beneath the city. The servers no one is supposed to know about. But you couldn't monitor things from the inside without a network tunnel to the outside, and I found it. You aren't half as smart as you think you are."

"Honestly, Charlie. I don't know what you're talking about."

She laughed. "You wouldn't know honesty if it bit you in the ass."

The sheriff shrugged. "So what did you see?"

Benning surprised Caleb by quickly glancing up at the corner of the room. She knew there was a camera there, and that she answered the question when she seemed certain she couldn't trust the sheriff suggested she already had a plan to collect the video later.

"The research lab outside of Metro. Or should I call it your nursery? Where you grow new slugs, or whatever the creatures are that the Royal Space Force brought on board with them. You should know what they're called. You are one."

The sheriff laughed. "Charlie, your story gets more preposterous every time you add to it. Why did you kill the Mayor?"

"I told you, I found the servers. I've seen the recordings and read the files. The first Mayor Pine was an RSF plant. A Colonel, not a civilian. He never should have been in charge. He was still working for the RSF. They brought the creatures on board. They set up the nursery and the research. What I don't know is if the creatures already compromised the RSF, or if they lost control later. The Mayor was selecting people to become hosts to them. He was smuggling the things into the city."

"But Mayor Pine was the fourth generation of Pines to be elected. Even if your claims were true, which they clearly aren't, that still doesn't explain why you killed the current mayor. It also doesn't explain what you hoped to gain by doing so, if the conspiracy stretches beyond Metro to the outside."

"He was in charge of the whole thing. I'm not stupid, Sheriff. I know I can't stop whatever it is you're planning. But I've also noticed the patterns. You can't reproduce quickly enough to replace everyone on board, and you can't stop the people you replace from aging out. Perhaps Mayor Pine was the fourth generation human, but the creature inside him was the same one as the one in Colonel Pine. I have no idea how old you are."

"I'm thirty-three."

"Poppycock."

"That still doesn't answer my question. If there's a secretive RSF plot to replace the people of Metro with slugs, how would killing one man stop it?"

"It won't. But I had to do something. I knew Doctor

Rhimes wasn't infected. I thought perhaps she would find the slug and begin asking questions. Perhaps in time, she would help me reveal the truth. And without the mayor to pull her off the autopsy, it would be difficult to stop her. But you bastards found a way. You poisoned her, didn't you?"

The sheriff sighed. "Of course. We've poisoned hundreds of people over the years, and replaced hundreds more with slugs. That's exactly it. You got us, Charlie. Congratulations."

"You can be a smart ass with me if you want, sheriff. That's not all you're guilty of, though I don't think your second crime is fully intentional. Pathfinder's captain was supposed to reset the ship's course to go to Alpha Centauri. But no one passed on the directives. Colonel Pine suppressed the comms and ensured we would continue to Trappist. But not because Trappist is habitable. There's something else out there that caught your interest. What I don't understand is what or why?"

"I'm surprised you don't have all the answers, since you're making all this up. You're delusional, Charlie. Unstable. The good news is, I doubt Judge Anderson will have you put to death if you aren't competent."

"I'm more than competent," Benning snapped. "A lot more than you. Whatever happens to me, tell your new boss, whoever that is, that the calculations are wrong. Pathfinder will never make it through the wormhole. You'll be smashed against the rocks, or run aground against an iceberg. And all your plans will be for nothing."

Caleb wasn't that surprised to see the sheriff react negatively to that news. He leaned back in his seat, rubbing his neck and suddenly looking very uncomfortable.

Charlie laughed. "You don't need to look so distraught. I solved the equation. The corrections are on my terminal, in my apartment. If you want to survive, you'll use them."

"If you think I'm some evil slug or something, why would you do a thing like that?"

"I already told you. It's obvious you can't reproduce quickly enough to take the entire ship. I might want you to die, but I don't want everyone on board to die."

"Especially your son."

"You leave him out of this."

"You're making it awful hard to do that, Charlie. Maybe he can tell us why his mother is crazy."

"If you hurt him—" Benning said, face twisted in anger.

"Why would I hurt him? He's just a boy. And he isn't responsible for the sins of his mother." The sheriff stood up. "There's no sense continuing this conversation. You have nothing useful, nothing even based in reality, to say. You'll remain locked up until Judge Anderson has time to deal with you."

"I'm sure he'll be very fair, since he's one of your kind, too."

The sheriff shook his head, exiting the room. Benning glanced at the camera again before the recording ended.

# CHAPTER 35

Tae was right. The video left Caleb speechless. Nobody else in the briefing room spoke either. All of them needed a moment to absorb what they had just seen and heard.

After the law office recording ended, Caleb stared sightlessly at the list of video files that replaced it. He had been under the assumption that the Relyeh had found Pathfinder and its settlers when they arrived in this galaxy, not that the khoron had come with them. Worse, the Royal Space Force had been breeding them. And if Colonel Pine was a host to a khoron before boarding Pathfinder, that would change everything anyone had ever thought about the origins of the war against the Relyeh.

It could change everything.

Elena was the first to break the pregnant silence. "Let me see if I understand this. Pathfinder is the starship that brought humans to this part of the galaxy. Humans were running away from Earth because it was being attacked by the Relyeh. Except, the Relyeh sneaked at least one of their kind on board in a position of power. That Relyeh then started a conspiracy to create more Relyeh and infect as many of the settlers as they could, while simultaneously sending the ship through a wormhole they had discovered in order to reach this part of the universe. Am I following so far?"

"That sounds about right," Caleb agreed.

"How did they know about the wormhole? And why did they want to come here?"

"I don't know about the first question. The second? There aren't any other Relyeh here. They came to conquer this part of the universe before an Ancient could do it."

*Or they were working for an Ancient.*

"Or they were working for an Ancient," Caleb parroted. "Arluthu?"

*It is unlikely.*

"Benning said they couldn't reproduce fast enough to replace everyone on the ship," Tae said. "But they had a hundred years. How slowly are khoron made?"

"It took them another four hundred years to have substantial numbers to launch an attack," Caleb replied. "And that's with a process that Ishek and I believe is enhanced."

"Why does it take so long to make a slug?" Orin asked. "It is tiny. And simple. It is true."

*It isn't true. Our DNA is much more complex than a human's. Also, our genetics have built-in error correction, so if any of the cells are defective, they're destroyed and replicated before maturation continues. The typical khoron requires eight months of gestation, typically in an incubator. The complexity of our composition also makes us impossible to clone using Relyeh technology.*

"Ish says it takes eight months, and it's more complicated than it seems," Caleb relayed.

"Even if the nursery had twenty pods, at eight months a pop that's only twelve-thousand khoron," Tae said. "Thirty percent of the population of Metro."

"Okay, so that explains why they couldn't just take

over," Elena said. "I suppose once Pathfinder arrived here, it took time before the khoron could set up a larger nursery somewhere. They would need to build more starships, discover more planets, and do the construction. Figure at least a hundred years."

"Probably more," Damian said.

"Meanwhile, the khoron are living among the people the entire time," Caleb said. "While the Spiral expands and the kingdoms are formed, the Relyeh are working behind the scenes to build their power, just waiting for the day they can finally overwhelm humankind." He paused, the pieces beginning to fall into place for him. "Only it's not enough to wait. If they want to defeat humankind in the future, what better way than by making things as difficult as possible, especially since no one knows they're not human but Relyeh. They allow technology to advance in ways that will help both humans and Relyeh to populate the galaxy, like hyperdrives, but stifle it in ways that will make it harder for humanity to win any wars."

"Only the Legion has Nightmares and Specters and other ships," Orin said. "That is not stifled technology."

"No, but look where it came from. I'm willing to bet it was the khoron who arrived on Pathfinder who made sure the history of the ship, and their involvement on board, was erased."

"This whole time," Penn said. "We believed the Relyeh were an alien race discovered by Crux, who allied with him. But Crux didn't introduce the khoron, the khoron introduced him."

"I just had another mind-blowing thought," Tae said. "What if Lord Crux is a host to a khoron? And not just any khoron. What if he's host to the same khoron who infected Colonel Pine?"

The room fell silent as they all stared at Tae. "What?" he asked.

"It makes sense," Penn said. "This is the culmination of all his planning, starting four hundred years ago. The endgame. We never stood a chance."

"Maybe not before," Caleb said. "But you do now. I don't want to sound arrogant, but you have Ish and me."

"That sounds very arrogant," Orin said.

"It is true," Penn agreed with a smile.

"But also accurate," Damian countered.

*Your theory is interesting, but I believe there is one detail you have gotten wrong.*

"What detail, Ish?" Caleb asked.

*Do you recall what the Empress said about the alloy? Crux gifted armor to her and her family made of the material. She was convinced he was already plotting her downfall then. But what if the gift was given as intended? What if the creation of the armor drew my brethren's attention and led to his capture or recruitment by the Relyeh?*

"You don't think he's being controlled by Pine?"

*I know he isn't being controlled by Pine. He is Sanctified. He is too strong for any khoron, whether basic, mutated, or Advocate, to overpower. His conquest of this galaxy is his own doing.*

Caleb swallowed hard before relaying the information to the others.

"That doesn't change anything," Penn said.

"It changes one thing," Elena disagreed. "We have no reason to assume that Colonel Pine's khoron was ever destroyed. So where is he?"

"Or more importantly, *who* is he?" Damian said.

"Captain," Tae said. "I haven't reviewed all the files, but there were a couple more I wanted to show you that I think you will find interesting."

"Maybe once we've entered hyperspace," Caleb replied. "I have enough to think about for now, and a mission to plan. What you've discovered is a genuine revelation and not just for me. For all of us. From here forward, Tae, I need you to focus on the wormhole traversal algorithm. Once you have that sorted, we can continue piecing together specifically what happened on Pathfinder."

"Aye, Captain," Tae said. "I'll get on it right away."

Caleb put up his hand. "One more thing. Like it or not, you're all part of my inner circle now. We need to talk about what comes next."

"Me? I am part of your inner circle?" Orin asked, obviously surprised. "Once this mission is over, I am still required to kill you."

The statement drew shocked gasps from the others. Caleb pegged Orin with a hard look. "But I can trust you in the meantime, right?"

"Yes.. You spared my life. I am also in your debt."

"Good. Standby, I'm going to give Ish control."

*You are?*

Caleb sensed Ishek's excitement.

"I could pick the information you snatched from Gareshk out of your brain, but it's more efficient if you lead the briefing." *Trust earned is trust given,* he added silently.

Ishek pressed into his mind, attempting to seize control. Rather than resist, Caleb allowed his own consciousness to fade into the background.

"Greetings," Ishek said to the others through Caleb. "Let me begin by summarizing our Advocate prisoner, Gareshk. He is a high-level operative within the hierarchy of Relyeh active in the Manticore Spiral. His orders were to use the Consortium, as well as Aroon's communications and data networks, to root out opposition to the new Empire. All with the expectation that increasingly desperate loyalists would turn to the dark networks for supplies. This included the activation of a counter-piracy Legionnaire interdiction force to intercept genuine pirate ships. So far, this force has accounted for the destruction of three pirate vessels, whose crews were turned into hosts or interrogated before being killed. They transferred anything valuable on board before they scuttled the ships and left them for salvagers, to make it appear as though the pirates were attacked by other pirates."

*That sounds familiar,* Caleb mentioned, with regards to how he had wound up on Gorgon.

"Do we know if the loyalists were using Aroon in that manner?" Damian asked.

"They were," Elena replied.

"How can you be sure?" Tae asked.

"Because I was one of their contacts. That's how I knew about the Empress."

*But she doesn't know we killed Lo'ane,* Caleb commented to Ish.

"I was high-ranking enough in the Consortium's security forces to have clearance to certain systems," Elena continued, "but unimportant enough to avoid notice. I know there were others, but none of us knew who the others were. It was safer for everyone that way. In any case, I worked with loyalist rebels from different parts of the Spiral, arranging for ships to deliver supplies to secret locations." She paused, her expression tensing. "If Gareshk was using Jack Jr.'s access to the systems, it's possible he eavesdropped on those communications and intercepted those ships before they ever arrived."

"What were the ships carrying?" Damian asked.

"General supplies. Food, clothing, medicine, equipment."

"Military equipment? Ordnance?"

"Of course. All of it was supply that made it into dark market circulation during the war. Small arms, mostly. I'm more concerned about the rebels. Those ships were delivering critical supplies. If they never arrived…" She trailed off as the somber sentiment rippled through the gathered crew.

"Why did they not use the Dark Exchange?" Orin asked. "The rebels could have created anonymous contracts through already established secure channels."

"I know the exchange is supposed to be anonymous, but jobs to move unspecified cargo to unspecified places are always going to arouse suspicion. In the past, that suspicion might have been the beginning and end of things. But now? There's little guarantee that Crux will honor the nature of the exchange. Any job like that could be a trap meant to identify potential sympathizers. Not to mention, with no control over the contractors, it would be more lucrative for them to bring the job to Crux and collect a nice fat reward than to continue operating on the exchange. So the loyalists turned to people like me. Former military they believed they could trust to hire ships we believed we could trust."

"That's still a risk," Tae said.

"Yes. The more links in the chain, the more chances there are for one to break. I'm sure Crux would have paid well for the betrayal." She paused again. "I did my best to build a strong chain, but the crews I hired probably died thinking I betrayed them. The rebels too. I know I would've thought so. Son of a bitch."

"It's not your fault," Penn said. "You were trying to help."

"It should have occurred to me that the Relyeh would have infiltrated the Consortium. They worm their way into everything, it seems."

"Pun intended?" Ishek asked.

The comment broke the tension, eliciting laughs from the group, including Caleb.

"If the khoron can be anyone, anywhere, how do you trust anyone?" Orin asked. "And how do you accomplish anything when you can trust no one?"

"You do the best you can with the information you

have," Penn answered. "How many people could have listened in on those comms?"

"Only leadership, and they have better things to do than eavesdrop. Besides, plausible deniability is a leading tenet among pirates, and especially among the Consortium. The more you know, the more dangerous that knowledge can become."

"You had no reason to believe Jack Jr. of all people would be compromised," Penn continued. "You used the safest channel you could. And right now, we have no proof that those ships were the ships the Legion attacked."

"What were the names of the vessels?" Ishek asked.

"Northstar was one of them," Elena replied.

"Captain Ng," Damian said. "But Northstar isn't a pirate vessel."

"I didn't say I only hired pirates. I said I hired ships I trusted. I've known Captain Ng for a long time. My father worked for his father when he founded the Every Ng Transport Company."

"The interdiction force destroyed Northstar three days ago," Ishek said, his voice completely lacking in empathy or compassion. "They tortured Captain Ng before ejecting him from an airlock." He looked at Elena. "You are fortunate. In his pain and terror, he did not reveal the identity of the person who hired him."

"He didn't know my identity," Elena countered, obviously angry with Ishek for his lack of tact. "I'm not that reckless or stupid."

*Ish, take it easy,* Caleb warned.

"Apologies," Ishek spat out. "I should not have underestimated you."

*What about the Legion's ships? Caleb asked. Do we know where they went?*

"The ships involved in the interdictions are under orders to return to a stardock controlled by the Empire, approximately sixteen hours from Aroon. Gareshk was planning to travel there personally when we arrived.

*Why would he physically go there? Didn't he get reports from the ship's captains?*

"Yes, he got reports from the ship's captains. It is unclear why he wished to travel to the stardock. Perhaps there is something on the station that he desires or requires."

"Does anyone else think it's weird that he's talking to himself?" Tae asked.

"You get used to it," Penn replied.

*Like?*

"If his mutations are unstable, he would need to be Sanctified again. That is one potential reason. Does it matter?"

"We were looking for a target," Damian said. "Something of Crux's to hit. Something important enough that it would sting, while also providing us with some income. I don't know about you, but I think a stardock and three ships carrying pirate booty is perfect."

"Almost too perfect," Penn replied. "Ishek, are you sure Gareshk didn't implant false memories to lead us into a trap?"

Ishek stared at her, his surprised expression reflecting both his and Caleb's reaction to the question.

*Is that possible?*

"I...I do not know. He had time to prepare, in the event Caleb penetrated his defenses. But I've never considered that form of defense before. Is it possible that he has considered it? Is it possible he has learned how to do it? I cannot guarantee that he hasn't."

"Maybe it isn't a perfect target," Orin said.

"Do you have any other intel that might give us a different option?" Elena questioned.

"If some of the intel is questionable, then all the intel is questionable," Ishek answered.

"I think we might be missing an angle here," Tae said. "Even if it isn't a trap, you're talking about three ships against one. Plus a stardock that may or may not be heavily armed."

"They are regular pirate vessels, not Specters," Ishek replied. "Gorgon outclasses them."

"Individually, maybe. What about as a group? And what if the station has starfighters? Because we don't."

"I will fly Kitara," Orin said. "She is a good ship, and beautiful in a fight. It is true."

"We also have Medusa," Damian added.

"And the Nightmare, if we need it," Ishek said. "But only Caleb and I can fly it."

*We need to be on the boarding team.*

"Caleb insists we should be on the boarding team."

"I agree," Penn said.

"I don't really want to die just yet," Tae said. "Maybe we can find a different target that isn't such high risk."

*Ish, pass me my body back.*

*But—*

*Don't argue, or you'll never have the stick again.*

*Fine.* Ishek's consciousness faded, leaving Caleb back in control of his body. "I've swapped back with Ishek." He looked at Tae. "That's our target. Trap or not. Risky or not. We only get one first impression, and I intend to make it count."

Orin laughed. "I am ready, Captain Cayheb. It will be beautiful."

"Ish, pass me the coordinates so I can relay them to Rufus. We're out of here as soon as the last transfer ship breaks the seal on the interlock. We have about twenty hours to prepare. I'm sure you all know what to do. Dismissed."

# CHAPTER 36

"The last transfer ship just arrived, Captain," Sasha said from her station on the bridge.

"How many crew are waiting for this one?" Caleb asked.

"Sixteen," Damian replied.

"All lower deckers?"

"Aye."

"How many did we lose?"

"More than we kept, after you told the crew about our plans, which if you recall, I argued against."

*So did I.*

"The good news is that with only seventy-three souls left on board, even after paying for transport, we can stretch our current funds by another three weeks. The bad news is there won't be anyone to clean the heads."

"With fewer people using them, they won't need cleaning as often. The remaining crew will just have to take turns," Caleb said. "Myself included."

"What?" Naya asked, offering him a shocked look. "Captain, if you do it, then I'll have to do it."

"There are still a few seats left on the transfer ship if you want to leave."

She wrinkled her nose at him. "When I'm this close…" She showed him her thumb and forefinger, the space between them less than an inch. "…to unlocking Graystone's accounts? Not a chance."

"Rufus, are the coordinates locked in?"

"Aye, Captain," he replied, glancing back over his shoulder. "Locked and loaded. Just say the word and we can head out of orbit to make a clean jump."

"It should only be a few more minutes."

"It's already been too long," Elena said, having replaced the officer Graystone had killed at his station. "You said Relyeh like Gareshk can communicate with all the other Relyeh through the Collective. Don't you think he told them he was captured? Don't you think Crux will send the Legion after us here?"

"Yes," Caleb replied. "Ishek already raised that point. But if he sends the Specters from where they attacked the Empress, it will be hours before they arrive. Even if he sends ships from the station we intend to rob, he's still an hour short."

"What if they come from somewhere else?"

"They would have had to be en route already, or have an unlisted stardock to deploy from. The next settled planet is nearly forty-one hours away. And look." He pointed to the surface, where groups of transports rose into orbit. "The Consortium spent the time packing since we returned to Gorgon. They and all the visitors are on their way out."

"They're abandoning Aroon?" Sasha asked, surprised.

"Crux knows we killed the khoron and captured Gareshk. He won't be happy about it. Aroon isn't safe for anyone whose loyalties are questionable. The Consortium knew it when they let us leave. They know Crux will put them out of business either way. But that's better than being attacked and killed."

"It's suddenly getting very crowded out here," Rufus said. Caleb glanced at the forward viewscreen. The Consortium members' ships were larger and better armed than any other ship in orbit, including Gorgon. Even larger ships dropped out of hyperspace, coming to retrieve the transports leaving the surface. Within a minute, nearly forty newcomers had appeared. "I'll have to adjust our tack out of this mess, and delta the hyperspace path."

"Is that difficult?" Caleb asked.

"Not at all, as long as the other ships follow procedure and maintain their travel lanes."

"Sir, we're being hailed by one of the transports," Sasha said.

"Open the comms."

"Aye, Captain. Comms open."

"Captain Card," Leighton said. "I didn't expect you would still be here. Are you waiting to take on the Specters when they arrive?"

"Nothing as noble, or foolish," Caleb replied. "Just unloading the last of my crew who didn't want to stick around. We'll be out of here well before the Legion arrives."

"I bet I'll beat you to it. How's my son treating you?"

Caleb smiled at the question. "Don't you mean how are we treating your son?"

"Not based on the last time I saw him. Have you made any progress with him?"

"Not yet. We haven't had time to bond. At least not in a friendly way."

"I'm transmitting my personal comms identifier to you now. If you have any news, or need to get in touch, please use it. But if you just need more coin, don't use it. My source of income just took a major hit."

"Understood. You did well convincing Oslo and the others to abandon the planet."

"It took little convincing. They may be greedy, but they haven't lost their minds."

"Where are you heading?" Caleb asked.

"That's a trade secret. Needless to say, Crux won't find me there, and I'll be quite comfortable, at least for a while. But make sure you take care of that son of a bitch, both because of what he did to my boy and because I'm not eager to learn what squalor is like."

"I'll do my best."

"I have a feeling you always do, Captain. Until the stars align to bring us together again, fare—"

The transmission cut off at the same time a flash of light guided Caleb's attention to the forward viewscreen. Not a flash. A beam. It had swept across space from nearly a thousand kilometers away. At its tip, Leighton's transport had gone dark, instantly split in two by the razor of energy.

"Shields!" Caleb cried before Damian had a chance to warn him of incoming warships. "Sound the red alert."

*You'll never learn not to underestimate us, will you?*

Damian tapped on his station's controls, activating the shields and the firing system before opening the ship's internal comms. "All hands to battle stations. All hands to battle stations."

"What's the count?" Caleb cried, unable to see the dark warships against the darkness of space. They had yet to appear on the threat projection either, despite their close range. "And why can't we see them?"

"There's something wrong with the sensors," Naya answered, her voice calm. "I'm trying to nail down the problem now."

"We can't fight what we can't target," Damian said.

"I know! I'm doing the best I can."

"Rufus, get us underway."

"Captain, the last transfer ship is still docked."

"We're sitting ducks right now. Do it."

A flash of light slammed into Gorgon's bow, the shields flickering but settling back in and holding.

"Point made," Rufus said. "On our way."

More energy beams slashed across space, revealing four approaching Specters. They targeted the fleeing transports, easily blasting through the smaller ships' armor and ripping them apart. Caleb didn't know which ones belonged to Consortium members. He had only identified Leighton's transport because of the synchronicity of his failed comms and the destruction of the ship he had witnessed.

Gorgon's thrusters flared, the starship beginning to move through space. Rufus fired vectoring thrusters, turning the ship away from the incoming Specters. A second blast hit their shields, which continued to hold.

"We can't take many more shots like that," Damian warned.

"I'm doing the best I can," Rufus replied. "It's a mess out there." As if to stress the point, the remains of one transport spun into the front of Gorgon, smacking off the shields and ricocheting away. "Not to mention, I can't maneuver too hard with the transfer ship connected. We'll rip it right off the interlock."

"We need them to finish up and stop leeching off us," Damian said. "Moss, how long until the ferry cuts loose?" He looked back at Caleb. "Twenty seconds. Almost there."

"Those Specters will be here in twenty seconds," Rufus said.

"Can you get us into hyperspace?" Caleb asked.

"In this? Only if you want to risk cutting one of these other ships in half."

Caleb surveyed the camera views on the surround. "Like that one?" he asked, pointing to the starboard feed, where a hyperspace field had formed around one of the Consortium ships. It would catch at least two other craft in its expansion if they didn't move aside.

"That crazy son of a bitch," Damian growled. "As if things aren't bad enough."

The Specters loosed more volleys, beams smashing into the ships arranged in orbit, another blast hitting Gorgon's shields. A follow up strike missed by a couple of meters, the light bright enough to burn momentarily into the feed.

"Damn!" Damian snarled. "We just lost the ferry."

Under normal circumstances, it was bad news. But these weren't normal circumstances. "Rufus, pick up the pace and get us out of here!"

"Hold on to your—oh crap!"

Another pair of flashes revealed two more Specters, their location leaving them in a position to box Gorgon in. Once the Specters closed ranks, their fight would be over.

"Naya, sensor status!" Caleb shouted.

"I sent Tae to look at the system. I don't know how the hell this happened."

*I can give you two guesses, but you probably only need one.*

Caleb's jaw clenched. Someone had clearly sabotaged the sensors. Was it a disgruntled lower decker or someone still on board?

The barrage of enemy fire continued, but the Specters failed to stop every transport from reaching their larger vessel. Like Gorgon, most were making a run for it, but a few opened fire against Crux's warships, hurling ion blasts and projectile rounds at the dark vessels.

"You're just wasting ammo," Caleb heard Damian mutter. He could see the same himself as the warship's shields absorbed the attacks as if they were light tickles.

"Captain, we're being hailed!" Sasha snapped.

"By the Legion?" Caleb replied.

"No. The captain of the transport ship Sojourner.

They're asking for an escort out of the area, seeing as how so many of our crew are on board."

*Well, they have some nerve.*

"Bring them up on the..." Caleb trailed off. The threat projection was offline, the sensors dead. They couldn't help Sojourner even if they wanted to. They would have to find the ship visually, and considering the number of vessels and the distances, that would be like looking for a needle in a haystack. "Tell them our sensors are damaged. We won't be able to find them."

"Aye, Captain," Sasha said.

Caleb surveyed the visible field, wincing as they hit another nearby ship. At least the energy beams gave him a chance to locate the Specters. His eyes snapped from one feed to another, the gap between them closing quickly. Based on his observations, he assembled a rudimentary threat grid in his mind, identifying the paths the Specters would take to reach them. He might have wondered how they knew exactly which ship to target, but he already had the answer. Gareshk had told them. Ish couldn't block the Advocate twenty-four seven without opening himself up to attack.

Still eyeing the video feeds, he spotted a rectangular ship angling away from the fight, forced to push through the debris field of an already destroyed vessel to reach a safe jump position. The pilot constantly changed vectors, the ship rising, falling, tilting, and rotating in space as a pair of energy beams zapped over the top of it. When two more missed, he thought the ship might actually clear the battlefield.

A final beam hit in the aft, the energy weapon cutting right through the ship's apparently meager shields. Minor explosions sent debris shooting out of the impact point, followed by a much larger explosion two seconds later that tore off the entire back-half off the ship.

"That was Sojourner," Sasha said, her voice tense.

Caleb's heart clenched, his eyes shifting to Damian, whose face hardened in response. Lucy and Linx were on that ship. There was no time now to mourn them or to even wonder if they may still be alive. It was time to go. Gathering himself, he returned his attention to the Specters.

Multiple beams lashed out at Gorgon. Two of them hit, the force of the energy shaking the ship. Damian's screen lit up, the flashing red glow from it not a good sign.

"Starboard shields are down, Cap."

"Rufus, get us a hyperspace path."

"We aren't clear," he replied.

"I don't care. If you need to override something, do it."

"Captain, hyperspace doesn't remove what's in the space in our path, it just shifts relative time so we move through it faster," Damian said. "Anything that hits us will go through us like we're made of paper."

"I'm aware of that," Caleb growled as Gorgon took another hit. "Rufus, turn us toward that Specter." He pointed to one on the port side. "Full speed ahead. Do the calculation."

"Aye, Captain."

"What are you thinking?" Damian asked.

"We'll destroy anything we hit like it was paper," he replied.

"You want us to slam into a Specter?" Rufus asked.

"No. But I want them to think we're going to slam into them. Do it."

Rufus followed the instructions, quickly bringing Gorgon in line with the Specter. A shrill collision warning echoed across the bridge, quickly stifled by the pilot. He glanced at Caleb, brow soaked in sweat. "Path complete."

A beam from the targeted ship hit the bow.

"Forward shields are critical," Damian announced.

"Full speed ahead!" Caleb shouted. "Initiate the jump!"

"Aye, aye, Captain," Rufus replied. Caleb was pushed back in his seat at the huge rear ion thrusters opened up to their limits, throwing Gorgon forward. The next round from the Specters missed, their firing solutions failing to account for the sudden change in speed. Meanwhile, the hyperspace field began forming around them, the bubble spreading away.

The Specter reacted at once, vectoring thrusters pushing it sideways while retro thrusters worked to slow its forward momentum.

"Keep on it!" Caleb shouted.

"Captain?" Rufus asked fearfully.

*Now this is getting interesting.*

"Do it!" Caleb snapped.

Rufus angled the ship toward the Specter. The field continued growing, but there was no way they would pass the ship before it fully enveloped them. The bend in the light stole their forward view, the lack of sensors leaving them suddenly blind.

"What if the Specter doesn't get out of the way?" Rufus said.

"It will," Caleb answered.

"But...what if it doesn't?" Naya said softly as Gorgon streaked across space like a lightning bolt.

Caleb was pretty sure the warship would move. If it didn't, this would be a quick trip. Leaning back in his seat, he closed his eyes. Either they would all be dead five seconds from now, or they would be home free.

He counted down in silence. Five. Four. Three. Two. One...

# CHAPTER 37

An hour had passed since Gorgon successfully skirted the Specters that Lord Crux had sent to Aroon. As he'd expected, the ship in their path navigated out of the way before they could collide, though just barely. The hyperspace field had sheared pieces of the ship's port flank off, sending debris ricocheting off the shields and back out of the field. There was a slim but real chance the maneuver destroyed the enemy ship. In fact, the crew had already started calling the strategy the 'Wild Card.' The Specter's crew may have been composed of spacers hosting khoron, but even they hadn't been eager to die.

Caleb's inner circle had already gathered around the holotable in the briefing room when he arrived. A schematic of what he assumed was Gorgon's sensor array occupied the screen.

"Any updates?" he asked, the assembled inner circle finally taking notice of him as he moved into an open spot around the table

"Captain," Penn said, coming to attention. "I didn't hear you."

"As you were," he replied. "We're pirates, we don't need to be too formal."

"I thought we were rebels now?" Naya asked.

"Rebel pirates, then. Or pirate rebels, whichever works."

"As long as Crux gets what he has coming to him, I don't care what we call ourselves," Damian growled softly. "They didn't have to target Sojourner. They didn't have to kill children!" He slammed his fist on the holotable, causing the schematic to flicker.

"It's not the first time the Legion has done something so horrible," Elena said. "And it won't be the last."

"Khoron have no regard for humans beyond their utility," Caleb said, bitterness strong in his voice. "It's likely Crux had nothing to do with it, unless every shred of his humanity is gone."

"We may have taken out a Specter," Damian added, glowering at the thought before looking at Caleb. "It doesn't feel like any sort of victory, though. We didn't just lose Lucy, Linx, and the other crewmen. We lost all the coin we paid them."

"And our greatest supporter in the Consortium," Caleb said. "Leighton's dead, and I saw at least two other Consortium ships cut apart by the Specter's energy beams. Whoever's left will no doubt lie low and lick their wounds, maybe for the rest of their lives. Which means our chance for additional funding is gone too. Not to suggest that outweighs the losses on Sojourner or the transfer ship, but it's all part of the equation."

"Agreed," Elena said. "We still have a war to fight, and it'll be harder to do it without coin."

Caleb motioned to the schematic. "I assume this is the sensor array?"

"A magnified cross-section of the logic board," Tae replied. "Do you see that soldered piece there?" He used his hands to manipulate the schematic, magnifying the area. "Someone definitely sabotaged this component controlling the primary sensor array."

"Do you have any idea who might have done it?"

"It's a clean job. Professional. Whoever did it knew exactly how to take the primaries offline without making a mess or leaving any clues. I already had Butcher scan it for prints or DNA. Nada."

"The list of people with the skill to do this must be pretty small."

"Yeah. A list of one," Tae agreed. "Me."

"Did you do it?" Orin asked.

"What do you think?" Tae quipped back.

"I don't know you that well. I cannot rule it out. It is true."

"It would be pretty slick for the person who committed the crime to be the one to identify the crime and point to themselves as the only suspect," Naya said. "Because who would believe that? But don't be so high on yourself, Tae. I could do that work. So could anyone in engineering."

"Not that well," Tae argued.

"With my eyes closed," Naya countered.

"Are you two arguing over who is more likely to have committed treason that led to the destruction of Sojourner and nearly got us killed?" Penn asked.

"I need a list of suspects," Caleb said. "If you want to put yourselves on it, be my guest. Damien, Elena, I'll need you to review the list and question the potentials. Tae, is it possible the person who did this left the ship?"

"Over half the crew left, Cap. Including two engineers. It's possible."

"We can't afford for something like this to happen again. We were lucky this time, but we might not be so lucky next time. I assume you can fix the damage?"

"I already did," Tae replied. "Took less than a minute

once I found the problem. Sensor arrays are back in business, not that there's anything to see right now."

"Thank you for your quick work. Does anyone have a guess where the hell those Specters might have come from?"

None of the assembled crew spoke up at first. Damian was the first to offer anything. "Your math was right on, Captain. The only way the Specters could have arrived when they did was if they had left their origin before Gorgon came out of hyperspace off Aroon. The only way they could have known where we were headed was if a member of the crew warned them ahead of time."

*Ish, are you sure there are no other khoron on this ship besides you and Gareshk?*

*You were in the Collective. You would have known.*

"Ish confirms there are no unexpected Relyeh on board," Caleb said. "Whoever the spy is, they're human, and they may or may not still be on board."

"And they may have already sent word to the stardock that we're on our way," Damian said. "You told the entire crew we were planning an attack on Crux."

"I wasn't that specific," Caleb replied. "I didn't mention the stardock. Our mole would need to know as much as Gareshk to guess that exact target."

"It's probably Granger," Penn said. "He hates your guts, and he's still on board."

"I don't think hating me is enough evidence to convict him outright. He's probably waiting for a shot at taking over, but he's smart enough not to force it."

"You haven't actually met Granger, have you?"

The comment drew a laugh from Damian, Tae, and Naya.

"It stands to reason the spy and the saboteur are the same or in league with each other," Damian said. "And since we came pretty close to being ripped apart by the

Specters, I think the odds are good that they abandoned ship to Sojourner. It would ease the sting a little if that's the case."

"Good odds aren't good enough," Caleb said.

"Aye, Captain," Damian agreed. "Elena and I will work on that, too. Naya, I'll need you and Sasha to help me sort through the comms logs."

"No problem, Sarge," Naya replied, glancing at Caleb. "Is this more important than Graystone's accounts?"

"Yes," Caleb answered. "Highest priority. We need to remove the internal threats asap. What about the damage to the ship, and the shields?"

"We'll have to send a crew out onto the hull to assess the armor damage," Naya said. "And to repair the shield conduits that burned out during the attack. We have a good supply of them on board, so we can get our defenses back to one hundred percent given enough time. The problem is that we're already en route to the enemy's stardock. We don't have enough time. A pause halfway and a few more hours to prepare would help."

Caleb shook his head. "No. If it weren't for our spy, I would do it. But every minute we waste is another minute they have to prepare. And if they do already know our destination, I'm sure those Specters will be right on our tails. We don't want them getting there ahead of us. It's bad enough we'll have to bug out right away if they show. Is there anything that will help the repairs move along faster?"

"Having back the two engineers who left would help," Naya scoffed. "Since that's not an option, the only recourse is to work faster."

"I can assist, if you show me what to do," Caleb offered.

Naya jerked with surprise. "I appreciate the offer, sir. But it will take time to train you, which will distract from the task at hand. We'll get the shields settled in time, if it's the last thing I do."

"Without shields, it will be the last thing you do," Orin said. "It is true."

"Sometimes I'm not sure if it's your translator acting up or you're really adding that to the end of your sentences," Penn said.

Orin shrugged, refusing to offer any clues.

"Penn, I want all the boarding crews ready for action. I'm putting you in charge of preparing them. Drag the other crews down to the obstacle course and put them through their paces. Six hours max, and then I want you all resting up for the next eight. After that, I expect the crews to be locked and loaded. Edge and I will go in first in the Spikes, while the rest of the boarding team will deploy once we get Gorgon docked. Orin, you'll provide cover for the Splinters in Kitara."

"I will do it," Orin agreed.

"Damian, while I'm off the ship, you have the bridge, with Elena taking over your role as tactical officer. You'll lead the attack on the stardock and any of the ships that try to stop us."

"Aye, Captain."

"We'll discuss our plans in more detail closer to arrival. For now, you all know what to do."

"Uh, Cap?" Tae said. "I don't have a job yet."

"How are you at fixing shield conduits?"

"Spacewalks make me queasy."

"Does Butcher have anything for that?"

"No," Tae replied.

"Yes," Naya countered. "Come on Tae, we need all the help we can get."

He made a face while sighing. "Fine. But if I blow chunks in my helmet, you agree to clean it out."

"Deal," Naya agreed.

"With your tongue," he added.

"That's disgusting. We don't need your help that badly."

"Aren't you his superior officer, Naya?" Caleb asked.

"As if that would ever mean anything to him."

"Cap, I had enough trouble with chain-of-command in the Royal Armed Forces. You're fortunate I listen to you at all."

"There are alternatives to following orders," Caleb replied. "Alternatives I know you wouldn't like."

Tae looked to Naya. "What time are we meeting at the airlock?"

"Thirty minutes."

"Aye, Nye."

"Okay, now you all know what to do," Caleb said. "Go do it. Dismissed."

He remained in the briefing room while the rest of the crew filed out, off to complete their tasks.

*I'm sure you don't want to hear me say it, but your next idea is bad.*

"What else is new?"

*Not doing it anyway would be a novel approach.*

"Maybe next time."

# CHAPTER 38

Gareshk looked up from his bunk as soon as Caleb entered the brig. A wide grin quickly spread across his face. Caleb knew what the Advocate planned to hit him with before he started speaking.

"A shame about Sojourner," Gareshk commented. "And about Junior's father. I let him know we executed him."

"A shame you didn't manage to execute me," Caleb replied flatly. He didn't intend to give the Relyeh the satisfaction of an emotional response.

"Tell me where we're headed, and I'll correct that mistake."

Now Caleb cracked a smile. "I bet you would. Here's the thing. I didn't come here to talk to you. I came to speak to Jack."

"I don't allow Jack to talk. He's quite irritating when he does."

"Ish would say the same thing about me, I'm sure. But I really need to talk to Jack. Don't make me hurt you."

"As if you could."

"Our escape from Aroon scared the crap out of my

bridge crew. Ishek's not as weak as he was the last time we talked. Neither am I."

The threat didn't impress Gareshk. "Give it your best try, Card. I'd like to watch you stumble out of here again."

*Ish, are you ready?*

*More than ready. I owe him for his insults.*

Caleb sensed Ishek fade from his mind, the symbiote focusing his energy on the Collective instead. Gareshk convulsed suddenly, pressing a hand against the cell wall to steady himself. His grin faded, his eyes vacant.

"Jack, can you hear me?" Caleb asked. His own head throbbed slightly, a sign of Ishek's war against the Advocate. "Jack, Gareshk's control is like a wall. You need to punch through it. Hit it as hard as possible, with all your willpower."

Jack grimaced, squeezing his eyes shut, apparently able to hear Caleb's instructions. His body tensed, veins bulging in his neck and forehead. Caleb could see the massive effort Jack was exerting, desperately fighting against the Advocate to regain control. Meanwhile, the pressure against his mind intensified. Ish was fully engaged in the collux battle, leaving Caleb to endure the backlash through their bond. He leaned against the bulkhead, steadying himself against a fresh wave of pain.

"Get out of my head," Jack snarled, eyes snapping open, glaring angrily at Caleb. "Get it out of my head!"

"Only you can get him out, and keep him out," Caleb replied. "Ishek is helping you, but he can't be there forever. You need to find your strength. You need to take charge. Force Gareshk to do what you want him to do."

"How?" Jack asked, face twisting with rage. He grunted, grabbing at his head as Caleb did the same, the Advocate's vicious assault stretching through Ishek and into his mind. Of course, Ishek was right. Weakening both of them right now was a terrible idea, but he'd never been good at waiting. Still, he'd neglected to have something left in the cell that could help him achieve his goal. It was better to give up now, cut his losses, and try again after finishing with the Legion's stardock.

*Ish*, he called out, ready to order the retreat. Before he could get that far, his eyes focused on the electrified mesh that formed the front of the prison cell. "Jack," he pushed out through his pain. "Walk into the mesh. Try to escape."

"What?" Jack growled back. "I can't get out. That's impossible."

"You need to hurt yourself. Make him help you. Make him heal you. The effort will weaken him, giving you a chance to overcome him and regain control permanently."

"Are you crazy? I can't." He stared at Caleb with wild eyes before doubling over in pain. Caleb's pressure increased too, but he stood his ground, refusing to give up.

"You can. If you ever want to be free again, you have to do it."

Jack looked up at him. "O...okay," he decided, his fear palpable. Caleb sensed Ishek's pleasure as the symbiote subconsciously picked up on the impending meal. Unfortunately, Gareshk fed on the same fear, threatening to allow him to regain his footing.

"Now, Jack!" Caleb snapped. "You need to do it now."

Jack looked at him, and then the mesh. He reached out gingerly, recoiling when his fingertip got close enough to feel the power of the charge. "No," he said. "I...I can't."

"Damn it, Jack!" Caleb shouted. "Do you want to be a slave to a khoron forever? You can break out, right now. You have a chance."

Jack's body coiled, suggesting to Caleb that he was about to throw himself into the mesh, to wound himself so grievously Gareshk would exhaust himself healing the damage. Then the kid shook, his eyes widening in fear.

"Come on, Jack! Set yourself free." His face still twisting

in fear and confusion, the kid lifted his hand and reached out, his fingertips drawing nearer and nearer to the mesh. "That's it, Jack." Grimacing, Caleb moved closer too, letting the electricity burn his fingertips and then his entire hand as he flattened his palm against the wire. "Lay your hand against mine," he ground out. "That's right. Come on. If I can do it, you can too."

Jack nodded, but he hesitated, his face growing more and more red, fear and fury in his eyes. Caleb could taste that fear, which had yet to subside. That wasn't a problem. Fear was normal. But what would he do with it?

"Come on, Jack," he repeated, pressing his hand harder into the mesh. He could smell his own burning flesh, but he didn't pull back. He couldn't afford to. Not now. "You don't need to be a slave. You're a human being. You're stronger than a worm. You can do it."

Their eyes met, and Caleb's heart dropped, his hopes vanishing in an instant as the tension fled Jack's body. "No," he whispered, tears streaming down his cheeks. "I can't." He slumped back onto his mattress.

Without warning, the pressure in Caleb's head lifted entirely. He gasped as Ishek's full consciousness returned and he was left slumping back against the bulkhead. Both relief from the pain as Ishek healed his hand and frustration with Jack swept through him.

When he looked up, Jack was gone.

Only Gareshk remained.

"Nice try, Card," he said. "Jack Senior may have been the self-styled Pirate King. His son is a pathetic waste of molecules, made serviceable only because of me. Now that you know it's true, what are you going to do about it?"

Caleb stared at Gareshk, angry with himself for pushing too hard. Angry with Jack for his failure. But the Advocate was right. He could tell the kid how to set himself free, but only Jack could cut the rope, something he couldn't or wouldn't do when he was more afraid of pain than he was of the Relyeh living in his armpit.

"I guess there's only one thing I can do," Caleb replied, reaching for his sidearm.

Gareshk's smug expression vanished. "What are you doing? You need me."

"What for?" Caleb replied. "If Jack can't free himself, you're both useless to me." He pulled the blaster from its holster and leveled it where he knew Gareshk to be. "I don't need to worry about upsetting his powerful father, because thanks to your friends, his father is dead."

"But...I'm sure we can work something out."

"Both you and Jack proved your worth," Caleb said, finger depressing on the trigger. "At this point, it's zero." He shifted his aim at the last second before pulling the trigger. The ion blast burned right through the mesh and then through Jack's clothes and into his heart. The sudden stoppage of the major organ knocked Jack off the bunk, where he landed face-down on the deck.

*You cheated.*

"He needed an extra push."

*Do you think he can do it?*

"I guess we'll find out."

Satisfied, Caleb holstered the blaster, turned, and left the room.

# CHAPTER 39

"Captain, we're two minutes out from the enemy stardock," Damian announced, his voice loud and clear in Caleb's helmet. "The last shield conduit just came online, the crew's on their way back inside from making repairs."

"They'd better hurry," Caleb replied, impressed with the crew's performance. Even down a couple of engineers, they had completed all the repairs as promised, and just in the nick of time. "We need to launch," he said, his thoughts straying to Jack, leaving him wondering what he'd find when he got back. As relevant as that was, he shook the thought out of his head. There wasn't time to think about Jack now.

"Aye," Damian replied. "Fire control system is online and ready for action. Berserkers and Headcrushers are standing by at the forward and rear interlocks. Kitana and Medusa are prepared for launch, and all Splinters are loaded and ready to go."

Even though the Splinters looked small and sleek from the outside, he hadn't realized how small they really were until he'd boarded one to have a look at its controls and capabilities. Now, as he crawled forward on his belly from the rear entrance, he moved past the first of the three back-less seats in the rear to the front position, just behind the hardened tip of the vehicle that gave the craft its name. Setting his rifle on the floor to his left and Hiro's sword on his right, he drew his legs up knees-to-chest and grabbed hold of the hand grip above his head. Turning himself around, he slid butt down into the pilot's seat. Though he wore lighter and thinner tactical armor specially designed for a Splinter instead of the Prince's armor Lo'ane had gifted him, it was still a tight fit.

Similar to wearing a second underlay, rather than a plated overlay, the tactical gear was lined with electromagnetic threads that, when activated, allowed every part to stick to the unpadded metal seat. The feature was especially useful during flight, when the magnetized grip worked in place of a harness to keep him and the other three Edgers boarding behind him from being jostled around a lot inside the fuselage.

The controls for the Splinter were between his legs, a simple control stick and throttle that would collapse flat once he opened the front of the ship for ingress to the target. A wire ran from behind the control stick to his helmet, projecting a forward-only view on the small screen directly in front of his helmet. The camera would be destroyed the moment they impacted the stardock, but at that point he wouldn't need it anymore. Splinters were one-way craft, intended for retrieval or abandonment after use.

"It sounds like everything's in place," Caleb replied. "Sasha, broadcast me on general comms."

"Aye, Captain," she replied.

"Attention all hands," he said. "This is Captain Card. You've all been briefed on this mission. You all know what to do. This is our chance to not only take a bite out of Crux and his Legion, but also to potentially make a shipload of coin doing so. I understand we've lost a fair number of ship's crew since I became Captain. That doesn't mean we're at a disadvantage. In fact, it's only made us stronger. If you're here, it means you're committed to the mission. It means you're focused. It means you're willing to work hard, whether it's for the Empire that Crux stole from you or because you love money. You're still here because you're some of the best damn pirates the Spiral has to offer. And together, we're going to make history. Knuckle up, spacers. It's go time. Card out."

Roy patted Caleb on the shoulder from directly behind him, offering a thumbs up before taking his seat. After activating the Splinter's reactor, Caleb could hear every little whine and feel every small vibration from the battery-powered engines as they came to life.

"Splinter One online and ready for launch," he said, the camera screen coming to life and showing him a feed of the hangar bay doors directly in front of him.

"Splinter Two online and ready for launch," Penn said a moment later.

"Splinter Three online and ready for launch," Fitz confirmed.

"One minute to hyperspace field collapse," Damian announced. "We won't know how close we'll be to the stardock until we leave the field."

"Copy that," Caleb replied. If luck was on their side, they would be near enough to launch immediately. If the jump calculations had left them over ten minutes away from the target, they would kill the Splinters' engines again to conserve their batteries. They would have plenty of time to start them back up again before they reached the mission launch point.

"Thirty seconds," Damian advised.

Caleb closed his hands on the tiny ship's controls. He probably shouldn't be the one piloting the craft, but Roy had insisted his experience made him better suited for the job since he was used to more fluid situations than just flying a Splinter in a straight line from point A to point B. That was typically all they needed. The target, the defenses, everything was planned out to the last detail. This time, they knew what the target was, but they didn't know what it looked like, or what kind of opposition they might run into. Caleb was better suited to making snap decisions in this kind of situation.

Behind him, he could sense the nervousness of the Edgers. As former military, they had all done this kind of thing before, but it had been awhile for them, and they had never followed Caleb into combat. His inherent abilities weren't an unknown quantity to them, but their association with him as their leader was still new. Sometimes it was good to be nervous. He wanted everyone on their toes.

"Ten seconds," Damian said, counting the single digits down out loud. When he hit one, Caleb felt the shift as a passing wave of pressure caused by the collapse of the hyperspace field. Eagerly awaiting Damian's read on the scene, his heart rate jumped as the words he wanted to hear echoed over the comms. "Target acquired. We're in range. Go! Go! Go!"

Warning lights began flashing, the bay doors immediately beginning to slide open. With the Splinters arranged in a single line centered with the doors, Caleb only needed to wait a few seconds before he was clear. "Splinter One is go," he said, punching the throttle. He immediately felt the pull on his legs as inertia pushed him back into Roy in a domino effect until the Edgers ran out of room. His arms tensed, threatening to be ripped loose of the seat and the controls by the sudden inertia. Holding fast, the Splinter shot toward the opening doors, exploding out into space within seconds.

"Splinter Two is go," Penn said, following the same tack. Fitz announced the third ship's launch soon after.

He had a limited view from the Splinter, but Caleb's immediate impression was that they had taken the enemy by surprise. There were no Specters waiting for them. No patrol ships circling. Everything was calm. Even better, all three interdiction starships were offline, each linked to three long spokes out of the sixteen jutting out from the tall, narrow cylinder that composed the dock's body. The ships weren't built using the dark alloy like the Specters. They appeared to be standard starcraft of three different designs. Relatively unimposing and impossible to identify as Legion, Caleb was certain the vessels had to have some tricks up their sleeves. Based solely on their outward appearance, he was certain Gorgon could dispatch all three without too much difficulty.

*Ish, what do you have?* He asked.

*There are sixty Legion on the station. We're too far out for me to judge their precise locations. Considering the three ships, it stands to reason that unbonded humans assist them.*

Caleb wondered briefly why any human would help the Relyeh. Of course, he already knew the answer.

*Money and power are intoxicating promises.*

*You hit that nail right on the head.*

"Captain, that dock's a Huntsman Corporation build," Damian said. "There are a pair of reactors at either end offering full power redundancy. The control room is in the middle, behind thick energy and physical shields."

"Can the Splinters punch through the middle?" Caleb asked.

"Not a chance. The closest safe impact zone is just below the second row of docking arms."

Caleb looked out at the dock, eyeballing the target. His HUD informed him they were two minutes out. "Copy that. Splinters, follow my lead. Gorgon, stay sharp. It won't stay this quiet for long."

"I hope you haven't jinxed us,Cap," Penn said as fixed

gun and missile batteries spaced across the body of the dock swiveled in their direction.

"Evasive maneuvers!" Caleb barked as they opened fire.

He yanked the controls, juking the Splinter sideways as searing beams of energy sliced past. The other two Splinters veered off as well, avoiding the initial volley. It was relatively easy to avoid the beams at this distance. Once they got in close, it would be a different story. And they had more than just beams to deal with. Already, nearly three dozen missiles streaked toward them, their blue contrails giving them away as they rapidly gained velocity.

"No fear," Fitz said over the comms. "Splinters were made for this."

Caleb watched the missiles approach. The HUD feed in his helmet marked every projectile, beeping once as the onboard computer determined a defensive solution. All he had to do was tap the thumb trigger to activate it. "Going auto," he announced before pressing on the trigger. The moment he did so, all three Splinters moved in unison, tightening their formation as the missiles neared. They broke apart suddenly, splintering into separate ships and making hard maneuvers that tested the Edgers' constitutions.

The missiles closed in on their original target, half of them colliding while the others missed the Splinters by a dozen meters or more. Those projectiles didn't give up. Calculating that they had missed the primary target, the missiles redirected toward Gorgon, coming in behind the much faster boarding ships.

Just in time, Caleb tapped his thumb-trigger a second time to deactivate the automatic maneuvering system. The batteries opened up again, dividing their side of the universe with bright flashes. The Splinters avoided that attack too, continually drawing nearer to the dock.

"Cap, one interdictor just warmed up," Damian warned.

"It's time for reinforcements," he replied. "Get Kitana and Medusa out here."

"Aye, Captain, they're on their way."

The batteries continued firing, but now that the initial surprise had been spent and the fire teams were organized, the missiles launched in unison with the beams, creating a denser field the AMS couldn't quickly find a solution to take them out.. Left to his own devices, Caleb's eyes narrowed as he eyeballed the marked threats. Like Fitz had said, the Splinters existed to punch through enemy defenses like these. He used the thumb stick to select the missile defense system, waiting to depress the trigger.

As the projectiles closed in, he rolled the Splinter sideways, putting it into a tight corkscrew. He tracked the missiles as they closed within a few seconds. Pushing upward, he avoided an energy beam.. Penn and Fitz had already fired their MDS, but Fitz had waited until the last moment to save as many of his rounds as possible.

Small guns positioned in a ring around the center of the Splinter opened fire, spraying the missiles as they came in. The rounds smashed into the projectiles, and they detonated on contact, quickly exploding in fireballs all around Caleb's Splinter, none of them making contact.

"Gorgon, we need a little help out here," he said, barely avoiding another energy beam.

"I have you, Captain," Orin said as a swarm of rockets flew past the Splinters, splitting up, each targeting a different gun. In some cases, the fire control system wasted a beam on the missile. In others, they hit the shields around the weapons. In either case, it slowed the rate of fire, allowing the Splinters to get that much closer to the stardock.

"Secondary interdictor is online," Damian announced. "The first is nearly ready to depart."

"You need to do something about them," Caleb growled

back. "Get Gorgon in the fight."

"We're almost in position, Captain. Trust me."

Caleb didn't have time to argue. Less than thirty seconds out from impact, he kept his attention focused on the dock and its defenses, which continued to take fire from Kitana and Medusa. The two support ships made it much more difficult for the enemy weapons to target the Splinters, taking a lot of the pressure off.

Still, he was about to register a fresh complaint with Damian about Gorgon's lack of action when the ship finally targeted the second interdictor rather than go for the station's guns. With it's reactor still coming online, it had no shields. The volley smashed through the vessel, ripping a dozen holes in it that immediately began venting spacers and atmosphere.

"Sarge is destroying our booty," Roy complained.

"Odds are the ships were unloaded prior to their next departure," Caleb replied. "There's a good chance that ship was empty."

"He'd better hope so."

Caleb made one last maneuver, juking up and to the side before cutting back down. A sense of satisfaction washed over him as he broke through the effective minimum range of the gun batteries, the upper portion of the dock looming ahead.

*One of the khoron is outside the station!*

Ishek's sudden warning came too late. The Splinter's computer blared the emergency, also too late. The blast that hit the ship punched into the rear thrusters, shoving the ship forward like a surfboard riding an ocean wave. Reacting to the reactor's overheating warning blaring through the Splinter, Caleb deactivated his tactical underlay's electromagnetic threads. He had just enough time left to open the nose of the ship, grab his rifle and Hiro's sword and make his move before the power source exploded.

# CHAPTER 40

The concussion of the Splinter's explosion sent Caleb and Roy tumbling toward the side of the stardock like a pair of cannonballs. Caleb knew right away that the other two Edgers, Bryce and Vani, hadn't made it. Two of the Edge's newest recruits, their position in the rear had led to them being vaporized.

Fortunately for Caleb and Roy, their tactical gear was space worthy. Packed in a pair of tiny canisters housed in the bulge on the back of their suits, each had a three-hour supply of compressed air and five minutes of maneuvering thrust.. Unfortunately, despite the Splinter's slowed approach, their velocity was still high enough that survival was hardly guaranteed.

The fireball that had been their Splinter vanished quickly in the airless vacuum, revealing a Nightmare streaking past and angling into a turn to make another run at them. A quick glance to where the other two Splinters should be confirmed they were on target and only a handful of seconds away from impact.

Caleb locked his attention on the rapidly approaching station.

"Roy, go horizontal!" he snapped over the comms., quickly sticking his rifle and sword to his back. He burned small vectoring ports at his suit's wrists and ankles, laying himself out perpendicular to the stardock's surface, right where Damien had said its skin was the thinnest. Shifting all the thrust to the vectoring ports at his ankles, he slowed his velocity. He was certain Roy, veteran Edger that he was, would do the same. "Sarge," he continued, "Splinter One is on target. Bryce and Vani are gone, and there's a Nightmare out here."

"I have him on my target screen," Orin replied. "I will hunt this hunter. It is true."

"Atrice, stay on the batteries," Damian said, "Keep Orin clear to engage the Nightmare. Captain, are you injured?"

"Negative. I'm set to impact the station in five." The surface was close enough he could make out a couple of individual pebble-sized chunks of debris embedded in the metal. Checking his velocity, he knew a direct landing would be risky. Too risky. "Roy, close the angle," he barked, rolling over and firing the wrist ports to change his vector. He didn't have time to alter it over sixty degrees, but the shift was enough to lessen the force of his impact.

He hit hard on his stomach, knocking the breath out of himself. Planting his hands, he activated their magnetic grip to keep from bouncing back into space. Like a cat sliding down a curtain, his back half slid down along the side of the station, arm muscles flexing as his hands slowed his momentum until he could finally lock his boots to the station surface and stop completely. He saw that Roy, further up the stardock's surface, had already come to a stop.

"The third interdictor is toast," Damian announced. "Looks like the second is launching."

Caleb spotted Gorgon below the station already exchanging fire with the remaining interdiction starship. He could tell Gorgon's fire control system struggled to lock onto the craft, which was half the size of the larger spaceship but much more maneuverable. Gorgon's salvos were more tentative than the enemy fire pummeling its shields. It didn't help that the batteries on the station also targeted Gorgon, creating a nearly overwhelming attack.

"Sarge, back off!" Caleb snapped, the big ship's maneuver around the station's energy beams too difficult to accomplish at its current close range.

"Aye, Captain," Damian replied, though there was no immediate sign of a change in its heading.

"Splinter Two is in," Penn reported. "Disembarking now. Clear so far. Oops. Spoke too soon. Engaging. Don't dally out there forever, Cap. You're going to miss all the fun."

"Hey, having tons of fun here," Caleb sarcastically quipped back. "Nearly got blown up!"

"Splinter Three is in," Fitz said. "I get blown up every day."

*Three more Nightmares are launching.*

*If you can sense them, why don't you disable them?*

*Because you didn't ask.*

*Are you seriously...*

Pressure in Caleb's head signaled Ishek was fighting to overwhelm the first of the Nightmare pilots. The release of that pressure a few seconds later suggested he had succeeded.

*Two more Nightmares are launching.*

*Killing them is really that easy?*

*Yes, it — no.*

Caleb's jaw clenched, sudden pain ripping at his temples. It was a familiar pain. A familiar attack. He knew the Relyeh that had launched it. Not by name, but by action. The assassin.

*He's here. On the stardock. I can't hold him back for long alone.*

"Roy, we need to find an airlock." Caleb shouted.

"Already on it," Roy replied. "Follow me, Bossman."

The pressure in Caleb's mind intensified, as did the pain. "Roy, wait." *Ish, I'm coming.* "I need a ride."

"What?" Roy replied.

"Just grab me and carry me to the airlock."

Roy still seemed confused, but he vaulted the gap to Caleb in a matter of seconds. "Lock your hands on my shoulders and release your boots," he said.

Caleb did as he asked, fighting through the pain of the assassin's assault. The moment Roy began pulling him across the stardock's exterior, he surrendered his consciousness to Ishek and the Collective. Dark tendrils snaked all across the light as he came to Ishek's aid, trying a hundred different paths to break through. Ish had been doing well, but losing ground. With Caleb's help, they quickly pushed the assassin back to the edge of the light.

But that didn't stop the attack.

*I need to get back to what I have facing me here*, Caleb said. *We can't let him lock us down.*

*That's exactly what he's trying to do. If you return, I will lose, and we will both be subject to his will.*

*If I don't return, I'm nothing more than a huge wart on Roy's ass. We need a solution. Fast!*

A too-long silence followed as they both tried to come up with a way out of the stalemate. Ishek finally spoke up.

*You will need to hold him on your own.*

*Am I strong enough?*

*I don't know. You have to do it, or we're stuck like this, at least until someone finds him on the stardock and ends his life.*

*In that case, I'm strong enough. I want to be the one to end his life.*

He sensed Ishek's amused pleasure. *I knew you would say that. Are you ready?*

*As ready as—*

Ishek was suddenly gone from his mind, black tendrils crackling out like lightning in a dozen different directions.. He had more experience now after the hours of practicing against Gareshk. A lot more. Though the initial attack didn't break him, it came damn close. Pushing with all his might, he shoved the assassin's attack back, slowly building a new wall between them.

*Any day now, Ish.*

He couldn't hold the wall forever. Whatever his Advocate planned, he needed to do it now.

Just like that, he did. The darkness vanished, clearing the field. His sense of Ishek returned.

*What did you do?* Caleb asked.

*I nearly had him. He didn't expect my attack while you defended. It is a powerful strategy, one you are becoming much more adept at.*

*I'll take that as a compliment.*

*It almost is.*

*Should we expect another attack?*

*It isn't likely. He cannot simultaneously assault you and protect himself from me.*

*Copy that.*

Caleb looked past Roy, spotting a small airlock up ahead. A service hatch, it rested just above one of the docking arms. Roy skipped off the station, launching the two of them about a dozen meters through space before engaging his wrist thrusters to push them back to the surface. His feet locked on, waiting for the next step, which would bring them all the way to the hatch.

Less than half a kilometer higher up, Kitana screamed past the side of the stardock, vectoring toward cover behind the docking arms. A pair of Nightmares trailed after Orin, pulsed energy blasts targeting the rear of his ship. Shields absorbed what didn't sizzle past into space, but even from a distance, Caleb could tell the Jiba-ki was struggling against the Nightmares.

*Ish?*

*I am growing tired after dealing with the other Relyeh. I do not know if I can overpower them both.*

*Can you at least distract them?*

*Yes. The closer one.*

"Orin, Ishek will temporarily take the closer Nightmare behind you out of the fight. Get ready to reverse your heading to take it out."

"Yes! I will do it," Orin growled back.

*Now.*

"Now!" Caleb snapped. He craned his neck, barely catching the action out of the corner of his eye.

Orin flipped Kitana over, cutting the main thrusters and drifting backward to target his primary guns on the Nightmares. The closer one maintained its velocity and course, allowing Orin to zero in on it. Pouring both ion blasts and missiles into the ship, the heavy barrage punched through its shields and the dark alloy hull, turning it into a sudden fireball. The second Nightmare flew right through it, its shields catching a ton of debris.

Still floating with Roy toward the docking arm, Caleb thought for a moment that Kitana would crash into the stardock. At the last possible moment, Orin's vectoring thrusters pitched the starship over. The Nightmare, already distracted by the first ship's explosion, was slow to react. The edge of its delta wing caught the structure, tearing a piece out of the arm. A flash, quickly extinguished in the vacuum, signaled the demise of the ship's shields.

"Thank you for the help, Ishek," Orin said. "I will take it from here. It is true."

Still tracking Kitana as Orin darted away from the

Nightmare, Caleb saw the third enemy ship circling the other side of the stardock. Medusa was right on its tail, hitting it the way the Nightmares had been hitting Kitana. He noticed something else, too. Gorgon was still closer to the stardock than he expected, engaged with the second interdictor. At a glance, Damian appeared to be winning the fight. Even better, the ship was no longer taking fire from the station's fixed batteries. Every one of them had gone silent.

"Cap, we're here," Roy announced, landing them next to the hatch. "Now we just need to figure out how to get inside."

"What happened to the dock's guns?" he asked.

Roy's head swiveled to take in the scene. "Greaser must have reached the fire control systems."

"How?"

"We don't call her Greaser for nothing. I'm surprised she didn't tell you her trick."

Caleb wanted to ask more, but there was no time. The airlock just ahead of their feet was locked up tight, and they had no easy way to break through it.

*Ish, I need beast mode. Ish?*

He realized Ishek wasn't present in his consciousness. But what was he up to?

The red light on the outside of the airlock switched to green. The hatch slid open. Before he and Roy could enter, a half dozen dead Legionnaires vented out into space, and Ishek returned to him, cackling with dark laughter.

*I'm beginning to truly enjoy fighting on the human side.*

# CHAPTER 41

Caleb slid down off Roy's back as the Edger ducked into the station's airlock. Roy headed directly to the controls on the far side of the airlock, closing the outer hatch, and equalizing the interior pressure before opening the inner hatch.

"Penn, Fitz, sitrep," Caleb ordered as he and Roy slipped into the stardock. The interior was exactly what he expected. A narrow passageway with drab metal walls, a grated metal floor, with pipes, wires, and lighting running overhead.

"We're halfway to the control room, Captain," Penn replied. "The defenses are pretty light. They definitely weren't expecting anyone to come knocking."

"I wouldn't call four Nightmares light," Roy said. "We lost two Edgers."

"And we'll mourn them the way we do all our dead," Penn answered. "With plenty of booze and exaggerated tales of greatness."

"Aye," Roy agreed.

"We've nearly reached the reactors," Fitz announced on behalf of his four Edgers. "More light defenses, though we've had to push back the dock workers. They're unarmored and lightly armed, yet they've been coming at us like their lives depended on it."

"They do," Caleb answered. "Whoever their master is, these khoron will be destroyed if they lose the dock."

"Damned if you do, damned if you don't," Fitz laughed. "Anyway, we should have the power supply under control within a few minutes."

"It's already under control," Greaser said. "I have full physical access to their servers. I disconnected their guns. I can also unplug the gravity, if you'd like."

"Maybe later," Caleb said, realizing he could have asked Greaser to open the airlock for them. But then, Ishek wouldn't have had the chance to overpower one of the Legionnaires inside and use him to direct the others to their doom.

*Penn was right. You missed all the fun.*

*Not until that bastard who killed the Empress is dead, I haven't. Find him for me.* "Sarge, sitrep."

"Three up and three down, Cap," Damian replied. "We're moving into docking position, ready to unload the other boarding crews."

"Copy that. Have them search both ends of the stardock for stragglers. We're nearly finished up here."

*Caleb, I've lost the assassin.*

*What do you mean, you lost him?*

*He is no longer on the Collective.*

*You mean he's dead?*

*It would seem so. If the others had encountered a Relyeh as powerful as him, it is likely they would have reported it.*

"Penn, Fitz, have either of your teams seen anything out of the ordinary?" Caleb asked. "Like a Legionnaire or worker unlike any of the others?"

"Negative," Penn replied. "All the Legion I've encountered are just like the bastards I've killed so far."

"Same for me," Fitz added.

*So where the hell did he go, and how did he disappear?*

Footsteps coming toward Caleb pulled his attention away from Ishek before he could answer. "We've got company," Caleb murmured, grabbing the rifle from his back and leveling in toward the junction in the corridor a few dozen meters away.

Right beside him, Roy did the same as a handful of workers charged into the passageway, led by a slender woman with a shoulder-length braid dropping from under a hard hat. She wore grease-stained coveralls, a desperate look on her face.

"Should I cut them down?" Roy asked.

*Ish?* Caleb asked.

*They are not khoron.*

"Negative. Hold your fire," Caleb replied. "Ish says they're clean."

"Oh, thank goodness!" the woman exclaimed, rushing toward them.

"Stop right there!" Caleb barked, bringing the group to a halt. "Who are you?"

"I'm Sarah," she replied. "I'm a mechanic. This is my team. You're here from Huntsman Corporation, aren't you?" She didn't wait for him to answer before continuing. "We took a job to complete the station's systems. A six-month contract. We've been here for over a year. The dock commander, Skaram, refused to let us go." She shook her head, tears welling. "He even killed Danny when he complained. This was supposed to be my dream job, but the whole thing's been a nightmare. Please tell us you'll get us off this station."

"We'll get you off," Caleb replied. "But you can't go this way. You need to head down to the lower level arms. Our ship is docking there."

"We don't want to go alone. The Legion is out of control.

Please, can you escort us down?"

"I'm sorry, we don't have time for that."

"But you came to rescue us, didn't you?"

"Not exactly, lady," Roy answered. "We're nice guys. We'll give you a free ride out. But we're here for the take."

"You're pirates?" one of the other workers asked.

"This here is Captain Card," Roy said. "You may not have heard of him yet, but soon enough the entire Spiral will know his name."

"Roy," Caleb chided. "We need to move."

"We have to go past them to reach the control room."

*Ish, still no sign of the assassin?*

*No. And it's pissing me off. I can disguise myself on the Collective and make my presence difficult to detect. He has vanished without a trace.*

I guess that's what makes him a good assassin.

"Penn, we're coming to you."

"Aye, Captain."

"We've reached the reactor," Fitz announced. "We're in command of the control room."

"Nice work, Edgers. Roy, let's go."

Caleb advanced toward the workers, shouldering his rifle as he neared.

"The lift is back that way," Sarah said, pointing in the direction they had come. "Can we follow you?"

"It might not be safe," Caleb said.

"Nowhere is safe," she replied.

Caleb nodded, moving through the group.

"Just try to stay out of the way," Roy said gruffly, pushing past them.

They made their way down the corridor, slowing at the junction. With the connecting passageway clear, they started down it. Another second intersection waited a few dozen meters down. Rifles leveled, they skirted along the bulkhead. The workers followed their lead, sticking tight to Roy's back as they advanced.

*There are Legionnaires approaching in the passageway on the right.*

Caleb brought the group to a stop. *How many?*

*Six.*

"Roy, Ish says we have six tangos incoming. Cross to the opposite side. I'll cover you."

"Copy."

Caleb swung his rifle around the corner, leaning his head out for a peek. A half dozen Legionnaires were running down the passageway. They started shooting the moment they saw him. Maintaining his composure, Caleb didn't flinch. Instead, he returned fire, covering Roy as he crossed the passageway. Once out of the line of fire, the Edger ducked back out to fire on the Legionnaires. One of them dropped to the deck, though none of Roy's hits penetrated their armor.

*Another one for me. I'm at seven so far.*

*We're not keeping score.*

*I am. Eight.*

Caleb heard the thud a moment later. "Roy, I'm going to charge them with the alloy blade. Cover me."

"Aye, Captain."

Roy leaned out again, firing on the advancing Legionnaires, his rounds doing nothing but creating a few dents in their alloy armor. Caleb reached back for Hiro's sword with his free hand, grasping at air where the handle should have been.

"Are you looking for this?" Sarah asked, the tip of the blade pressing against his back.

# CHAPTER 42

Caleb froze. *Ish?*

*He's back on the Collective.*

Caleb cursed violently under his breath, angry with himself for trusting Sarah. He didn't have time for this. *Can you beast mode me, at least?* He angled his chin back toward Sarah, but not far enough to see her. "What do you want from me?"

*Nine. And help you even the score?*

"A full surrender. All of your forces. Now."

Roy ducked back, looking over at Caleb and freezing too when he saw the situation. The three remaining Legionnaires reached the intersection, two turning toward Roy, one aiming a rifle at him.

*Come on, Ish.*

"It should be a pretty simple choice, Card," Sarah said. "You and your second are dead if you don't."

*All right, all right. But only because I don't want to die.*

Caleb immediately felt the boost of chemicals heating his system.

*I'll take the one in front of you.*

*No*, Caleb countered. *Help Roy first. On my go.*

*Aye, Captain.*

"But my crew will still take this stardock and all the booty you lifted from the pirate ships you attacked."

Sarah laughed. "You traveled infinite light years just to become a pirate. That's pretty sad."

The mention of his crossing surprised him. He tensed, the reaction amusing Sarah even more.

"You're a terrible pirate, Card. You didn't even sniff out my scam. Hayden would be ashamed."

"How do you know about Sheriff Duke?"

"I've been in your head, Card. I know a lot about you. How did it feel when we stabbed Empress Lo'ane?"

Caleb saw Roy's eyes widen through his faceplate. He hadn't told anyone besides Damian about that. At least now he knew who he was dealing with. But how had she disguised her presence?

"*You* stabbed Empress Lo'ane," he replied. "I couldn't do anything but watch. That won't happen again."

"Won't it?"

The question was more of a signal than Sarah realized. Before she could order the Legionnaire facing Roy to shoot him, silently or otherwise, Ishek cut his strings. As he fell dead, Caleb dropped his rifle and lunged at the other two, beating Sarah's attempt to stab him in the back. He drove his open palm against the first Legionnaire's chest, his enhanced strength driving him back off his feet. He grabbed the second Legionnaire with his other hand, tugging him into the path of Sarah's second attempt to stab him. The blade went through the Legionnaire's armor and deep into his chest. It snagged there, embedded in one of the man's ribs, pulling it from Sarah's hand as he fell.

Sarah leaped at Caleb unarmed, and Roy opened fire at the last Legionnaire. Caleb had no time to wait for the outcome. He turned, bringing his hands up to block Sarah's attack, the force of her blow pushing his forearms all the way back, straining them near to breaking. She ducked past him, going after Roy as the other workers charged Caleb, preventing him from blocking her.

Instead, he threw himself at the oncoming workers, hitting the first one with a hard right hook, that broke his jaw with a loud crack. As he crashed into the bulkhead, Caleb kicked the next worker in the gut, doubling him over, before moving past him to drive his elbow back between the man's shoulder blades. He doubled over, gasping for air. A woman leaped past him, awkwardly trying to throat punch Caleb. He grabbed her by the arm and threw her into the bulkhead. Knocked out, she slid down the bulkhead and out of his way.

No way were these workers like Sarah. She had hit him like a bullet train. Still, they were helping Crux. Human or not, that made them the enemy.

He whirled around to help Roy. Sarah was on top of him, hands pinning his arms. She'd ripped his helmet off and had her mouth close to his. *Something* was coming out of her mouth with her breath, difficult to see, but definitely there.

*Ish, what is she —*

His body ran cold in response to Ishek's trembling fear.

*Oh no.*

*Ish?*

*Kill them both. Now!*

Caleb dropped to grab the sword and yank it from the fallen Legionnaire. By the time he straightened up, Sarah was on her feet, facing him. Roy was getting up too.

"Roy?" he said.

The Edger answered by swinging his rifle at Caleb. He barely had time to close the gap, knocking the rifle aside with his hand as he drove the blade into the other man's gut. He braced as he did, Sarah's expected punch slamming into his helmet and knocking him sideways where he crashed into the bulkhead. Roy gasped and grabbed at the blade while Sarah again came at Caleb.

*Don't let her breathe into your mouth.*

Caleb didn't need Ishek's warning. Somehow, that simple act had turned Roy against him in a matter of seconds. He jerked his head aside as Sarah threw another punch at his helmet. Her fist cracked against the flange fastening on the left side of his head, her knuckles scraping open. Going on the offensive, Caleb head-butted her.

Blood flew from her broken nose. She tumbled back, catching his leg as he kicked at her chest and lifting it until he went down flat on his back. She stomped his faceplate, her boot cracking the transparency. He grabbed her calf, twisting until she dropped on her side, allowing him to roll back to his feet.

She leaped up and threw herself at him, lips curled in a snarl as she pounded him with a series of short, hard punches. He finally caught her arm, twisting and breaking it before shoving her into the opposite bulkhead. Bouncing off, she sidestepped his follow-up punch and shattered his faceplate with the butt of her good hand.

Forcing him back against the other bulkhead, she spun, kneeing him in his kidney and knocking him to his knees, the pain so intense all he could do was cringe. She leaned down, bringing her mouth close to his, but before she could breathe into his mouth, Caleb wrapped her in a bear hug. Holding his breath and turning his head aside, he squeezed her tightly, shutting off her air. What little she exhaled felt cold instead of warm against his cheek before dissipating.

He continued squeezing, turning the fight into a contest of lung capacity and willpower. She grabbed at his head, trying to force it straight, but he clamped his jaw shut, refusing to inhale. Staring into one another's eyes, he saw only death and chaos in hers as they silently battled.

His lungs beginning to burn, her breath cut off, and he

felt her ribs give under the strain. By her face, he could tell she was much closer to death than he was.

She resorted to punching him in the sternum; her blows still landing like hammers as she tried to knock the wind out of him, forcing him to breathe. It was hard for him to keep a tight grip on her under her relentless pounding, but he refused to let her go. Instead, he took her to the deck, dropping on top of her. The added pressure was enough to break her spine, and though she was still alive, her arms fell dead beside her.

"Well…fought…Card," she wheezed out, just before she died.

Caleb breathed heavily as he removed his arms from beneath her, lifting himself to kneel over her. *Ish, what the hell?*

*Yes. Hell is a good way to describe it.*

*I don't understand.*

*I don't completely understand, either. Check her arm.*

Caleb unzipped the front of Sarah's coveralls. She wore a white tank top underneath, the edges yellowed with sweat. Lifting her arm, he found an Advocate bonded to her. But it wasn't like any other Advocate he had ever seen. Different from both Ishek and Gareshk, it had an almost metallic sheen to its skin. Still alive, it shifted slowly in whorls of gradation, rippling like liquid mercury.

"What the hell?" Caleb whispered, sensing Ishek's concern.

*This Advocate is infected with a moiety. This is bad. Very bad. We need to destroy it.*

*How?*

*Burn it.*

*I have nothing to burn it with.*

*Then throw it from the airlock, but you must contain it immediately. Do not let it escape. And do not touch it.*

Caleb wasn't sure what Ishek meant until the metal-like

moiety pooled on her skin and streamed slowly down toward the grating in the deck. He quickly removed his helmet and placed it under the moiety stream.

*Cut the Advocate off her.*

He did as Ishek said, using the sword to remove the Advocate completely. It fell into the helmet, along with the moiety. He didn't waste any time from there, jumping to his feet and running back to the airlock.

*I still don't understand.*

*Khoron are not advanced Relyeh. They cannot organize on their own. We have always known there must be another Relyeh guiding them. A more powerful Relyeh. This is worse than I would have ever expected.*

*So you know who's running this show. That makes things easier, doesn't it?*

*Not with what we have seen. Too many khoron. Crux is Sanctified. And now this. I wish it were Arluthu guiding the Relyeh in this part of the universe.*

*What's the Ancient's name?*

*Iagorth the Devourer.*

A chill ran down Caleb's spine from Ishek's reaction to the name. Rather than explaining Iagorth's infamy, Ishek passed him the knowledge through his thoughts, filling in the blanks in a matter of seconds.

By the time Ishek was done, the chill Caleb felt was his own.

Reaching the airlock, Caleb opened it and placed the helmet inside. The moiety was moving inside it, tendrils of metal stretching away from its main mass in an attempt to locate an escape from the headgear.

*Hurry.*

Caleb closed the inner airlock and activated the outer one. The vacuum immediately sucked the helmet out into space, sending it hurtling away with the moiety still inside.

"Will that kill it?"

*No. But if we are fortunate, it will float out there for a long, long time to come.*

Caleb exhaled, dwindling adrenaline leaving him drained.

"Cap, Gorgon just docked," Damian said. "Head-crushers and Berserkers are sweeping the decks."

"Copy. Don't trust anyone who isn't from our crew, and have them report anything unusual immediately."

"Aye, Captain."

By the time he returned to the corridor, Penn was there, kneeling over Roy.

"I'm sorry," Caleb said.

She looked back at him before her eyes danced across the still unconscious workers. "What happened here?"

"I got the answer to one of my questions. Only now I'm not sure I wanted the answer."

"That bad, huh?"

"It's not good."

"I came running when it seemed like you were in trouble. We've claimed the control room. The stardock is ours."

Caleb nodded. He would have liked to enjoy the moment more, but Ishek's revelations about Iagorth had ruined that. "We need to grab what we can asap. I want us gone in eight hours."

"Aye, Captain."

"Sarge, once the boarding crews finish their sweep, escort Naya to the control room. I want as much data from the stardock's servers as we can grab."

"Aye, Captain."

"After that, meet me in the cargo hold to get a look at our bounty."

"Aye, Captain," Damian repeated happily. "Here's to the start of a beautiful and profitable uprising."

Caleb knew he wouldn't be so happy once he understood the full scope of their undertaking. Still, they had won today, and they would be more prepared for tomorrow.

*I don't give a damn about Iagorth,* he decided. *Knuckle up, Ish. The fight may have just gotten harder, but it's far from over.*

Ishek responded with a pleased chuckle, finishing Caleb's thought for him.

*And we don't quit until we're dead.*

———

Thank you so much for reading Galaxy Unstable! For more information on Book Three, please visit mrforbes.com/ forgottengalaxy3. Also, please continue to the next page for more information on Caleb and other books by M.R. Forbes. Thank you again!

# THANK YOU!

**Thank you for reading Galaxy Unknown!**

Did you know there are more books that take place in the Forgotten Universe, including Caleb's origin story?

A lot more.

Want to read them, but don't know where to start?

If you're looking for Caleb's first series, go here: mrforbes.com/forgottencolony

Otherwise, head on over to mrforbes.com/forgottenuniverse to see a list of all the books.

**Looking for something outside of the Forgotten Universe?**

I love writing, and release a new book every 6 weeks or so. I've been doing it for over ten years now, so I've got a pretty decent-sized catalogue. If you love sci-fi, you're sure to find something you'll enjoy. Flip to the next section in this book or head on over to mrforbes.com/books to see everything on my web site, or hit up mrforbes.com/amazon to look at my stuff there, including most popular titles, reviews, etc.

By the way, you can also sign up for my mailing list at mrforbes.com/notify to be alerted to all of my new releases. No spam, just books. Guaranteed!

# OTHER BOOKS BY M.R FORBES

**Want more M.R. Forbes? Of course you do!**
**View my complete catalog here**
mrforbes.com/books
Or on Amazon:
mrforbes.com/amazon

**Forgotten (The Forgotten)**
mrforbes.com/theforgotten
Complete series box set:
mrforbes.com/theforgottentrilogy

**Some things are better off FORGOTTEN.**

Sheriff Hayden Duke was born on the Pilgrim, and he expects to die on the Pilgrim, like his father, and his father before him.

That's the way things are on a generation starship centuries from home. He's never questioned it. Never thought about it. And why bother? Access points to the ship's controls are sealed, the systems that guide her automated and out of reach. It isn't perfect, but he has all he needs to be content.

Until a malfunction forces his wife to the edge of the habitable zone to inspect the damage.

Until she contacts him, breathless and terrified, to tell him she found a body, and it doesn't belong to anyone on board.

Until he arrives at the scene and discovers both his wife and the body are gone.

The only clue? A bloody handprint beneath a hatch that hasn't opened in hundreds of years.

Until now.

### Deliverance (Forgotten Colony)
mrforbes.com/deliverance
Complete series box set:

**The war is over. Earth is lost. Running is the only option.**

It may already be too late.

Caleb is a former Marine Raider and commander of the Vultures, a search and rescue team that's spent the last two years pulling high-value targets out of alien-ravaged cities and shipping them off-world.

When his new orders call for him to join forty-thousand survivors aboard the last starship out, he thinks his days of fighting are over. The Deliverance represents a fresh start and a chance to leave the war behind for good.

Except the war won't be as easy to escape as he thought.

And the colony will need a man like Caleb more than he ever imagined...

### Starship For Sale (Starship For Sale)
mrforbes.com/starshipforsale

**When Ben Murdock receives a text message offering a fully operational starship for sale, he's certain it has to be a joke.**

Already trapped in the worst day of his life and desperate for a way out, he decides to play along. Except there is no joke. The starship is real. And Ben's life is going to change in ways he never dreamed possible.

**All he has to do is sign the contract.**

Joined by his streetwise best friend and a bizarre tenant with an unseverable lease, he'll soon discover that the universe is more volatile, treacherous, and awesome than he ever imagined.

**And the only thing harder than owning a starship is staying alive.**

### Man of War (Rebellion)
mrforbes.com / manofwar
Complete series box set:
mrforbes.com / rebellion-web

In the year 2280, an alien fleet attacked the Earth.

Their weapons were unstoppable, their defenses unbreakable.

Our technology was inferior, our militaries overwhelmed.

Only one starship escaped before civilization fell.

Earth was lost.

It was never forgotten.

Fifty-two years have passed.

A message from home has been received.

The time to fight for what is ours has come.

Welcome to the rebellion.

### Hell's Rejects (Chaos of the Covenant)
mrforbes.com / hellsrejects

The most powerful starships ever constructed are gone. Thousands are dead. A fleet is in ruins. The attackers are unknown. The orders are clear: *Recover the ships. Bury the bastards who stole them.*

Lieutenant Abigail Cage never expected to find herself in Hell. As a Highly Specialized Operational Combatant, she was one of the most respected Marines in the military. Now she's doing hard labor on the most miserable planet in the universe.

Not for long.

The Earth Republic is looking for the most dangerous individuals it can control. The best of the worst, and Abbey happens to be one of them. The deal is simple: *Bring back the starships, earn your freedom. Try to run, you die.* It's a suicide mission, but she has nothing to lose.

The only problem? There's a new threat in the galaxy. One with a power unlike anything anyone has ever seen. One that's been waiting for this moment for a very, very, long time. And they want Abbey, too.

Be careful what you wish for.

They say Hell hath no fury like a woman scorned. They have no idea.

# ABOUT THE AUTHOR

M.R. Forbes is the mind behind a growing number of Amazon best-selling science fiction series. He currently resides with his family and friends on the west cost of the United States, including a cat who thinks she's a dog and a dog who thinks she's a cat.

He maintains a true appreciation for his readers and is always happy to hear from them.

To learn more about me or just say hello:

Visit my website:
mrforbes.com

Send me an e-mail:
michael@mrforbes.com

Check out my Facebook page:
facebook.com/mrforbes.author

Join my Facebook fan group:
facebook.com/groups/mrforbes

Follow me on Instagram:
instagram.com/mrforbes_author

Find me on Goodreads:
goodreads.com/mrforbes

Follow me on Bookbub:
bookbub.com/authors/m-r-forbes

Made in the USA
Las Vegas, NV
29 November 2023

81815132R00184